MW01135833

Christine Zolendz

Fall From Grace

Cover Design by okaycreations.net

"Piece of My Heart," lyrics written by Bert Berns and Jerry Ragovoy © 1968, recorded by Janis Joplin on her "Cheap Thrills" album

Editor extraordinaire: Frankie Sutton
http://frankiesfreelanceediting.blogspot.com/

This book is dedicated to everyone who has ever been told they can't. Let's jump off the cliff together.

And to my girls. Always dream big.

Chapter 1

What woke me was the insistent beep-beep-beep of the little machine that was monitoring his dying heart. I opened my eyes slowly, and as always, he lay there watching me.

I got up from where I was sitting and leaned in close to him, placing my hand on his cheek. "Let go. I understand."

He struggled for breath and mumbled something I couldn't hear. I smiled anyway. "Go, Jake. I'll be fine, don't hold on for me."

A lone tear escaped from his eye and his breathing stilled. The monitors screamed their piercing sirens.

I stepped back as nurses and doctors flooded the room, but I knew it was too late. He was gone and I was completely alone again.

Voices blurred and time seemed to slow down as I made my way towards the hall. God, I don't belong here anymore. This is my own personal hell.

Someone cut off the horrific screams of the heart monitor and the sudden realization that Jacob was dead shot waves of horror through me. *Does life ever get any easier?*

For so long, I helplessly watched as a vicious disease sucked the life out of his once strong spirit. Jacob's trembling hands, and jaundice skin showed his inability to fight the invisible murderous enemy. *How much more powerless and insignificant can a person feel when watching someone they love slowly die?* I wished each night to take his place, yet I was still standing there and Jacob was gone. I never believed in wishes anyway.

I placed my hand on the doorframe and looked back once. Do not resuscitate. Do not grieve for me when this cancer wins. Do not give me a funeral to remember what killed me. They were calling the time; it was 3:16. The numbers made my frown tighten, or maybe it was just the knowledge that Gabriel would be standing right outside the door.

"Hello, Gabriel," I whispered, even before I stepped through the doorway. My insides twisted themselves into knots as I stood before him.

"Grace."

I looked up and tried my best to smile; trying to hold in the tears that I knew would soon flow like a great flood from my eyes. Gabriel was always so beautiful to look at. No matter when or where he showed up, he was perfect. He was leaning against the white walls of the hospital hallway and his perfection made them seem dirty against his bronzed flawless skin.

"What is your plan now, Grace?"

"Oh, Gabriel, it's the same as always. Just keep breathing and put one foot in front of the other. Now, if you would please excuse me, I just lost my brother and I'd like to be alone." I brushed past him, accidentally touching the edge of his arm, and I shivered.

Gabriel reached out his arm and gently touched my shoulder. "I'm sorry about your brother, Grace. I'm sorry about all of this."

I stopped and turned towards him. Even though his voice had sounded full of tenderness, his ice-cold blue eyes held no emotion. "Thank you, Gabriel. I'm sure that one day, I'll meet up with him again. After all, we all gotta die sometime, don't we?" My sarcasm dripped thickly off every word. I couldn't say what I wanted to. *How many times can you say I'm sorry? How many times will I watch death take everyone, leaving me here? How much more can I endure when I've endured so much more than others have? How many times have I wished death would come for me? Even in death, I would not be allowed to rest, would I?* Sorrow seeped through my veins. This is all I knew; all I'd ever know; an eternity here on earth.

His long elegant fingers brushed up against my cheek. "I really am sorry about Jacob, Grace. I wish I could do something. I know how special he's been to you." For a single nanosecond, or maybe even less, his eyes offered a smoldering glance, as if they were trying to tell me something separate from his blank expression.

He turned to leave, but I felt his halfhearted attempt at being able to do something, hang heavy and linger in the air between us.

"This has nothing to do with Jacob, Gabriel. Yes, my brother is gone now, and I will miss him, but this has to do with my being here, still alone. I'm relieved Jacob is gone. He's been dying for years with that cancer. No human being should suffer as he did. Being here is excruciating, Gabriel, but I'm still *here*! So please, do not patronize me. Do not visit every so often, glare at me with those cold dead eyes, and tell me how you wish you could do something, when I know for a fact that you could. Unless you have something to offer me in way of advice or counsel, I'll be doing what I've always done, putting one foot in front of the other and moving on." My eyes welled up when I turned from him. Of course, I would miss Jacob. Someone like Gabriel would never understand any of these horrible human emotions and all this pain. I just wished it would end; I would just like not to exist in this world anymore or in any world. I just wanted, well, it doesn't matter what I wanted, did it?

In one quick movement, Gabriel grabbed me and spun me to face him. His stern fatherly expression dissolved into a tender smile. The behavior startled me in such a way that my knees gave out from underneath me. I had never seen

Gabriel smile like that. He embraced me in his huge bronze arms and whispered into my ears without saying a word.

"You are the strongest person that I have ever known. You've been broken more times than anyone, and yet you keep...I want so much to save you..." His embrace calmed me. I slowly pushed myself off and out of his arms, trying to distance myself from him.

The tenderness was gone and the stern father figure was standing before me as if that little slip in time of encouragement and tenderness never happened.

"Thank you, Gabriel." And, that's where I left him. Standing in a hospital hallway, in the middle of nowhere, thinking that I was the strongest person he'd known. *As if I had a choice in that.*

Chapter 2

I kept walking until I found myself standing in the middle of the hospice parking lot, but I couldn't remember where my Jeep was. I couldn't remember the last time I was outside of the hospice walls. The rays of the sun felt as if they were assaulting me for hiding for so long. Rummaging in my pockets for my keys, I wondered if I should go back inside to the room they had given Jacob to get my belongings.

Clicking the alarm on the keys helped me find my Jeep, and after climbing in, I sat heavily into the driver's seat. I glanced in the backseat where my guitar case was propped up against the back window. Just whom was I kidding? Everything I owned was in this vehicle. I just needed to leave, so I started the engine.

I peeled out of the parking lot as if my tailpipes were on fire. I had more than 400 miles to cover and I wanted to do it as fast as I possibly could. Heading straight to the I-90 New York State Thruway, I stepped on the gas as hard as I could.

I placed my phone in the speaker cradle on my dashboard and called Lea hands-free.

"Grace? What's wrong?" the disembodied voice of my best friend answered.

"Jake's gone, so I'm coming back. My room still empty?"

"Oh, Gray." Her pet name for me touched my heart. "Of course, it's empty. I don't even know what to say. Jake was..."

"Please don't. It's over and he's not in any more pain. I'll be back sometime tonight."

"Conner and I are going to watch his friend's band play later. Text me when you get in and I'll message you the address, in case you feel up to going out." *Oh Lea, you're so used to my stoic episodes. Maybe a night of music and drinking would be the answer to my prayers, or at least it would numb my mind of this harsh life.*

"Conner, huh? Sounds like a plan. I'm almost on I-390 now. I'll see you in a few."

"Oh man, you're doing about 90, aren't you? Don't kill yourself, please, I know you have a death wish, but I'd like to see you again, and in one piece, please. Besides, I really want you to meet Conner." Her voice did nothing to hide her feelings for him and it made me smile. Lea was such a beautiful soul. She deserved to find someone who could make her smile.

"I'm not driving anywhere near 90," I replied. *Well, 120 was nowhere near 90 in my mind.* "I can't wait to meet Conner too." I clicked off the phone and pushed the Jeep to go even faster. The traffic was uncharacteristically thin and I found myself weaving through cars as if I was invisible. *If only I could be invisible, or at least not feel this sad world. If only I didn't have to be so...human.*

In the solace and loneliness of my front seat, while I sped through the world in a blur, my tears fell free. I separated my mind from my body as I always do, and let the sorrow wash over my soul. The sky slowly grew darker as my world tilted itself towards the moon. Great dark clouds assembled above, crowding the heavens and it opened up. Hail pelted my windshield and the rain poured down, matching my mood. All of it was making me feel as if the heavens were mocking me.

I made the seven-hour trip in five hours, crying all the way. At exactly 9:15, I had my few belongings back in the small Manhattan apartment that I began renting with Lea so long ago. I sat down on the big brown couch we bought at a secondhand store downtown and looked around. Everything was the same. It was as if I hadn't left six months ago and Jake was still kicking pancreatic cancer's ass. *One foot in front of the other, just keep moving forward.*

Lea had texted directions to the bar to me, which read, Walk out door. Turn right. Walk around corner. Find big sign that says Boozer's. Get smashed for Jake.

I walked back to my room and stripped out of my clothes. My shirt had gotten soaked with my tears. I changed into an old comfortable pair of jeans and a small white T-shirt, thinking Lea would complain about how plain I looked. Then, I slipped on a pair of black stilettos that had been left in my closet. I hoped the bar wasn't too far, because I had a feeling that later on I'd be stumbling home barefoot.

Splashing water on my face in the bathroom was the only thing I did to freshen up. I didn't even bother looking in the mirror. I grabbed my jacket and ran my fingers through my hair to tame the tangles as I walked out the door. I was never one to care about how I looked on the outside. That wasn't the real me anyway. Not that I didn't appreciate the way I looked now, I just didn't feel it mattered, because how you look doesn't change what's in your soul.

Making my way down the street, I found comfort in the busy New York City sounds; the taxis flying through the streets, people talking, laughing, and shouting. Like me, everything felt raw and alive in this city. *Raw and still very much alive.*

Boozer's kept an enormously cheesy neon light over its open front doors and the music from inside was drifting out into the street. I was enamored with it before I even walked inside. The front windows were made of small panes of glass that were foggy from the cold February night. Old-fashioned lanterns hung from the old world brick façade, making the building look as if it belonged in a small romantic Tuscany village, and not on a New York City Street.

An enormously chiseled looking man stood inside the opening of the bar and winked at me as I walked in. A bright red STAFF shirt clung to his body as if it was painted on; his expression looked like he wanted me for dinner. *Too arrogant.* However, that didn't stop me from wondering if he'd thought I'd be a main course or just an appetizer.

I scanned the crowded room for Lea and spotted her right away. Of course, she was the one dancing on top of the table in a booth near the stage against the wall. Everyone was talking and watching the band play music that was a mix between rock, blues and alternative. Nothing spectacular; average music, and I tuned them out.

I expertly navigated myself through the crowds of people; the sound of the music drowned away from my ears; I barely noticed when they stopped playing. When Lea saw me, she grabbed me in her arms and pulled me up onto the table with her. "You're home! Oh God, Gray, I'm so sorry. Come on, talk to me!"

I held her at arm's length and gave her a small smile. "There's nothing to say that hasn't already been said. Let's not talk about it, okay?"

She took a flying leap off the table and dragged me with her. I almost fell flat on my face, but she thunderously dragged me to a small crowd of guys who were looking at me in confusion.

Lea marched me right up to a tall blond guy. "Conner! This is my best friend in the whole entire universe. Grace." She turned her head to me and yelled over the crowd, "Gray, this is Conner. *The One!*" Mad giggling ensued and with it came an exact measurement of just how drunk she already was.

Conner, aka *The One*, arched his eyebrows slightly towards Lea, and then gave me a huge smile. I couldn't help but smirk at her, sighing inwardly. Yes. The way he looked at Lea, well, most girls would kill for a guy to look at them the way he looked at her. My heart leapt for my friend, because she deserved to find her *One*, as she called him. I reached my hand out to shake his and instead he grabbed me in a bear hug and lifted me off the ground. "Welcome home! Lea's been talking about you nonstop for the last six months. I was beginning to think that she actually made you up!"

I laughed. "Well, thanks. I'm happy to meet you too!"

He gently settled my feet on the floor and wrapped his arms around Lea, who was looking up at him lovingly, and swaying a bit. "I'm really sorry to hear about your brother. Lea's been crying since you called."

What could I say to that? Nothing, really. Lea knew Jacob her whole life. If I really wanted to think about it, the truth was that Lea knew Jacob even longer than I had. I didn't think about it though. The second the thought entered, I wiped it from my mind. I couldn't think about those things. Right now, I just really needed a drink.

Lea staggered closer to the table and grabbed two beers. "Where's my pitcher of margaritas?" she yelled to nobody in particular.

Conner shook his head and laughed. "You drank it all. Have some beer for now, because you're going to pass out on me if you keep this up."

Around us, the movement of the crowd escalated with excitement. I looked around the room to find the cause. A man stood in front of the room on the small stage with a microphone in one hand and a beer in the other. "Are we having fun yet?" he screamed at the audience. Not waiting for the yells of replies to die down the man keep talking. "Welcome to Boozer's! Drink until you pass out, and we'll let you sleep on the floor! Let's give it up for our house band, Mad World! Ladies, stay off the stage, but you may throw as much of your clothes at them that you want!"

I laughed out loud at the absurdity of the emcee, and then stopped when I noticed all the bras and underwear haphazardly hanging from the rafters on the ceiling. *Wow*.

Cheering erupted as a group of three guys ran onto the stage. The volume exploded to an ear-piercing decibel and a small lacy black bra went sailing from the crowd, landing in the hands of the fourth member of the band, who strolled, relaxed and unaffected into the middle of the stage.

Lea grabbed me around the waist and pulled me through the crowd. "This is the band. Come on; let's stand on the side over here. In a minute, we won't be able to see through the sea of half-naked girls!"

Wobbly, she climbed back on top of the table we had occupied earlier and held out her hand for me to follow. I followed her up and still grasping my hand, she continued climbing over the leathery cushions of the booth, right onto a wooden shelf in the wall and we plopped down on a deep-set windowsill.

I sat next to her and wondered how many times in the last six months, she sat there and listened to her boyfriend's friend's band play. How long had she smiled that *satisfied with her life* smile? I wondered what contentment felt like. I shut down the thoughts again. I was worn out, but I was definitely happy that Lea had that smile on her face.

I followed her glance to Conner, who stood in the crowd of people and looked back at her with a matching smile. It felt as if I was in the room alone with them and I was intruding in a private moment.

The crowd was in a complete frenzy, when a rough, sexy voice poured a velvety haunting song into the microphone. I couldn't help but look up to see the match to the voice. How I had been capable of not noticing him before was beyond me. He was perfection. I couldn't even have matched an adjective to him if I'd tried, but perfect would be the closest fit, and it still wasn't good enough to describe him.

He was looking through the crowd with intense eyes, as if he was searching for something. Then his expression eased into a sexy smoldering smile. His short dark hair hung thick and unruly, cut in uneven layers. It looked tousled, as if some lucky girl had just run her hands through it backstage. *Ah, maybe that's who it was that he was searching for.*

Lean toned muscles stretched beneath the skin of his tattooed arms. One perfectly sculpted hand caressed the mic stand; the other ran through his perfect hair. His husky voice whispered its song. It silenced the crowd as if he was a god.

What use is a tomorrow?

I've endured forever

There's little hope.

I drown my sorrow.

His voice slowed and stopped; a sad melody began on a piano. He stepped back from the mic, never taking his eyes from the crowd, leaned back and reached for a jet-black guitar.

A fast drumbeat broke through the silence, followed by a bass and his soul retching guitar rhythm took my breath away. His voice entwined with an anguished piano chorus and the crowd roared to life. They sang along with the words, as if it was the most popular song on the radio.

Lea nudged me, "They're mind-blowing, aren't they?"

It took a moment for me to find my voice. "Yeah, mind-blowing." Just listening to that voice was sending shivers through my body, and the way his hands moved over that guitar, *holy crap*!

She gave me a knowing smile. "Yeah, the first time Conner brought me here and I heard Shane play, I thought of you. Inspiring, isn't he?" She understood how much music could move me. How many nights did I play for her to go to sleep when we were younger, for every heartbreak and every tear?

Stretched in front of us, the crowd seemed to double. Girls sat on top of their date's shoulders. People danced on top of tables and a long line of scantily clad females were writhing against each other on the bar, vying for the band's attention.

Lea and I looked at each other and fell into each other laughing. "Come on, Grace, let's take our shirts and bras off and show these girls how it's done!"

I shook my head and laughed even harder, "Girl, you take your bra off over here, and those puppies of yours will knock your friends off the stage!"

She smiled with pride, "Hey, you're just as boobilicious as me! Come to the bathroom with me. The room is spinning and I don't wanna ask Conner to carry me in!"

Boobilicious? I nodded my head and helped her down. We passed Conner and all his friends, who were sitting around a table at the edge of the crowd. He waved me over and handed me two icy cold frozen margaritas. Lea stumbled ahead of me through the crowds, wobbling through a hallway towards what I guessed were the bathrooms.

I tried to follow her, inching my way through the crowd, and carefully holding on to the two drinks. Of course, I lost sight of her and was stranded in the middle of a crowd of hot, sweaty dancing strangers. *Great.*

Before I knew where I was, I heard a loud commotion in the crowd behind me. A fight had broken out among a group of extremely drunk guys. I continued to move forward in the direction I thought Lea had drunkenly walked. She had to be even drunker than I thought to have lost me and not realized it.

As the brawl got more out of control, I found myself smack in front of the stage. A smaller blonde haired girl and I found ourselves trapped between the stage and the fight, when an elbow from one of the guys rammed into her and she bounced off me, causing both of the ice cold drinks to spill down the front of my very white tee shirt.

The crowd was chanting and screaming at the brawlers, but all I could look at was the icy cold fabric clinging to my skin. Of course, there was the fact that I had a lacy red bra on which now could be seen through my now very wet tee shirt. I threw the empty plastic cups down to the floor. "Crap! Son of a..."

Black leather motorcycle boots jumped from somewhere above me and landed at my feet. Startled, I stepped back. The lead singer, Shane, had jumped off the stage and was now staring down at me with a flirty smile on his face. "Wow," he smirked.

I rolled my eyes, backed up another step, only to be shoved from the fight that was going on behind me, right into his arms. I pushed off him as if I landed on fire. His eyes were ice cold blue.

He pulled me away from the group of guys who were wrestling with the bouncer now. I covered my wet shirt with my arms, feeling completely naked.

One of the other guys from the band, the drummer, jumped off the stage next. "Come on, Shane!" He grabbed Shane by the shoulder and pulled him towards the fight.

"Yeah, one sec, bro," he answered his friend, but never took his eyes off of mine. He grabbed his tee shirt from his waist and pulled it over his head. He was all smooth muscle, as if he was painstakingly chiseled from marble. *Oh my, I hope I'm not drooling.*

He shoved his shirt into my hands and smiled a wicked smile. "Sorry your drinks spilled...but not really." Then he winked and dove into the fight behind me to help the bouncer and he disappeared into a crowd of flying fists and legs.

As everyone around us continued to cheer on the fight, I headed for what I hoped was the bathroom and found Lea on the floor of a stall hugging a toilet. When she heard the door close, she lifted her head and gave me a half smile of embarrassment. "Gracie. I've been chemically inconvenienced and I don't think I can ever leave this toilet. Take a picture of this so I remember never to do it again."

"Lea, I have a huge file folder of those pictures on my computer. It won't stop you." I knelt down next to my best friend and pulled her blonde hair from her face. I grabbed a ponytail holder from the front pocket of my jeans and tied her hair back.

Her big brown eyes looked into mine and I saw tears fill the edges of them. "Jake's really gone?"

I nodded. Saying anything would make me start crying again.

She moaned, heaved into the toilet again, and I just rubbed her back. "How do you do it,

Gray? How can you watch people die over and over again? I can't even imagine him not in this world anymore."

I sat back and leaned against the door of the stall. My eyes flitted over the small space, amazed at how clean it actually was for a bar. I didn't want to talk about this; about anything. I didn't want to feel anymore. This was hell. "Lea. He suffered. He was too good for this world; no one should feel that pain. I wish it were me, Lea. I don't know how I do this. I don't know anything. I'm sorry, I don't know what to say."

"I don't want you to say you wished it was you. I almost lost you once, you were my miracle."

I hugged her tight. "Let's get off this floor, okay." I helped her up, took her to the sink, and helped her wash up. I hoped she would drop the subject, but I knew she had to grieve somehow for Jacob. After all, we were closer than family.

We grew up next door to each other, born the same day, she five minutes before me. Our families said we were destined to be best friends; like sisters. Our mothers and fathers were best friends. When I was fourteen, I lost my parents in a horrific car accident and I almost died. I did, actually. For two minutes, I clinically died. Months later, when I opened my eyes, I was a different person. I remembered Grace's childhood, I knew all her friends, her crushes, her pains. However, the real Grace moved on, her beautiful spirit evaporating like raindrops into the heavens.

Only I stayed behind, stuck here, as if I was super-glued to the earth. *My soul's punishment for something that happened so long ago.*

After my hospital stay and my rehabilitation, Lea's parents took Jacob and me in, not that we needed for anything. My parents had a life insurance policy that was astronomical, so Jacob and I would never want for anything. Ever.

Jake didn't live with us long though. He was eighteen, used some of our inheritance to go to Cornell University in Ithaca, and lived on campus. Lea and I visited him as much as we could and he came home every holiday. We were a family.

I knew she needed to grieve.

"Hey, what happened to your shirt? You're sopping wet! Nice bra."

I looked down, remembering the spilled drinks and I laughed. "A fight broke out in the middle of the bar and I kind of got caught in it. I spilled our drinks all over myself."

"Ah, man, our drinks spilled? Were they margaritas? Did you kick their asses?"

Leave it to Lea to think that I should kick someone's ass over a spilled drink. I stripped off my wet shirt and put on Shane's dry one.

"Where did you get a shirt? Did you come with extra clothes? Did you go shopping without me? What the..."

"The singer, Shane, right? He took off his shirt and gave it to me." I cut her off before she asked anymore of her dumb drunk questions.

"Shane gave you the shirt off his back?" Her expression was sheer confusion. "Be careful of that one. He's slippery like a fish."

I wrapped one arm around her waist and helped her drunk-walk out of the bathroom. "I think I can safely say that you have nothing to worry about there, because he's definitely not my type."

She leaned her head against mine as we exited the bathroom and she giggled. "Gray, there's no such thing as your type, that's for fairytales. You gotta just hook up with a bunch of wrong guys for a while and have fun."

I missed her drunken soliloquies. It hadn't been the same being so far from her and listening to her being a mother hen to me over the phone.

Conner was obediently standing outside in the hallway and looked beyond relieved when we finally emerged from the bathroom. He grabbed her and helped her walk over to the table where the rest of the people he was with were sitting. The crowd in the bar seemed to have thinned out and the stage was empty. I wondered how long we had been on that bathroom floor.

We sat around the table and Conner gave Lea a bottle of water that she sipped continuously.

Lea politely introduced me to Conner's friend Tucker.

Conner worked in a large accounting firm; Tucker had just finished law school and he was working in his father's firm. The two of them and all the members of the band had known each other since high school.

To confuse me even more, Conner and Tucker were explaining to me that most of them were roommates and they all lived in the same apartment building. It all sounded like a bad episode of *Friends* to me.

"Hey, how'd you like the brawl?" a voice called from behind us.

We all turned to see Shane, pulling a chair to the table between Lea and me, with a confused looking blonde who stood next to him. The blonde looked around and seemed to wonder if she should sit or stand, then decided to sit on his lap and start nibbling on his ear. He was still shirtless and the blonde had the biggest set of silicone breasts I had ever seen in real life. They were so enormous, I wanted to see if they'd make a big pop if I poked them with a fork.

"Ugh, Shane, get a kennel for your lapdog. The sounds of her slopping your ear is making me wanna hurl again," Lea muttered.

The blonde stopped and looked at Lea. "Jealous much?"

I watched Lea's knuckles turn white with the force of her grip on the table. "Yeah, I'm always jealous of Shane's conquests. They are the equivalent of a blow up doll with the brains to match."

"What the hell does that mean?" Blondie snapped.

"See, you just proved my point." Lea looked at me and smiled. "Maybe if we use big words, it will leave?"

I shrugged and laughed. "Lea, you know you should never have a battle of wits with an unarmed opponent."

"Shut up, skanks! You're both just jealous." Blondie yelped, puffing her giant silicone chest out at us.

"Slut," Lea smiled.

I gave the blonde a serious face. "Yeah, listen you should really stop now, because I'm betting on the smartest thing that ever could come out of your mouth is a penis."

Lea lost it and the water she was drinking burst from her mouth and landed all over blonde Amazon breast girl. She jumped off Shane's lap and scrambled to her feet. "Shane! Stick up for me! She just got me all wet!" she whined and then she stomped her foot like a kid having a tantrum.

Lea and I bumped heads laughing. I tried not to, but I looked at Shane and he was staring right at me. I held his gaze. His eyes were crystal clear blue and breathtaking. I wasn't used to seeing people with eyes so piercing. Usually people mentioned it about my eyes, which were light gray, almost silver.

He smiled at me with what I guessed was the smile he used to make most girls act as if they'd suddenly dropped fifty IQ points. I felt nothing. *Truthfully, I felt bad for the blonde.*

The muscles of his chest flexed, but I pretended not to notice it. He wore his sex appeal like a medal, mentally undressing me. I rolled my eyes at him and shook my head. "Hey, thanks for the shirt before. Would have been cold walking home like that."

Blondie stomped her foot again to get his attention, but he didn't seem to notice. "This is the one you gave your shirt to? I want a shirt too!"

I looked to Lea and gave her the let's get outta this bad soap opera signal and stood up. I turned to blondie and smiled. "Just think of it like this, I got him half-naked for you already. Try to enjoy yourself. He looks like someone who has a land mine in his pants."

"Huh?" She gave me a really confused look.

"You know a land mine; small, hidden, and explodes on contact."

Shane's eyes widened for a split second, and then he stood up and leaned against the table blocking my way past. "So you must be Lea's best friend, the one she grew up with and talks about all the time, huh?"

"Must be," I snapped.

His grin became wider. "Do you have a name?"

"Yes, I do," I replied, but not telling him.

Lea started laughing at our standoff. She folded her arms and watched. "Conner, watch her outwit him, just watch." Her slurred words made her sound like a cartoon character.

Shane glared at Lea and back to me and smiled devilishly. Ice cold eyes. "I'll just call you Red then, since I can't get my mind off that sexy little bra I saw you in before." His smile lifted up in one corner challenging me.

I leaned in really close to him and slowly lifted my eyes to meet his. "Why not Lacy? Or, did you miss out on the soft silk and lace material it was made from? Too bad, you'll only get to see the color. You know, if you're going to be a smart ass you should start with being smart, otherwise, you're really just an ass. Enjoy the rest of your night."

I held my palm up to his face when he tried to talk. "Please, save your breath, because you might need it to blow up your date later." I walked past him and out the front door.

Lea was giggling behind me. "Gray, I think you made history in there, as the first girl ever not to jump into bed with Shane Maxton after he gave one of his Coochie Award winning smiles."

Chapter 3

Conner and Tucker walked Lea and me back to our apartment like gentlemen. The conversation between the four of us never strayed from Shane's antics of the night or the fact that he paid an interest in me. The warnings to stay away from him from the two guys made me feel like a sixteen year old.

When we reached our apartment, I wasn't surprised that Tucker and Conner came inside with us.

Conner draped himself over the couch as if he owned the place, and Lea curled up next to him, moaning about the room spinning. That left Tucker and me on opposite sides of the couch sitting in our two side chairs. Tucker leaned forward with his elbows on his knees and hands dangling between them, watching me.

Tucker had a young boyish face - and he was attractive, very attractive. His dark copper colored hair matched the exact shade of his eyes, which were still staring at me. "Can't say I blame Shane though," he smiled. "Grace was the prettiest girl in that whole bar."

"Grace *and* Lea," Conner added.

Lea moaned in response and lifted her head. "Thanks, babe," she muttered.

Conner turned to look at me and regarded me with a serious expression. "You should steer clear of Shane, though. I mean, don't get me wrong, he's one of my best friends and I love the guy. You know, like a brother, but he's got some major baggage with women and I just don't think he'll ever be capable of having more than a quick sexual relationship with a girl."

Lea snorted and laughed. "Um, yeah. Well, gentlemen, thank you for all the warning labels you just plastered all over Shane, but there's definitely nothing to worry about with Grace. Without a doubt, Shane is not a thought in Grace's mind; definitely not her type at all." She started giggling uncontrollably. "Although, I think a great one night stand here and there might be good for her, but trust me, boys, Grace is a nut that'll never be cracked!" She gave me a wink and stumbled to the bathroom.

I smiled and settled back into my chair more. It felt comforting that I had Lea in my life. She knew me; she knew who I really was. To everyone else, I was just a regular twenty-something; indistinguishable from anyone else, and that's what I wanted. No one but Lea and Jacob knew about my past and my secrets. Now Jake was gone and Lea was the only person in the world who knew who I really was. I sighed in relief. "I appreciate the Shane warnings, but I'm really not interested in being a notch on a bedpost, so I'm really not interested in him." *Like a narcissistic little boy would get under my skin.* I had to be honest though, Shane was insanely attractive, but looks fade and they are just a covering. Even if the outside of a building looks beautiful and structurally sound, it doesn't mean that once you step inside, the building wouldn't be rotten and crumble down around you; crushing you. I was way beyond that. I had been broken so many times, no one needed to remind me of getting hurt. I just smiled and reassured them the existence of the possibility that I was just an ordinary girl.

Lea wobbled back into the room. "Really. Like, how much did I drink, and why can't I get a normal hangover like everyone else? Why do I have to suffer 'the puke until you're sober situation?" She plopped the bathroom wastebasket on the floor next to her and collapsed back unto the couch.

Conner bolted upright seeing the bucket. "Sweetie, if you puke in front of me I'm gonna blow too. I can't stand the sight of someone vomiting!" He eyed her nervously.

She rolled her eyes. "I think I'm good. This is just in case, and you really should be the one that holds my hair back. That's the sign of a good boyfriend!"

My eyes wandered up to the clock, and I saw that it was four in the morning. I yawned loudly, and announced, "Well, I'm beat. I'm going to bed. Conner, I'm positive that I will be seeing you in the morning, and knowing Lea, many mornings to come," I smiled. A bubble of giggles escaped Lea's lips. "Tucker, it was nice to meet you."

Tucker stood up when I did, which I thought was sweet. "Good night, Grace."

I think I fell asleep on the walk to my room, because the next thing I knew, it was two o'clock the next afternoon and I was still wearing Shane's shirt. The subtle scent of him still lingered on it causing me to jump out of my bed thinking he was there with me.

Chapter 4

I heard Lea's laughter in the kitchen and smelled the fresh aroma of dark brewing coffee. My mouth watered. I had missed Lea's muddy strong coffee.

I still had my heels on. So I slipped out of them, changed my jeans for a pair of boy shorts and just left Shane's shirt on. Then I walked out into the hallway and into the bathroom. I wondered if Conner was still here. Well, it wouldn't be the first time I walked out of my room to run into one of Lea's friends. I laughed remembering the time one of them tried to jump in the shower with me. The poor guy didn't know what hit him, but the way he screamed like a girl, made Lea and me both laugh for days. I could tell that Conner was different for Lea though, she was serious about him. As long as he didn't try to bathe with me, I figured he was golden.

I floated into the kitchen, grabbed a mug, filled it with coffee and turned around to find Shane leaning up against the sink, watching me. He ran his hand through his mass of sweaty hair and wiped his forehead with the tee shirt he had hanging around his neck. He wore nothing else except a pair of black running pants and sneakers.

Conner came into the kitchen dressed the same way. Apparently, they went jogging together every day, Conner was explaining to me, but I was too distracted by the sight of Shane to listen. He was ridiculous to look at; every single muscle on his body was clearly defined. The only word that popped in my mind was *delicious*.

Shane cocked his head and gave me a sideways smile. His eyes were the lightest shade of blue I'd ever seen. They were intense and alarming. They reminded me of something from long ago. "Red, you still have my shirt on." His voice was low and raspy, wrapping itself around me. I could understand perfectly how any girl could fall for him; he was dangerously beautiful.

Embarrassment spiked through my veins. I was standing in front of him with his shirt still on and a pair of tiny boy shorts. I saw him smiling and appraising me. There was no way I could let this man know how he affected me. There's no way, I could let any man affect me, period.

His eyes continued to sweep over my legs, and I could swear that everywhere his eyes locked on me, I could feel a slight touch. I kept my gaze steady on his eyes until he locked back onto mine. An alarmingly gorgeous half-smile stared back at me.

"Would you like it back right now?" I asked daringly.

Conner had stopped talking at some point during our conversation, but neither Shane nor I noticed when. I only noticed Shane's slight forward movement at the thought of me returning his shirt at that moment. *Like I would fall into his trap and take my shirt off for him.*

"Sure thing," I said and bounced my way out of the kitchen and back into my bedroom. I change into an oversized sweatshirt and sweat pants, ran back into the kitchen and tossed the shirt at him. "Thanks again," I called to him as I left the kitchen.

Lea was laying on the couch in the living room in the same exact place I left her the night before. She had her Kindle eReader on and was probably devouring some cheesy romance novel. I sat down next to her and sighed. "What are you reading now?"

"Vampire romance. It's pretty hot, you should read it after me, and get away from reality for a while."

I barked out a laugh. "Nothing can make me forget my reality," I answered flatly.

Looking up Lea asked, "Why do you have an aversion to reading all of a sudden?"

"Why bother? There's no book; fictional, horror, fairytale, anything that could come even close to the warped disturbing reality of my horrible existence," I shuddered.

"Gray," she leaned forward and hugged me. "Why don't you just try to live a little? Do what makes you smile. Stop looking for things that aren't here. Just enjoy the things that *are* here."

If only it were that easy. I leaned back and smiled at my friend. In a blink of an eye, this life would be over.

Conner and Shane strolled in and stopped abruptly, feeling the seriousness of our conversation. I stood up and without a word walked back down the hallway and into the kitchen to reclaim the coffee I had left there. I needed to escape before anyone saw me cry.

"Everything okay?" I heard Conner ask.

Shane chuckled. "Did I piss her off? Shit, I didn't make her cry or anything, did I? She just asked if I wanted my shirt back. I thought I'd get to look at her half naked again!"

I heard Lea stomp off the couch. "Shane, you are the biggest egotistical self-centered man I have ever met. If you think for one minute, someone like Grace would spend more than a minute with you on her mind, you're more than stupid." Her voice got louder. "Her brother died yesterday. Ass hat!"

She stormed through the hallway. The sound of the bathroom door slamming shook the walls.

Within two seconds, Conner's voice was murmuring to her through the locked door. I leaned my hands on the kitchen countertop letting the cool granite calm me.

The floor creaked softly behind me. Shane leaned against the counter next to me. He was so close that I felt his breath on my temple. It took all the control I possessed in my body not to scream at him to get away from me. "I'm sorry...Grace, I didn't mean to be a smart ass. I didn't know about your brother. I didn't mean to..."

I shook my head and sighed. I didn't even turn to look at him.

"I'm being serious, Grace. I know how much it sucks to lose someone you care about." I felt him lean in closer and it made me dizzy. "Look at me."

I met his eyes with mine, and then his gaze traveled down to my lips. Of all the male egotistical, crappiest things to do, he was trying to use my grief to get me to kiss him! *I swear, if he leans in and tries to kiss me, I'll bite his lip right off!*

His eyes lifted back up to meet mine. He had to have seen the disgusted expression on my face. "It is what it is. You said nothing that affected me Shane. Thanks for the condolences for my brother. And, do yourself a favor, don't bother trying to mess with my head, it'll be a waste of your time. I won't sleep with you. Just treat me like one of the guys and we'll get along fine and then you won't have to stand over me in a kitchen pretending you give a shit about anyone other than yourself."

He blinked and hesitated for what seemed like an eternity. Then a devilish smile crept across his face, "Who said I wanted to sleep with you? You're just one of the guys. I don't *do* guys."

I burst into laughter and matched his smile. Leave it to an egotistical man to make a joke about it.

He slid his hands off the countertop and dropped them to his sides. His smile lingered for just a moment and he backed away. "Although, I have to admit. You are the sexist guy I've ever met."

The totally goofy grin that was plastered on his face right before he walked out of the kitchen made being mad at him almost impossible. *Almost*.

After a few minutes, the four of us converged back into the living room and hung ourselves over the furniture. For some odd reason, Shane and I found ourselves sitting next to each other on the couch. Lea was cuddled on Conner's lap in one of the chairs, and she was spastically flipping through the channels on the television. Shane was continuously texting someone, or a bunch of someones, and smiling like an ass.

Every so often, he'd read a message from off his phone and brush his arm against me and laugh. I forced myself to ignore him, but he still hadn't put his shirt on and the closeness of him made me want to reach out and feel his skin. He really was ridiculously beautiful. Too bad, he wasn't much more then eye candy.

Another twenty minutes was all I could stand. I jumped up, grabbed my sneakers, and put them on.

Lea sat up. "Where are you going? We were going to go to the bar again tonight around ten." She gave a nod towards Shane. "His band is playing another gig there. Want to hang out again? I'll let you get drunk this time and hold your hair back," she pleaded.

I tightened my laces and stood up. "I'm getting antsy. I thought I'd go for a run."

Shane put his phone on the table and watched me.

"Well, what about hanging with me tonight? We haven't seen each other in six months, I missed you!" Lea whined.

"I don't know. I'll see how I feel after my run. If you're not here when I get back, I'll text you." I hurried out of the room and out of the front door. *I just needed to be outside.*

The minute I turned around to stretch my legs against my front steps, Shane was standing right next to me. I rolled my eyes and ignored him.

That is until he started stretching alongside me. "What are you doing?" I asked.

"I thought I'd run with you," he said laughing a little. "I figured you wouldn't care; you know, since you're just one of the guys, and this is what I do with the guys. Unless you don't think you could handle it."

Mentally flipping him the bird I smiled sweetly, "I'll try my best." I took off running along the street and headed towards Fifth Avenue; hooked a right and sped passed the Metropolitan Museum of Art. It had been a little over six months, but I could do this run in my sleep. Even at the hospice, I ran at least ten miles a day at the gym, just to separate myself from what was happening. I took up running after my accident when they taught me how to walk again in rehab and I never stopped. Running is as natural to me as breathing now.

Once in Central Park, I started on the Reservoir Loop around the Jacqueline Kennedy Onassis Reservoir. Shane kept pace with me silently. The only sound I focused on was my feet hitting the soft cinder pathway. My eyes stayed focused ahead of me, never once acknowledging Shane next to me.

The Jackie O Loop is about 1.5 miles long, and as soon I completed it, I started on one of the full loops through Central Park along the East side. I vaguely remembered each loop being about five miles long. I ran them twice. I think I hit my runner's high twice; it was pure bliss. Starting the second loop, my mind took over; my soul pushing me forward as it always does, my body just a machine.

Shane kept pace still. I decided that he wasn't human.

I ran through the 86th Street Transverse, out onto Fifth Ave, and slowed my pace. I continued to slow until I was cooled down and walking; breathing evenly. I walked towards my apartment steps, only then noticing night had fallen and the temperature had dropped to around 35 degrees. I stretched my legs against my steps; still remaining silent.

I guessed Shane was somewhere behind me doing the same thing. I didn't care to look at him until he cleared his throat, seemingly to get my attention.

I spun around to face him. He stood in the middle of the sidewalk glaring at me in what looked like disbelief.

"You're a runner, huh?"

I made a stupid face at him. "I said I was going for a run. You assumed that I wasn't man enough?" I snapped.

Shane shook his head at me and gave me an amused expression. "Not many people surprise me, Grace, but you just surprised the shit outta me."

Ignoring his statement, I got out my key and unlocked the front door.

I heard him sigh behind me. "Did my heart love till now? Forswear it sight, for I ne'er saw true beauty 'til this night," he murmured.

My hand released its grip from the doorknob and I looked back at him. One arm rested on the railing of the stairs, the other lay over his heart.

"Shakespeare," I whispered.

He nodded a sad smile at me and turned to walk away.

I opened the front door and stepped halfway inside.

"Hey, you coming to the bar tonight?" he called out after me.

I stopped and turned around, "Maybe, I don't know. I have to see how I feel after a shower."

A smile burst onto his face, making him more stunning than it was humanly possible. "Do you need help with that? I'd like to see how you feel after a shower too..."

I slammed the door on him, but I couldn't help smiling. *Crap*.

Less than an hour later, I was dressed in a pair of jeans, an off the shoulder sweater that Lea forced me to put on, and a pair of knee high leather boots that I had forgotten I bought last winter.

I was then locked in the bathroom and again forced to endure a complete hair and face make-over from Lea, who decided it would be her mission to get me to look, as she so eloquently put, *doable*.

My jet-black hair looked bouncy and wild, and she did the makeup around my eyes to make them look smoky and sexy. *Oh dear God, even I wanted to take me home!* She wasn't going to stop until I went out on a date with someone.

This wasn't the first time she did this either, it was probably more like the fifth. Each time, I ended up going out with some guy who was nice, but who just wasn't for me. I hated this game.

"Lea, I don't want to try to impress anyone, this isn't me," I said.

She rolled her eyes so expressively I thought they were going to pop out of her head. "Gray, I could cover your face in shit and make you wear tampons as earrings and you still would be the hottest girl in the bar. Besides me, of course."

"So why am I getting all dressed up. Where's the shit and tampons?"

She slapped me across the shoulder playfully. "Look, I just think you need to feel a little sexy and try to live a little, that's all." She sat down on the edge of the bathtub and a serious expression crossed her face. "Gray, all you got is me now. I just want you to have fun. Make this life the best you ever had. And, you know who was asking a ton of questions about you?"

I pretended to care, "Hmm...who?"

"Tucker. He's gorgeous, isn't he?"

"Sure. Come on. Let's go have some fun." I said pulling her out of the bathroom.

When we walked into the bar, the guys were already there. Tucker and Conner sat with their backs to the empty stage and waved at us. Shane was sitting on the right of them in between the longhaired drummer and bass player of his band. Leaning against his chair with a beer in one hand and his guitar in the other, he looked relaxed. I hoped that he was utterly exhausted from the run; it would serve him right.

Tucker stood up when we got to the table and gave me a broad smile. It made me want to throw up, and I didn't even understand why. Conner grabbed our coats and put them on the back of various chairs.

"Grace, you didn't get to meet the rest of the guys last night. Of course, you know Tucker and Conner," Lea said, sounding oh-so-dorky. "This is Ethan, the drummer," she pointed to an extremely blond guy who looked to be the size of two NFL football players. He saluted me with a drumstick. "And, this is Brayden, the bass player, and you know Shane already." Brayden nodded at Shane and me. Well, Shane just stared at me saying nothing. I chuckled inside; the run must have gotten to him!

The last band member, who was introduced as Alex, showed up with a huge bucket of ice-cold beers for everyone.

Lea grabbed me by the hand and shoved me into the seat next to Tucker, who promptly handed me a beer. I tried to twist my face into a smile. This was going to be a long night.

Tucker leaned closer to me and whispered into my ear, "You look incredible."

I leaned back and smiled. "Thank you." He was sweet. Very attractive too, but he just wasn't…well, I guess I'd give him a chance. *A small one*. I looked up to see Shane watching me. He didn't take his eyes off of me until the drummer, Ethan, hit him on the head with one of his drumsticks to let him know they needed to be on stage. Shane was definitely not used to a girl saying no to him. He looked pissed at me. *Oh well.*

"What the hell was that look?" Lea asked when Shane got up to leave. He had to have heard her, but he didn't acknowledge the question.

Tucker leaned in smiling, "Well, take a look at her, she's beautiful. Of course, Shane is going to look at her!"

I shook my head. "No. I think he's pissed at me. I sort of told him off this afternoon and then he challenged me to a run."

Lea's eyes widened. "He ran with you?"

I nodded my head and laughed.

Tucker and Conner both looked confused. "Why is that so funny?"

"I made him run about twenty miles without stopping. I didn't jog either. I ran. I think he's pissed, because his ego got a little wounded."

The guys burst out laughing. "That's awesome!"

A moment later, the emcee was introducing Mad World again and the crowd tripled before my eyes and went wild. Shane's unbelievably sexy voice cut through the noise of the screaming audience and silenced them. The power his voice had over everyone was crazy.

The music was absolutely moving. Whether they played a fast or slow song, they were talented. I found myself ignoring the conversations I was involved in with everyone at the table just to hear the words to the songs or the sweet chords thundering from Shane's guitar.

I was grateful when Tucker left to use the bathroom. I stood up and watched Mad World play. A slow piano melody drifted softly to my ears, I closed my eyes and listened. Lea walked over and grabbed my hand.

"Come on, Gray, let's go up and watch them. This is one of my favorite songs."

We made it up to the stage without getting into any brawls like the night before. I laughed at the thought. Lea stopped in front of Shane and he winked at her. As Alex played his keyboard, Shane walked to the back of the small stage, grabbed a guitar, and started playing an intricate melody.

My breath caught in my lungs. Shane was playing a twelve-string double neck harp guitar.

Lea watched my expression. I looked at her with my eyes wide. "Yeah, I know right, Shane's freaking talented." She laughed. "Gray, close your mouth, you're drooling. I would tell you to take a chance on that kid, but he's just as fucked up as you are. I just thought you'd get a kick out of him playing that. I figured you are the only other person on this planet to know what that instrument is."

Shane poured his soul into the rhythm, blending the notes perfectly with Alex's classical piano melody. You couldn't hear anything from the crowd of people who were watching the band, awestruck. Ethan slowly started a beat and Brayden's bass collided with the soulful sound of Shane's voice.

I stand there

And no one knew me

I reach for her

She looks right through me

I can search this world over

She can't see me

I drown in tears

They look right through me

From behind me, a strong hand grasped my shoulder and Tucker's face appeared next to my cheek. "I was wondering where you went. Do you want to dance?"

Without waiting for my answer, he spun me around and wrapped his hands around my shoulders. Conner had already grabbed Lea and she winked at me. I gave in and danced, swaying to the music.

When the song ended, Shane said goodnight to the crowd and bras and panties were thrown onto the stage. Shane grabbed a black lacy bra and held it up to his nose and the crowd roared. The band jumped off the stage and they were immediately surrounded by a group of blonde half-naked girls.

Canned music drifted from the speakers and people started dancing again, blocking my view of the band.

Tucker and Conner dragged us back to the table where Lea and I decided we should play a drinking game called Fuzzy Duck. It was definitely time to let loose.

Lea and I got the bartenders attention and he brought two bottles of Tequila and grabbed a handful of shot glasses. We got back to the table where each band member had returned to the table; each one had a hot blonde on their lap, except for Shane. He had two. I shook my head, smiled and raised the bottles of Tequila over my head.

"Okay, ladies and gentlemen, here's the first drinking game of the night. Fuzzy Duck!" I announced.

Everyone stared at me.

"Fuzzy Duck?" Tucker asked.

"Yes, Tucker. I said Fuzzy Duck," I replied. "Here are the rules. Everyone starts by taking one shot. Then we pour another. We go around the table and each person has to say Fuzzy Duck. The first person who messes up has to take a shot and around and around we go!"

"Fuzzy Duck?" Tucker asked. Again.

"Yes, Tucker. I said FUZZY DUCK."

I filled all the shot glasses and we all took a shot. The first round was hard. Not all the groupies could remember what they were supposed to say. Within an hour, and two more drinking games, everyone was pretty much buzzed; the blonde groupies more so than everyone else.

They fell over each other laughing and giggling. One of the girls who had occupied Shane's lap was aptly named Barbie. She abruptly caused the end of our drinking games when she heard a song she liked and began giving Shane a lap dance in front of everyone.

Lea rolled her eyes and pretended to dry heave. She threw a fistful of waded up napkins in their direction, hitting Barbie in the head. "Holy Strippers, Batman! Are you that desperate to make sure he goes home with you?"

Barbie didn't stop and she pretended not to hear Lea's question. She ground herself into Shane's lap, grabbing his hands and placing them over the edges of her hiked up skirt. He grabbed into the flesh on her legs and she arched back and let out a high-pitched moan. *Oh, crap.*

"Maybe she just needs a few dollar bills?" I said. Everyone laughed. But it didn't stop her. She moved his hands up over her breasts, and then making it worse, the other blonde who had been sitting on his lap before joined in too. Spikes of heat flamed through me. *No. This should not affect me.*

"Ah! Change the porn channel! You're gonna give me an STD over here!" Lea shouted.

That made Barbie stop and stand up. She put her hands on her hips, which made us all laugh because her skirt was still hiked up and we all saw her neon pink thong. "Why don't you mind your own business, skank!"

"Skank? Me? I'm not the one giving a guy I just met a lap dance in public." Lea jumped to her feet.

Barbie backed off a step and started to say something, but Lea cut her off. "Don't even try, because you might find me smacking the slut out of you in a minute!"

The song changed into one I knew and I pulled Lea towards the dance floor. "Let's dance. Who cares what she's doing."

With one hand on me, Lea grabbed for Conner with the other. "Well, I care. My boyfriend is watching it!" Conner didn't seem fazed though, which made me think he was probably used to Shane and his many friends.

Tucker followed us to the dance floor and we all moved to the music together. Well, all except for Tucker, who sort of bounced back and forth against the music. Lea and I giggled into each other, watching him and his Stereotypical White Guy Dance, forgetting about Shane and the blonde airhead Barbie.

We left after a few songs, and Conner and Tucker walked us home. When we rounded our corner, I started to feel nervous. Tucker was probably going to try to kiss me. The kiss didn't worry me as much as the feeling behind it. Would I feel anything? Or, would it be like every other time when I felt nothing but hollow; empty?

Lea fumbled with the keys to the front door as Conner gave her tiny butterfly kisses on the back of her neck. She laughed, opened the door and pulled him in by the collar. They disappeared into the darkness of the hallway and probably headed straight for her room.

I hesitated on the first step. Torn between finally wanting to feel whole again and yet knowing I never would. I climbed to the top step with Tucker right behind me. I swear time slowed as I turned to face him. His hand was already against my chin pulling me forward. His eyes gazed into mine; warm chocolate. I wanted to feel something; I wanted the longing to be over. Closing his eyes, he touched his lips to mine. *Dry and chapped.* His body leaned into mine, his tongue separating my lips. His kiss turned strong and rough, with the edge of his teeth sharp and lusty.

He pulled back and we held each other's gaze. A lifetime of averageness flashed before my eyes. Despair and sadness seeped through my veins. *Law firms, stuffy office parties, civil ceremony, miscarriages, suffering.* Not that he wouldn't love me enough, I just would never love him enough, and he would never be faithful. Why settle for something like that, when you've tasted heaven and you'll always know what you're missing? *I was still alone in this life.*

Tucker smiled down at me as if he had felt something different. "I'm sure you hear this every day, but you have the most beautiful eyes I've ever seen. They're almost silver."

All I could offer was a half-smile. I clutched his jacket tighter in fear that I might run and never come back. All I could think of was Lea and how I couldn't hurt her like that. Nevertheless, I wanted this life to be over. I would never stop longing for something that would never be real. The emptiness in my soul was physically painful.

Why couldn't Tucker be the one I've waited for?

"Could I take you out for dinner next weekend? Just you and me?" he whispered as he planted little kisses on my nose and my cheek. *Any girl would be happy about this!*

"Like a date?" I moved back, trying subtly to stop the continuous kissing. "Um...sure. That sounds...nice."

He smiled wide and waited for me to say something else. Did he think I was going to invite him in? God, the thought of sleeping with him made me want to gag. Don't get me wrong, my body was up for it, but my mind was screaming obscenities at it. Shane's haunting lyrics played in my mind.

I stand there

And no one knew me

I reach for her

She looks right through me

I can search this world over

She can't see me

I drown in tears

They look right through me

That's how it felt. As if Tucker looked right through me, I was invisible. He couldn't see the real me standing in front of him, just the body of a pretty girl with light gray eyes.

I was trapped; imprisoned.

I backed up and tried to give him my best Oscar winning smile. "I can't wait." I moved closer to the door and turned the knob.

For a split second, Tucker looked disappointed and then contentment covered his face. "Great. How about Friday night around seven? I'll pick you up."

I pulled myself through the front door. "Sounds like a date! I'll see you then. Goodnight, Tucker." I closed the door on him, but not before seeing another flash of disappointment cross his face.

I leaned my back against the door and hung my head in my hands. I don't even know how long I stood there. The only reason I remembered to move was because I heard Lea and Conner laughing from her bedroom.

The sounds of their happiness made my insides ache. I glanced at the clock; it was almost two in the morning. If it wasn't so early I'd run. I probably wouldn't even make it a mile. Best thing to do was sleep; figuring I'd weigh my options on what to do with Tucker in the morning.

I opened my bedroom door and froze. An icy cold breeze blew my curtains gently; casting shadows across the room from the moonlight. I flicked my light on; I never left my window open. Gabriel lay sprawled across my bed, his hands folded behind his head.

Relief flushed through me. I was afraid it might have been Tucker waiting for me.

"Gabriel," I greeted him. "What did you do, climb the fire escape? You couldn't use the front door?"

Gabriel frowned. "You were busy at the front door. You didn't even notice me standing on the sidewalk. How was your kiss? I thought you might vomit on the poor boy."

"Hmmm. Yeah, I guess I almost did. Do you think he noticed?"

"Mr. Kissy face? No, Grace. He's way too captivated by…what does he call it…your smokin' hot bod, to notice." The only emotion he showed was a slight hint of amusement.

"Yeah, I figured. Geez, did you really hear him say that about me?"

He ignored my question. He reached for my guitar case, opened it gently and took my guitar out. Closing his eyes, he strummed the strings creating a melancholy composition that hurt to listen to. The notes silently sung of longing and need. Tears filled my eyes.

"Why are you here, Gabriel?"

His eyes opened and the color in them made me want to curl into a ball and die a thousand deaths. They reminded me of the one I searched and longed for.

"I just wanted to see how you were. You looked fine outside. Moving along in your life, I see."

"Get out." I whispered. I walked over to where he lay and took my guitar from his hands. "Get out and don't come back. Ever." I placed my guitar back inside its case, and a million thoughts ran through my head of how I could possibly get away from all of this.

He was next to me in an instant, grabbing me by the shoulders. My skin burned uncomfortably under his touch. He forced me to look into his eyes.

"Gabriel, please. Leave. You can try to spin whatever you want to what I do, but I'm done. I want this to be over. I can't do this anymore. I'm looking for someone that doesn't exist; *he* doesn't exist. If I have to keep doing this, just let me quietly exist without coming here and making me question things further."

"Grace, you have never and will never quietly exist. You shine on earth as if the sun was born here. You have been a beacon for all of humanities sufferings and exhilarations." His voice became a whisper, "And you, my dear, have been steadfast in your belief of finding something that I know for a fact, does still exist."

His words brought me to my knees and I crashed to the floor. "Please, Gabriel. Please tell me where he is." I pleaded.

Embracing me tightly, he whispered against my cheek, his lips just brushing against my skin. "I've told you too much already, Grace. Just live this life of yours."

My head spun franticly. "Please, Gabriel. Please!" I begged. But in an instant, he was gone. Out the window, through the door, or into thin air, I had no clue. My heart pounded against my chest, remembering the words Gabriel said to me. I wondered what his punishment would be for helping me keep my faith.

Sleep came swiftly and heavy. Tucker's kisses and Shane's hands on Barbie haunted my dreams until my body could take no more of it and I woke at six. Three hours of sleep was not nearly enough, but my body wouldn't let me stay in bed any longer.

I slipped on my running gear and headed towards the front door. I ran down the steps and almost tripped over Shane who was sitting on the last step.

"Ouch!" He scrambled to his feet as I ran into him.

"What the hell are you doing here?" I demanded.

"I was going for a run and I thought you or Conner would be up for one."

I laughed. "Conner won't be up for a while. Shane, did you even sleep? I only got like three hours."

His face flushed. "Nah, I'll sleep later. I have too much energy."

I smiled, "Wow, that must have been a really great lap dance, huh?"

"Shut up!" he muttered elbowing me. He started running towards Central Park and I followed, laughing. Gabriel gave me hope last night and nothing Shane would do could make me feel bad.

We repeated the same trail as the day before, our feet hitting the ground in unison creating a calming rhythmic cadence.

Less than three hours later, we collapsed sweaty and exhausted on my couch. Shane aimed the remote toward the television and flicked through the channels. We settled on some unknown comedy show and laughed uncontrollably at the jokes we heard. That's exactly how Conner and Lea found us when they woke up and stumbled, groggy from sleep, into the room. Shane and I slumped over the couch, both of us sweaty, panting and laughing.

"Oh my God! Did you two just have sex out here? Ewww. Grace! Come on, Shane really?" Lea yelled.

We laughed even harder. "What? You seriously think that we just had sex? Here on the couch?" I asked.

Shane looked at Conner and gave him a thumb up. "Dude, if you guys look like this after you guys get freaky, that's awesome. But, no we just came back from a run. I wouldn't touch Grace if you paid me. She's really a man."

Shane stood up still chuckling. "I'm starving. Grace, you hungry, bro? I'll make you breakfast."

I narrowed my eyes at him, immediately suspicious. *What could this man possibly make me for breakfast?* "Are you even capable of pouring cereal into a bowl?"

He arched one eyebrow at my joke; eyes sparkling. "Are you insulting me?"

I shrugged. "Um. No, not really. It was an honest question."

He walked across the room and theatrically waved his arms toward the kitchen door. "C'mon. You have to be just as hungry as I am after all that sex…I mean all that running."

I threw a pillow at him. He ducked. "Oh, so now you're saying you *do* have sex with guys?" I laughed, following him into the kitchen.

Most of Shane's body was already deep in the refrigerator piling stuff into his arms. When he was satisfied with what he found, he dropped it all on the counter and reached for a frying pan. "So, honestly, why did you think I wouldn't be able to cook?" He was facing the stove pouring a cap full of vegetable oil into the pan, so I couldn't see his expression. He cracked three eggs at a time right into the pan. *I wonder how many shells just dropped in there?*

He flipped the top of the garbage pail open, tossed the shells in, and repeated the process. After chopping, dicing and adding all the ingredients, he turned the burner on. He lifted his sweatshirt over his head and wiped the sweat off his forehead with it.

Oh dear God, he *is* perfect! A large black tribal tattoo that began as a dragon at his elbow curled around his right shoulder and traveled onto his shoulder blade. The thick black tribal strokes exquisitely turning into a dove, wrapping its wings around itself. His skin was a soft bronze stretched over the ridged hardness of his muscles. It was completely understandable how girls threw themselves at him. I pitied him, wondering if he'd ever feel anything more than the sensations of his own skin.

He got out two plates from the cabinet as if he owned the kitchen. *Geez, how many times has he cooked in this kitchen in the last six months?*

Placing one plate in front of me and another in front of him, he sat down and shoved a fork full of food into his mouth. "Spinach, mushroom, green pepper and cheese omelet ala Shane," he said between chews. "You haven't answered me. What is it about me that made you think I can't cook?"

I stabbed the omelet with my fork and took a bite. *Crap, it was delicious.* "You just strike me as a shallow person who gets everything they want from other people. I would have bet that you've had a different blonde make you breakfast every morning of your life."

He gave me an amused look. "Well, you're half right. I am shallow, but I can cook, and honestly, I like chicks with jet black hair better than blondes," he laughed. His icy blue eyes regarded me. "Well? Is it good?"

Best freaking omelet I've ever had. I stopped the words from fumbling out of my mouth. "Yeah, sure. Thanks. I didn't realize how hungry I was," I grumbled.

He shoved another fork full of food in his mouth and chewed. He leaned forward with a serious expression on his face, "So, what's the deal with you? What's with the intense Shane revulsion? I've never had a girl not jump at the chance with me. Or, wait, are you into chicks?"

I laughed at his audacity. "So you think because I'm not falling for your crap that I'm a lesbian?"

"Bi? Maybe just playing hard to get?"

"You really are full of yourself. Brace yourself Shane, this might be hard to hear," I teased. "But you just don't do it for me. Sorry."

Shane's eyes brightened at my words. "So, who *does it* for you then?" He purposefully drew out the words, making me shake my head.

I stood up and placed my plate into the dishwasher. I leaned back, rested my elbows on the counter, and thought for a minute. "Someone who doesn't think of me as a walking vagina."

He howled with laughter. "A walking vagina! Oh, shit, if only there was such a thing!" He was laughing so hard he had to wipe tears from his eyes.

I smiled. "And what's your deal? What happened to you making you think that women were put here just to serve you? Maybe something happened that makes you so insecure that you would be incapable of having a relationship or normal friendship with a girl?"

His smile faded. He stared at me with those eyes. "There's no deep dark reason, no insecurity, nothing to read into. I just don't want anything more from someone. Ever. There is no need for it. Every girl I sleep with knows my intentions clearly. They want to fuck the lead singer of Mad World, so I give them want they want and get what I want from them. There's no need for more. None of them are worth more than that."

That was so sad.

He stood up, stretched his arms over his head, and yawned loudly. "So, what do you do? Where were you living all this time?" he asked, immediately ending his sad monologue.

I squirmed, not meaning to. "Jobless at the moment. I've been living with my brother in a hospice for the last few months, so my job was just trying to make him comfortable."

A sympathetic expression passed across his face. It didn't fit his self-proclaimed moral free ideals, making me think that there was way more to Shane Maxton than a pretty faced lead singer. But, what did it matter? I had my own problems, my own past to deal with, and I was positive mine was more unbelievable than his was.

"That's heavy. What about your parents? Did everybody in your family just move there to be with him?"

"Nope. My parents are both dead. It was just me and Jake." I wanted this Spanish inquisition off me. "How about you? What's your family like? Where are you from, what do you do?"

"Normal family. They all live in Florida now. Nothing dysfunctional. My parents are still married, no one had dependency problems, and no one ever hit me," he said flatly. "And being the lead singer for Mad World really pays all my bills." He seemed curt and uncomfortable.

I nodded. "Hmm. Sounds like you're put together all nicely. Even though you're standing here having a difficult time having an innocently normal conversation with someone of the opposite sex, knowing that there is no way in hell I'd ever sleep with you. No, Shane, you're not dysfunctional in any way." I pushed myself off the counter and walked out of the kitchen, done with the stupidity of our discussion.

Shane knocked the kitchen chairs against each other trying to make sure he'd get the last word in, "Hold on!" he yelped.

"Save it for someone who actually would care about what you had to say, Shane," I called from the next room.

I locked myself in my room, inserted my iPod into its speaker dock and melted into oblivion when the first sounds of music touched my ears. I was determined to spend this entire Sunday in bed, reliving Gabriel's words repeatedly in my head.

Chapter 5

The force of the front door smashing into the wall, causing the entire apartment to shake, jarred me from my sleep. I peered over at the window, dusk was settling. The neon red numbers on my clock said it was only four in the afternoon. *Ugh! I just wanted to sleep until next week!*

I listened at the door, wanting to make sure I wouldn't be walking out into a private spat between Lea and Conner. When I heard Shane's voice, I rolled my eyes. I laughed to myself. *Well, it can't be anything serious then.*

Still in my comfortable flannel pajamas, I walked into the living room. The whole band was there, bickering between each other, while Lea and Conner tried to make sense of what was going on. Alex the other guitarist and keyboardist of the band sat in the middle of all the commotion with both arms in casts.

Everyone stopped and looked at me when I came in. "Are you seriously wearing teddy bear pajamas?" Alex asked me. He raised one eyebrow, "That is incredibly adorable and sexy."

I couldn't help but smile and I lifted up my slippers to amuse him further. I pointed to them, "Complete with my comfy teddy bear slippers. What in the world is going on in here? Why are both your arms in casts?"

Brayden threw his hands into the air. "This loser spent the morning in the hospital after getting his ass kicked last night!"

I took a closer look at poor Alex's face. His bottom lip was red and swollen, there was a cut above his left eye, and reddish-purplish bruises were forming over both his cheeks and across his nose. *Ouch.*

"Holy Crap!" I yelled. "What the hell happened?"

"Seems that one of the bimbos from last night had a boyfriend. That said boyfriend introduced himself to Alex by way of his fists and a baseball bat," Lea said, handing out bottles of water and bowls of chips to everyone. *When did she become the model hostess?*

"A baseball bat?" I asked.

Alex's cheeks turned redder. "Yeah. The dude jumped out on me from the closet with the bat. I threw my hands up to block it and he broke both of my arms."

"Please tell me the boyfriend looks worse," I pleaded.

Ethan's deep laugh echoed throughout the room. He really was the biggest guy I had ever seen here, maybe 6' 7" and his voice matched. His pin straight long hair was so blond it was almost white. He reminded me of the guys in those hair bands from the 90s. "I think maybe Alex hit him with some splatters of blood, but that's about it!"

Everyone laughed, even Alex. *Well, no, not everyone.* Not Shane. Shane stood leaning against the front door with his arms and legs crossed. He had an angry expression on his face. "Yeah, well, that's all really funny, but who is going to play rhythm guitar this weekend, or next? Or, how about the week after that? Who the hell are we going to find who can play as good as Alex, *and* play his keyboard, sing, *and* learn all the fucking songs before Friday night?"

Once again, Shane's voice silenced a room. This time, it wasn't with the sounds of his singing, but with the anger, he had for a friend. *Jackass!*

Lea gave me a sideways glance.

I grimaced at her, warning her to keep me out of the situation.

Conner motioned for Shane to calm down. Impressively, he took control of the whole situation. "Listen, it's only Sunday. We have until Friday night. You know that there are shit loads of guitar players in New York City that have your CDs, knowing your music by heart. Let's ask around, make some flyers and have a small audition on, let's say, Thursday. You guys can pick the best player. You definitely won't find anyone who can play the piano and the guitar like Alex, but just don't do the songs that call for both. Alex, how long do you have to have the casts on?"

"Six weeks or so," he answered.

"Okay, so it's only for a few weeks. Just think of the exposure it'll get you with having auditions. If that's not good for you guys, then cancel the next six weekends. Take a break," Conner offered in all his level headedness.

Shane grumbled in the corner like a child. The rest of the band considered what Conner had said.

"We can always get Tucker to do it. It's been a while, but I bet he remembers how to play," Ethan said.

I followed Lea into the kitchen when she went to get more water. "Okay, number one, why the hell are you serving them like that? Are you now studying for a career in waitressing? And number two, isn't this like a personal band thing, why are they here talking about this? Don't they have like an entire apartment building they live in? And number three, Tucker can play the guitar?"

She offered me a goofy grin. "They always come to Conner for advice. He's the smartest one in the bunch."

"A raisin would be the smartest one in that bunch, Lea," I cut her off with a laugh. "Sorry, I didn't mean to cut you off. I couldn't pass that up, continue please."

"They have all known each other from high school. They were all in the high school band together in ninth grade. Conner used to play with them too. And they always end up coming here. Conner's here a lot. It makes me crazy, if I know they are having weird band orgy parties there and Conner is with them."

"Lea, have they ever had weird band orgy parties where they live?" I asked.

"No, but they might. Grace, I really like Conner and I don't want him to lose interest in me and end up with some random..."

"I got it. I'm not complaining that Conner is here. He's awesome, Lea, he is. And don't you dare volunteer me for anything to do with playing my guitar for them! I saw that face you made!"

She made a pouty face at me. "They may be jerks sometimes, but they are really great guys, even Shane."

"Even Shane what?" Shane's voice cut in.

Lea and I jumped at the sound of his voice. Lea composed herself quicker than I did. "We were just wondering what we could do to help, that's all? Um, how long were you standing there?"

His face gave nothing away. "Long enough to know that we are jerks, but really great guys, even me." He glanced at me.

Lea chuckled, "Yep, that's how I feel about you guys in a nutshell. So what can I do to help?"

He tilted his head. "Do you have markers and paper, so we can make some posters and put them up in all the local bars."

Lea jumped to it. She flew through the apartment gathering supplies for her little art project.

We ordered pizza and we all sat around and colored flyers for the auditions. We looked like a group of five year olds on a play date. When I mentioned that out loud, all hell broke loose.

Alex's face scrunched up and he shouted, "Brayden picks his nose and eats it!"

Almost choking on a bite of pizza, Brayden shouted, "Alex has got the cooties!"

"So we look like five years old, huh?" Ethan asked coming up behind me. He grabbed me in a gentle headlock and gave me noogies on my head.

I screamed and ran for my water bottle, and poured it all over Ethan's head. "Oh no," I teased. "Ethan just wet himself!"

Conner opened his water bottle up next and poured it all down the front of Lea's shirt. She screamed and tackled him, and poured the contents of her water bottle down the front of his pants.

Brayden climbed onto the coffee table and mooned everyone.

Shane just sat, watching the antics with a mischievous grin on his face. He held a full water bottle in his hand, cap off, eyes blazing at me. *Oh, crap!*

Our eyes locked and he sprang at me like a cougar on its prey. I tried to get out of the way, but I slammed into the now disabled Alex, who was chanting for Shane to get me. Thank God, his open water bottle flew out of his hands in the opposite direction of me. I bounced off Alex and landed sprawled out over Shane. I held my arms out over him, trying not to touch his body. Without a moment of hesitation, he flipped me over onto my back and while laughing, he pinned me down. Alex kicked over a closed water bottle to him and he fumbled for it. Grabbing it with his right hand, he brought it up to his mouth and tried to open it with his teeth.

I bucked hard underneath him, but he was so solid, I couldn't move him. He bent down, with his face hovering next to mine, and whispered, "She is a mortal danger to all men. She is beautiful without knowing it, and possesses charms that she's not even aware of. She is like a trap set by nature - a sweet perfumed rose in whose petals Cupid lurks in ambush! Anyone who has seen her smile has known perfection. She instills grace in every common thing and divinity in every careless gesture. Venus in her shell was never so lovely, and Diana in the forest never so graceful as you." He lifted his head slightly and his eyes looked deep into mine.

"Cyrano De Bergerac, Shane? For a self-serving man-whore, you know way too many romantic quotes," I whispered back. *How in the world would someone like Shane know a quote like that?*

I tried to move again, electricity shooting up through my body. *Oh my!* I grabbed the only thing I could, my slice of pizza, and smashed it in his face laughing.

He rolled off me laughing just as hard. "Oh shit, she got me good!"

For good measure, I threw a slice at Alex, catching him right in the middle of his forehead, where it stuck. Everyone was howling with laughter.

That is, until Lea screamed, "Who the hell is going to get the cheese off the ceiling?"

It took us an hour to clean up the mess that took us five minutes to make. We definitely acted like five year olds. However, we all laughed and we had a plan to help with the situation they were in. When there was no more cheese to be found on the furniture, we split into pairs to post up the pizza stained flyers.

Shane held the stack of flyers in his hands and gave out the orders as if he was elected president. "Conner and Lea, you guys hit the Bowery Ballroom and the bars around there. Brayden and Ethan, you guys hit the Highline and wherever else you can think of on the West Side. Alex, you go home. Both your arms are broken and you look like an idiot. Grace and I will hit the East side."

He looked over at me and smiled, "Ready?"

I tried to hide my horror of being stuck with him. I don't think I did a great job. "Uh...yeah...sure."

He chuckled, grabbed my coat and handed it to me. "Don't worry, I won't try anything, unless you've change your mind."

I shot him a look.

He put his hands up in the air as if a surrender. "Yeah, Grace I got it. You'll never have sex with me. Right. I know. Maybe I'll make up a few tee-shirts so there'll be no confusion for anyone who thinks my dysfunctional ass can't just innocently flirt."

I put my coat on, stuck my tongue at him and walked out the door with everyone. *Could he even be capable of flirting innocently?*

Shane followed me down the steps and we walked down the block in silence until we got to the corner. "Thank you for helping."

I looked up to him to see his expression, but there was none. No hidden meaning. Just a thank you. "No problem. Conner and his friends are very special to Lea, and I'd do anything for her." I looked ahead again. "Besides, it's just handing out a few flyers. I'm not playing a guitar for him, just helping you guys find someone who can."

"Yeah, that would be a hoot. Watching those delicate little hands of yours playing Alex's heavy riffs, now that would be hysterical to see."

I glanced up at him, but made no attempt to tell him I could play. I walked right over my pride and kept my mouth shut.

Taking Alex's place would cause people to ask questions about my past, and I just needed to move forward to find what I was looking for. Lea's friends were nice enough, but not worth me baring my soul in front of everyone.

We walked through the East side, hitting all the bars that held live bands. He regaled me with stories of all the guys when they were in high school, but never talked about himself. Before I knew it, we were sitting in a quiet corner in Boozer's, sipping beers and snacking on cheese fries with Alex who never went home, just straight to the bar. The waitress had given him a straw for his beer, so he wouldn't hurt himself any further. Not long after we arrived, Conner and Lea showed up. Brayden and Ethan strolled in last, followed by Tucker, who was feverishly trying to explain to the both of them that he couldn't play guitar for them on Friday, because he had a date with the *hottest girl of his dreams*. When he saw me, his cheeks turned deep red. He obviously hadn't known I would be there to hear that.

"Hey, Tucker," I nodded.

Tucker's eyes brightened when I said hello. He smiled broadly. "Hey, Grace." He moved through everyone, pushed Shane's chair over, with him still sitting on it and pulled up a chair next to me. "Hey, Shane, you don't mind right?"

Shane shrugged Tucker off, but for a fleeting second, I saw a tightness settle around his ice blue eyes.

Tucker's expression was full of elation at the sight of me. A brief thought flew through my mind. *Could Tucker be the one I was looking for?* Maybe I needed to give him a chance; maybe I had missed something?

"Wow, Tucker. What are you, like 12?" Alex teased.

Tucker smiled bashfully at me. "Dude, I just want to sit next to the prettiest girl in the bar, that's all."

I smiled up at him. *He couldn't be the one I was looking for, could he? Give him a chance. Give him a chance.*

Alex laughed at him. "Tuck, you think she looks pretty now? God, you should have seen her in her little pink teddy bear pajamas before. It made me start thinking of very indecent things," Alex whistled and gave me a wink.

Tucker looked down at me and raised one eyebrow. "Hmmm. Damn, I miss all the good stuff."

"Oh yeah," Alex continued. "She looked all sweet and innocent. I just wanted to corrupt her."

Lea softly chuckled, watching Alex flirt with me. "Corrupt her? What were you thinking of doing? Show her the smallest penis in the world? Make her dislike men forever?"

Shane choked on his beer laughing. "Yeah, dude. One night with you and she'll run screaming to a convent."

Alex laughed along with Shane, "Ahh. You're probably right. But, sorry Grace, watching you in those little pink pajamas, put pictures in my mind of how freaky I'd get with you."

Everyone laughed.

As always, Lea took it a step further. "So, Alex, what kind of freaky things go on in your place? Hmm? What's the freakiest thing you've ever done?" I think she asked the question to embarrass him, but it didn't work well. His face reddened, his eyes widened, and a huge smile broke out on his face. This was going to be a horrible conversation!

"I love bondage. I'd love to spank you, Lea," he said to embarrass her right back. "But what I'd really love is to know what freaky things you get up to, Lea," Alex replied politely. "And you too, Grace." Somehow, I knew this line of questioning was going to turn to us.

I laughed and gave him a wink.

Conner threw a handful of cheese fries at Alex. "Leave my girl's freakiness outta your thoughts!" He laughed.

Shane leaned across the table and crossed his arms. "Okay, Lea's off limits, because she's Conner's girl. I'd like to hear about Grace, though."

Tucker pushed Shane so hard that he almost shoved him off his chair. "Real nice, ass!"

I glared at Shane, who gave me an innocent look.

With the most serious expression I could make, I joked, "Some of my close friends have called me Black Widow, because after I sleep with someone, I kill them."

Shane looked at me evenly, matching my serious expression, "I have no doubt in my mind that you have had that effect on men, since I feel like I've died every time you've smiled at me."

I looked away and tried to gather up my composure. The way Shane just said what he did had made me feel uncomfortable. It felt more than some guy just trying to get in my pants. I grabbed a few of the empty bottles off the table, walked toward the trash, and tossed them in. I walked up to the bar and ordered something a little harder than beer; I wanted my insides to burn.

"May I have a shot of Jack, please?" I threw a few twenties on the bar. I figured I'd stay at the bar for a few minutes. It felt safer to do a couple of shots than try to figure out why Shane was trying to make me feel uncomfortable. Or, why it was getting me uncomfortable. *How many times have I smiled at him?*

"Hey, you okay?" Tucker's voice materialized beside me. He placed his hand on the small of my back and motioned for the bartender to pour two more shots. "Shane just says things to see how people react to them."

I picked up my second shot and he clinked his glass with mine. "Shane doesn't bother me."

He nodded and smiled down at me, "Well, that's good. He just hardly ever meets a girl that doesn't think he's a rock star. He's a good guy, he just knows that there are a lot of women who want to be with him because of what he does, not who he is. He's not used to beautiful girls not paying attention to him."

I desperately wanted to change the subject. *Why would I want to talk about Shane? Why did everyone around him feel the need to justify the things he does or says to me?* "Talking about rock stars, I heard that you play the guitar." I smiled.

Both his eyebrows raised in a questioning look. "I don't play often anymore. Where did you hear that?"

"Tonight. When the guys were freaking out about what they were going to do about Alex not being able to play. One of the things they said was that maybe you'd help them out, since you used to play with them." I signaled the bartender for another round.

He sighed, "Yeah, but I told them that Friday was out because I have a date. I don't want to cancel on you, Grace."

"Oh. Well, we could make it another night if you'd like to help them."

Tucker searched my face, I didn't know what he was looking for, but his eyes lingered on my lips the longest. "I would still have to audition for the jerks on Thursday."

I downed another shot. Numb. I just wanted to be numb. *Give Tucker a chance.* I wish Jacob were here, so I could have someone to tell about what Gabriel told me. "I wouldn't mind going out another time, Tucker, really."

"Would you like to go out another night this week? How about Wednesday? I could pick you up at like six?"

"That sounds great, Tucker," I lied.

He brought his hand up to my face and caressed my cheek with his hand. "You are so beautiful."

I grabbed another shot and welcomed the numbness. I turned around to walk back and join everyone at the table. Shane was watching me, looking forlorn and sad. My heart sank. *I don't care, I don't care, I won't care*.

"Hey, Tucker," I said pulling him back. "I think I'm going to go on home." I didn't want to be near Shane. I didn't want to ever see such sadness on a beautiful face. And I didn't like feeling that it had something to do with me and I *wanted* to comfort him.

"Sure, Grace. I'll go get your coat and I'll take you home. Are you okay?"

My eyes still held Shane's. "Yeah, Tucker. You know, I was just thinking about how I'd like to be somewhere else with you and not have an audience." I took my eyes off Shane's and looked up at Tucker smiling. *I needed to give him a chance*.

His eyes widened slightly and I swear he licked his lips. "That…that sounds like the best idea I have ever heard. I'll be right back." He ran to get our jackets and I started for the door. *I have to give him a chance*.

Tucker walked me towards his apartment building, but instead of taking me inside, he walked me up to a little red Jaguar XKR. He opened the passenger door and motioned for me to get in.

"Your car? You okay to drive?" I asked as I sighed in relief. I wanted to give Tucker a chance, but the thought of going back to his apartment scared the hell out of me. So I jumped into the car, going for a ride somewhere would be perfect.

"I'm absolutely fine. I thought we could go for a drive," he replied.

The interior of the car smelled like leather and a little too much cologne. I coughed, and my eyes stung.

"Wow, Tucker. This is a really nice car. I take it the lawyer racket pays well?" I joked.

Pulling out into the street, he turned and chuckled along with me. "You can definitely say that. Working for my father's firm, I'll be his partner within a year. So my future is pretty much set." He threw in a hearty laugh, "I just started looking for houses on Long Island. I think I need to get a little break from living with the guys. Some of us have matured a tad more than others."

I smiled at his pride, but inwardly frowned. *Oh, Tucker life can change in an instant.* "Wow, sounds like you have everything all set."

"Yeah, only thing that I've been missing is the beautiful girl, but I think that changed recently." He slowed his car to a stop, still watching me. I had no idea how he didn't crash into something, and as horrible as the thought of having an accident was, at the moment it was more than welcoming. I looked out through the windshield and saw the amazing view of Manhattan's skyline glowing against the dark sky. I hadn't noticed where he drove me, but we were in some sort of scenic parking lot like teenagers.

Tucker turned on his audio system and Joe Cocker's voice wafted through the speakers. "You are so beautiful to me." *Oh my God, I hated this song.*

Before I could even ask him to change the song, even though I had a strong feeling his whole playlist would be cheesy love songs, he leaned across the seat and kissed me. I was completely taken off guard and I gasped. He pulled me closer to him and let out a soft moan. *Give him a chance.*

"You are so beautiful to me," he sung the words into my lips. His tongue slipped into my mouth, while his hands deftly unzipped my jacket.

He leaned into me harder and I fell back against the window. His hot chapped lips traveled along my jaw, down my neck, lingering on my collarbone. I tried to push him away from me, but his kisses never stopped. His hands roamed all over me, lifting up my shirt, grabbing at me roughly with one hand, and ripping the button of my pants off with the other. The button went sailing through the car, smacking against his windshield. He tried to thrust his hand down the front of my pants. *Worst moves ever.*

Fast images flashed through my thoughts, someone smashing the car door open, screaming at Tucker to get off me; the one I've been looking for. *I wish.*

"Uh, Tucker. Whoa." I whispered.

He sat back immediately. "Grace, I'm, I'm sorry," he stammered. "I don't know what came over me." He reached out and lifted my chin to look in my eyes. "It's just that you drive me crazy. You are so beautiful and I want to be with you." He grabbed the back of his neck and rubbed it. "Grace, the way you were kissing me, I thought you wanted me too."

I sat up and fixed my shirt. I watched as irritation settled around his eyes. "I'm sorry, Tucker. This is just going too fast, that's all. I really am not the kind of girl who likes to get mauled over in a parked car," I said.

"I'm sorry. I just really wanted to be with you. I wanted to be with you before one of the other guys got to you. You've seen Shane look at you," he said flatly.

"Shane doesn't want me. He just wants another hole he hasn't stuck himself in yet. Tucker, do you really think it would be okay to have sex with me in a car? After knowing me for a whole...what...three days? Is that what you think of me?"

"Holy shit, Grace, no. No way. I'm so sorry." He flicked his hand through his hair and looked away. "I just really like you a lot. Please, give me another chance. Let me still take you out to dinner on Wednesday, and I promise I won't try anything."

"No harm done. Well, maybe just to my jeans, but sure, I'll still have dinner with you." I tried to give him a smile.

"I just ruined my chances with you, didn't I?" he whispered.

I turned my gaze from him and looked straight ahead at the expanse of the beautiful twinkling city laid out before me. *How could I explain anything to him?*

"Look, Tucker, I just haven't been with anyone for a long time, that's all. I'm rusty at this, and honestly, I kind of planned out my life without having any men involved in it," I grimaced.

"What? Why?"

"Let's just say, I once had my heart ripped from my soul. This isn't easy for me," I explained.

Tucker shook his head in understanding. "Sorry, Grace. I'll be much better behaved next time," he smiled. "I'll take you home, okay?"

Just like that, he pulled his little red jaguar out onto the street and sped towards the city. To my surprise, he didn't ask about my past or who broke my heart. I was thankful for the reprieve, but couldn't stop myself from thinking that he was selfish not to ask. Tucker was all about himself. He would be on his best behavior from now on, until he got what he wanted from me, whether it was just to sleep with me or make me the trophy wife to live in the house he planned to buy on Long Island, I didn't know. However, he was sneaky, and much more dangerous than someone like Shane, who would tell you straight out that what he wanted was nothing more than sex.

I'd go to dinner with him and that would be it, his chance was over. I should have known after that first gut wrenching kiss; he wasn't the one I'd been searching for.

Tucker purposely drove slowly. Making small talk. Weather, the band audition, and his law firm. When he finally pulled up to my apartment, he kissed me quickly goodnight on my cheek and apologized again.

Conner and Lea were curled up on the couch when I walked in. Shane and Ethan were sitting across from each other tossing a ball.

Shane straightened up when I walked in slamming the door behind me.

"Hey," I nodded to the room.

Lea gave me a smile thick with implications, "Hey, yourself. Where did you and Tucker go?"

I paused in the doorway, taking off my coat. "He took me for a ride in his car." I looked at Lea, "Can I talk to you for a minute?"

She jumped up with concern in her eyes and followed me into my room. I closed the door behind her and leaned up against it.

"Okay, what's going on?"

"I'm going out to dinner with Tucker on Wednesday night," I began. Lea's face burst into happy laughter and she clapped her hands together.

"Yea! I knew one of these hotties would..."

"Lea, I'm going to need you to help me figure out something to tell him to get him off my back," I cut her off.

Her smile faded and anger replaced it, "What did he do?"

I burst out laughing. "Nothing to me. Well, he literally tried to rip my pants off me," I showed her my busted jeans and she laughed along with me.

"Lea, I'm sorry. I know you wanted me to like him, so I tried to give him a chance. He was awful. He was like an octopus; his hands were all over me, telling me about how he thinks he found the perfect girl for his house in Long Island. I tried, but he's not the one for me."

Lea crossed her arms across her chest. "Nobody is the one for you, Grace. And what I want is to get you laid. I'm not asking you to get married to anyone."

I cringed. "Well, the thought of Tucker kissing me again makes me want to wash my mouth out with rubbing alcohol. Thank you very much."

"Ugh. That bad, huh?"

I nodded. "Not everyone is a Conner! Do you remember Harry McAllen in tenth grade? How we all dared you to kiss him at Traci's party. And when you did, he vomited from drinking the wine coolers we snuck in right, into your..."

"OKAY! Okay," she cut me off, waving her hands in front of her. "Don't remind me of that! Okay, I understand. But, Grace I just think that you are wasting your life by waiting for something that isn't..."

"Real?" I looked up at her. "*He's* real Lea. He's more real to me than you are standing right in front of me."

She sighed. "Okay, Grace. I get the point." She opened the door, and turned to look at me again, "But, can't you just think of it as practice for when Mr. Wonderful shows up? Really Grace, what if he's not the same person when you find him?"

My expression must have been bad, because she immediately apologized and ran to hug me. "I'm sorry, Grace, I just don't want you to waste your life." She walked out of my room not even able to look at me again and closing the door behind her.

I reached for the knob to go after her, but I stopped when I heard voices in the hallway. "Is she okay?" a mumbled voice asked.

"She's better than anybody I know. She just wants to alone, literally," Lea answered the voice. I couldn't tell who she was speaking to, but really why would I care?

Lea couldn't understand; why would she? How could she? All she knows is this. She can never comprehend what it is I have seen, felt, and have branded on my soul.

I needed to run to clear my head, thoughts of me leaving here for good were seeping into my skin. *It would be so easy.*

I changed into my sweats and laced up my sneakers. I walked through the house trying not to be noticed. The last thing that I needed was someone following me, but no one was around and whispers were coming from Lea's room. Relief flooded through me, a lone run.

I dashed through the streets making my way into Central Park. I started on one of the loops, but I stopped when I saw a familiar figure sitting on one of the park benches. His white jacket reflected in the moonlight, making him look more angelic than was needed.

"Gabriel," I greeted him. "I was just thinking about you."

He patted the bench and motioned for me to sit down. When I sat down, he grabbed my hands. The warmth radiating off him was almost sublime.

"Hmm. I find myself thinking of you too. Why were you thinking of me?"

"I'm so tired, Gabriel."

"I know. You're on the right path, though." *Did he mean Tucker?* He smiled rubbing his index finger along my knuckles. It was a strange gesture for him, he'd always gone out of his way not to touch me, and now every time he saw me, he made sure there was some sort of subtle physical contact before he left.

"Gabriel, I really need to..."

"I wish that I could do more," he cut me off with a kiss to my forehead. "I wish I could do so much more for you." Once again, he was gone, leaving me alone sitting on a cold park bench. I clasped my hands together and tried to hold onto the warmth that still lingered on my skin from Gabriel's touch.

Chapter 6

I woke up the next morning to Conner and Lea singing a duet in the shower. Laughing, I padded my way into the kitchen in my fluffy bear slippers. In my opinion, Conner was definitely living here now, and they sounded so happy.

Shane looked up at me from the kitchen table with an innocent look on his face. "Morning, Sunshine!"

Skimpy little tank top, boy shorts, floppy bear slippers and bed hair is not the way I wanted someone like Shane to see me. I was betting on at least two weeks of insults to follow, but, he didn't even look at my outfit and he didn't give any snide remarks.

I poured myself a cup of coffee and stirred in some sweetener, waiting for him to start with the teasing. "Good morning. Um, do you come here for coffee every day?"

Shane got up from the table and ran his hands through his hair. "We were going on a run, but he slept late. I'll be out of your way in a minute, unless you feel up to running with me?"

I eyed him curiously.

"Why the hell are you looking at me like that? No strings attached. I'm seriously just asking if you want to go running with me. Nothing else."

"And you're not going to start joking about me standing in front of you with this on," I pointed to my outfit.

His eyes never left mine. Never looking at where I pointed. "Well, I'm sure you'll change if you want to go running."

I smiled at him. *I think he's trying to be on his best behavior.* "Who are you and what have you done with that male chauvinist pig Shane?"

"Har, har, har. You coming or not?"

"Sure. Just let me change." I turned to walk back to my room, and immediately regretted giving him that view of me with my short boy shorts on. There was an audible sigh as soon as I did. When I got to my room, I realized I was smiling. *Oh, that's not good.*

We ran for a good two hours, not once speaking to each other. It was the most comfortable silence I had ever experienced.

We ended up back at my apartment. I took a shower, leaving Shane sitting in the living room watching television. The thought of Shane being in the next room and me in the shower made my mind go wild. I tried to focus on Tucker and about how I could get out of our date on Wednesday, but

Shane's beautifully sculpted shoulders kept taking center stage in my mind. *What the hell?*

I tried to relax myself under the hot water, but nothing helped wash away the images of Shane. I blasted the cold water on and stood under the stream shivering. *Why do people say this works? It doesn't.*

I leaned my forehead onto the cool tiles and closed my eyes. There was always one thing that I could focus on, one thing.

I let my mind open up and go back, remembering. Pale blue colored eyes. It hit me like a slow roar of thunder, my skin could still feel his touch and my body shivered. My knees felt weak; I sat under the icy cold stream. I could still feel his breath on my neck; the way those eyes looked at me; I was his everything.

I didn't know how long I sat there. I only got up when my skin looked a funny shade of blue. I wrapped myself in a towel and cursed out loud for not remembering to bring my clothes in the bathroom with me. Doubtful that Shane had stayed so long, I just wrapped the towel around myself tighter and walked out into the hallway.

I was still concentrating on those pale blue eyes when I noticed Shane was standing in the doorway to the kitchen, eyes wide and sparkling.

"I made lunch, if you're hungry." His voice was no more than a whisper.

Standing there like a deer caught in headlights, I felt the heat rising to my cheeks. "Yeah, sure. I'll be right there."

He said nothing more and walked back into the kitchen.

I dressed in a pair of black yoga pants and a plain purple tee shirt. I ran a brush through my hair and let it air dry. I put on my slippers and made my way into the kitchen.

Shane was grabbing water bottles for us from the refrigerator when I walked in. Two plates were on the table filled with turkey and lettuce wraps with a delicious looking olive salad on the side. *Wow.*

"Sorry, I took so long. I really didn't think you were going to stay," I said.

Shane shook his head, chuckled softly and looked up to the ceiling, as if he was searching for some divine intervention. "Is that why you took so long, so I'd leave? All you have to do is ask me to leave, Grace. I just thought after a two hour run on an empty stomach that you'd like some food."

I gave him a smile. "No, ass. I didn't stay in there because of you. Not everything in this world revolves around you, you know. And thanks, I'm starving," I said, sitting down.

He watched me closely as I took my first mouthful of food. *Delicious.* "Will you be joining me or are you just here to watch me eat? It's pretty good, by the way." I teased, motioning to his untouched plate.

Shane made no move to eat. He just sat and stared intently at my eyes. I stopped chewing and swallowed my food. I should have chewed more, because I immediately started coughing; my eyes tearing.

He jumped up and moved in front of me, "Are you okay? Is it that bad?"

I burst out laughing, and wiped my teary eyes. "Oh God, Shane. It's delicious. I'm choking because you're sitting there staring at me like the taste of your turkey wrap depends on your life."

Shane laughed too and sat back down.

"Man, you made my eyes tear up," I complained.

Leaning his elbows on the table, he moved closer to me, "Those are such gorgeous eyes, there should never be tears in them," he said. "Your purple shirt is reflecting into them. It's making them look lavender."

I smiled. "No wonder you were staring at me like that. Yeah, I can change my eye color if I wear certain colors, but most of the time they're dull gray."

It was his turn to burst out in laughter, choking, "Grace, there's nothing dull about those eyes, and you're right, this shit is delicious. You're welcome."

After we finished, I helped him clean up and we made our way into the living room.

He grabbed his coat and his bag and turned to me. "Have anything planned today?"

"No, not really."

"I was just going to play around at the studio, wanna come?"

"Studio?"

"Yeah, we have a sound proof studio apartment. That's where we practice every day." *Yes. Yes! I want to bring my guitar and play those notes that make you sing like that.*

"How many apartments do you guys have?" I wondered out loud.

"Tucker's father owns the building, so they're reasonable. So, do you want to hang out?"

I grabbed my coat, put on my shoes, and nodded. "Tucker and his family seem like they have it all, huh?"

Disappointment flashed across his features. "Yeah, Tucker has it all."

We stepped out into the windy February day and walked down the street towards his building.

He glanced at me sideways, "Did you have a good time with Tucker last night? I saw you leave the bar with him."

I looked at him and shrugged. "Yeah, he took me for a drive."

We stood on the corner waiting for the light to change, hands in pockets. "So, do you like him?"

"What? Why are you asking me these questions?" I asked. *No. He disgusted me and broke my favorite pair of jeans.* We walked across the street.

"I was just wondering. That's all. You just didn't look too happy with him sitting at the bar last night. I was surprised when you left with him."

I stopped walking and looked up at him. "What do you mean?"

"It was the way you responded to him," he replied.

"Shane, what the hell are you talking about? How did I respond to him?"

He looked up at the cloudy sky and squinted down at me. "He put his hand on the small of your back and you squirmed away from him every time he did. It looked like you were going to drink the whole bottle of Jack when he started rubbing his thumb on your back. The worst was when he touched your face and you cringed. Yet you left with him." He sighed and looked down, "I just didn't understand it at all."

"Strikes me as strange that you would notice all those things that you say I did. But, really, who I go home with isn't any of your business. I don't ask you about all the girls you take home."

"You can. I don't hide anything."

"Shane, I would probably get pregnant from you just telling me the things you do," I laughed.

His smile tightened.

We continued walking and at the end of the block, entered a narrow three-story apartment building. He guided me along the first floor and down a back stairwell into an enormous basement that had been turned into a fully equipped music studio. *Whoa*.

Ethan was sitting behind his drum kit. He gave me a huge smile and jumped up to kiss me hello. "Hey, Grace. Here to listen to us?"

I nodded smiling.

Ethan's smile got wider, "That's great. Shane never lets chicks come down here."

I glanced over at Shane, who was holding an acoustic guitar, and lowering himself onto the floor. "Girls shouldn't be allowed down here. I can't find my muse if some chick is trying to suck on my neck," he laughed. "Besides, it's Grace. She's just one of the guys." He never looked up at me when he said the words. Nevertheless, I felt there was something more to him asking me to come here. A single butterfly fluttered somewhere deep in me, in a place I thought was long dead.

A soft sad melody whispered through his guitar, slow and addictive.

Behind him, Ethan sat motionless, listening.

Shane's eyes closed and his voice drifted through the guitar notes; rising and reaching through my ears to the tips of my toes. It ached with a longing and a need. The words were pain and desire.

I watched as his whole body changed. His face twisted in agony and desolation, yet his body swayed gently to his music. It took every fiber of my being to not reach out my hand and touch his perfect face, to wipe away his sorrow.

I lowered myself to my knees where I stood. I couldn't trust my legs to hold me upright any longer.

He gazed up at me through impossibly long lashes, his eyes a scorching icy blue locked on mine. I couldn't tear myself away from looking at him.

Then at all once the music stopped, his voice holding a note for a single beat more; then silence. His torn expression stirred a fire in me. I felt warmth thunder through my veins under his intense glare.

His eyes tore away only when Ethan's voice cut through the room, "That was the most intense song I've ever heard, dude! That was crazy! Play that again and lemme find a good beat."

Shane looked back at me with no expression on his face. "Yea, sure, Ethan." They composed the song right in front of me. Shane hadn't looked at me again for the rest of the time. The strange personal moment he shared with me was over.

Sometime later, Brayden and Alex arrived and smiled at me. Brayden walked up behind me and hugged me, "Hey, Grace, it's nice to see a pretty face down here."

"Dude, I resent that. I have a very pretty face," Ethan chimed in.

Band practice turned out to be both entertaining and relaxing. An unfamiliar feeling of contentment settled over me. I stayed until my hunger overtook me, having not eaten since that morning. I said my goodbyes and walked out quietly. Shane never looked up from his guitar; just gave me a low, "Night Grace."

As I reached the stairs, I heard Shane call from behind me. He jogged over to me, hands running through his messy hair. "Sorry, I get really involved in there."

"Why would you be sorry? Listening to you guys play was epic. The music sounds even better without all the screaming half-naked girls," I teased.

His smile was amazing. We walked up the stairs to the front door. "I'll walk you home."

"That's not necessary, go back to practice," I insisted. *Oh, but I want him to take me home. Shut up, shut up. Do not think about Shane like that!*

"I'll walk her home for you," a voice said. A cold wind whipped through the front doors that Tucker was just coming through. His hair was slicked back and he was dressed in a long winter overcoat; unbuttoned it flaunted his Gucci suit. His briefcase matched. I didn't even bother to look at his shoes, no doubt they'd be made of gold.

"That's okay, it's only a few blocks." I said.

"Well, it's dark out and a beautiful girl like you should have someone to protect her," Tucker replied. His smile was genuine. *Protect me? This was coming from the guy who ripped the button off my pants?* "I'll get her home, Shane. You can go back to practice."

Shane's smile tightened; again. "Great. Thanks Tuck. Night, Grace," he said walking back down the stairs.

Tucker held the doors open for me and I was blasted with icy cold air. He ushered me out, "So, funny meeting you here," he smiled down at me. "Are you cold? Come here." He lifted his arm and wrapped it around my shoulder.

"Oh, that's okay. I'm fine," I said sliding out of his grasp.

Tucker didn't miss a beat; dropping his hands to my waist. "I don't mind. It's not every day that I get to walk down the street with a beautiful woman."

I stared straight ahead. "Thanks."

"So what were you doing here with Shane, anyway?"

"I was watching the guys practice. Why?"

"Oh, shit! I'm supposed to practice with them after work, which is now! Why the fuck is it every time I have something I want to do, these assholes have to depend on me to do other things!" His anger seemed extremely misplaced. He even threw down his Gucci bag. *Holy crap, he's having a tantrum!*

I tried to smile, "Tucker, I live like two blocks away. You go help them, I'm fine."

That made his pouting stop. He kissed me on the cheek. "I can't wait to take you out on Wednesday, but more than that, I can't wait for you to see me play on stage on Friday!"

"So go practice!" I pretended to be excited. *You insane psycho! I think I need to get a very contagious stomach virus before this date.*

I walked home alone; my small glimpse of contentment gone.

Chapter 7

Unfortunately, I woke up Wednesday healthy and perfectly able to go on a date with Tucker. I was so entirely against it that Lea stayed home from work to spend the day being Tucker's cheerleader. The more I tried to explain to her that I didn't want to go on the date, the more disappointed she seemed; she was killing me.

Lea always had this fairy-tale delusion of us marrying best friends or brothers. We would go on double dates, be each other's maid of honor and live next door to each other. She had an extensive map laid out of her life, with everything she had planned to do etched in with permanent marker. Little did she know that when people make plans for their lives, God just laughs and makes his own.

Lea whined continuously about giving Tucker a chance as she primped and prettied me up.

She dressed me in a dangerously low cut silver blouse that hugged my body like a glove. A pair of black stretch pants, *so no buttons would be broken* Lea reasoned, and my over the knee black leather boots. My long black hair fell in thick shiny soft waves and my eyes were smoky and sexy; a dangerous look for someone who really didn't want to go on a date.

At 5:45, I was presented to Conner, who had sat in the living room for the last hour conspiring with Lea in telling me all the wonderful attributes of Tucker Bevli.

"Very hot," Conner appraised me.

I stood in front of our full-length mirror. I groaned and leaned my head on his shoulder looking away. "You aren't helping me at all." I playfully punched him in the stomach. "I don't want to date Tucker."

Lea put her arm around my waist and turned me to face the mirror again. "You are going to go on this date, whether you like it or not. And you should let that insanely, rich, jaguar driving, Gucci wearing Greek god take you out more, and then you should pull the pole from up your ass and sleep with him." Then she smacked me on the ass. Hard.

I watched myself in the mirror jump from the slap and laugh.

Five minutes later, Tucker texted me on my cell phone to tell me he was outside. He didn't even come in to get me. Didn't even call, just texted. Prince Freaking Uncharming. *Strike one*. I shook the thought and dragged myself outside to his waiting car.

I was assaulted by cologne when I opened the passenger side door for myself. *Strike two*. He slid close to me and pecked me on the corner of my mouth with a kiss, wetly. I clasped my hands together to stop myself from wiping it away. *Strike three*.

"Are you ready for the best date of your life?" he asked; eyes sparkling, hair gelled to the sky.

"Well, aren't we filling me with expectations," I laughed. "Best date ever? Will I get to rate it after on a scale of 1 to 10?"

He gave me a thoughtful look and then smiled, "Nah, just a typed up report on my desk by morning." He laughed at his own joke.

"That would mean you'd have to make it worth writing about." I was a bit intrigued by what he might think the best date of my life would be, certain that it would be the furthest thing from the truth. "The question I have is whether you are trying to impress me, make me happy, or just make yourself immortal?"

"Immortal? What, like you're a vampire, I let you bite my neck and I'll get to live forever with a beautiful woman like you. I would. In a heartbeat."

I'd never met an ass like him before. *Strike four.* "No, immortal because I would write about you. Theoretically, writing about someone makes them immortal, because the words live beyond them, keeping them alive."

"That doesn't make sense, but any who, no. It would be impressing you and making you happy. Not that I wouldn't love to be immortal. I can think of some situations where that can be really useful."

He just said "any who." What strike is this?

I laughed, "Oh, really?"

He sped down the street. Within two minutes, he was pulling up to Columbus Circle, right in front of The Time Warner Center. We could have walked there.

Noticing my puzzled look he purred, "I got reservations for Masa."

I just stared at him. Blankly.

Tucker jumped out of the jaguar, ran around to my side of the car, and waited for me to open my door. *Strike twenty-something. Maybe he'd break a nail if he had opened it for me?* He hooked his arm around my waist and squeezed. "Masa, Grace! It's the most expensive place to eat in Manhattan. It's a two hour eating experience that you're going to love!"

Inside was simple and elegant. We were escorted to an exquisite bar and our coats were taken as if we were family visiting. Noticing me without my coat, Tucker's eyes filled with pride. His chest visibly puffed out and he glanced around the room. I hated it, and it made me feel dirty. *Why should he feel pride from me?*

A bottle of champagne was brought out for his approval; the staff called him by name. The champagne was poured. Tucker sipped his and motioned for me to do the same. It went down delicious and smooth; he smiled.

"Do you like it?" he asked.

"It tastes lovely, thank you."

"It's Gaston Chiquet Brut 1er Cru 2002. It's $150 a bottle. Drink as much as you want," he winked. *Oh, I fucking will.*

Without ordering, we were served food. Sushi. *Well, at least I had $150 champagne to fill me up.* I think that someone should warn you before taking you to a sushi bar, since it might be nice for a person to be able to tell you they HATED SUSHI!

Toro, uni, aoyagi, sayori...I kept drinking to make myself not think about what I was eating.

"This place is beautiful, isn't it?" he asked, leaning against the bar; eyeing me.

"Yes." *Does he know ANY other adjectives?*

"So tell me about *you*," he said.

"Like what?" I asked gulping my champagne.

"Where did you grow up, where'd you go to school? Stuff like that," he explained.

I swallowed hard, champagne going right to my head. *I could tell him everything; that would send him packing.* It almost made Jacob leave me and he was my brother. Tucker wouldn't believe me though; he wouldn't even hear me. "I grew up in Belle Harbor, a block away from the beach. Lea and I lived next door to each other." My knees started tingling from the champagne. "I've been to a couple of schools and I studied everything."

"I was thinking," he said, proving he did not intend to get to know any more about me. *Sure, you were thinking.* "Why don't I see if there's any room for an assistant in our office? I was thinking I could help you out, since you don't have a job right now." He smiled so wide, I noticed where all the sushi was stuck in his teeth.

"Like a secretary? I don't think that's for me. But, thank you for thinking of me." Another bottle of champagne came to the table.

"Nonsense. Grace, you need a job. My firm is the best place, and when I become partner you could be my personal secretary." His eyebrows moved up and down.

I barked out a laugh that was a little too loud. "Nope. I'm good where I'm at right now, thanks." More sips of champagne. *Does this come with an IV?*

"So what are your plans then?" he demanded. *Condescending jerk.*

"Just plan to keep breathing for now, that's about it. Well, until I stop, that is," I said laughing.

"Stop breathing? Don't be silly. God, this shit is delicious!"

I giggled. He was absurd and I was getting tipsy.

"So am I making myself immortal?" The question caught me so off guard, I sucked in my breath loudly.

"I take that as a YES!" He fist pumped. *YES, I just said he fist pumped! I needed to get the hell away from this spiked haired, sushi eating, fist pumping jackass as soon as it was humanly possible.*

I choked on my words laughing. "Tucker being immortal would suck, even for you."

"Bullshit!" He was getting drunk.

"Just think of everything you love and have now, slipping away from you. People you love getting sick, getting old, dying. Again and again. You wouldn't be able to stand the sorrow."

"Psf. I'd fuck a lot of girls. Ha. I'll be like Shane and Alex."

I shrugged, and then agreed. "Okay so immortality is good for having lots of sex. That's about it. This is a dumb conversation."

He spoke endlessly about the sushi, making it insanely hard not to picture myself eating the sushi. However, I stomached it, because he was holding the conversation quite well all by himself and I didn't feel like talking to him any longer. He ordered another bottle of champagne.

After an hour of the torture, Tucker's phone began ringing continuously; for fifteen minutes straight, until he shut it off, embarrassed. "Fucking assholes. Probably Shane or Alex trying to fuck up my date with you! They both wanna tap your ass."

"You curse a lot when you're drunk," I smiled. "Tap what?"

"Your ass, Grace. I wanna tap your ass...right in this fucking bar," he chuckled.

"No can do, there's way too much sushi, it would be weird."

My phone started ringing. I pressed my screen to see who it was. *Lea.* Something must have happened.

"Helllooo," I sang.

"Grace?" Shane's voiced echoed in my ears. *There's that butterfly again. What the hell is with the butterfly? Doesn't it know I can't let myself feel...human?*

"Shane?"

"Where's Tucker? He's not answering his phone? Where are you?" Shane demanded.

I heard the phone being yanked out of his hands and I flinched, accidentally pressing down on the screen. Lea's voice screamed through the restaurant. *Whoops, speakerphone.*

Seemingly humiliated by my loud conversation, Tucker tried to wrestle the phone out of my hands. His face was crimson and he looked like he was about to explode.

"What is wrong with you, Tucker? Give me my phone back!" I yelled, not caring who heard me in the restaurant. Lea and Shane's voices were still on speaker, loudly screaming profanities to the entire restaurant.

Tucker drunkenly poked the screen of my phone five times to get it off speaker. Everyone in the restaurant waited to see what would happen next. He looked around wildly; his knuckles were white from squeezing my phone so hard. "You are embarrassing me!" he snapped.

I looked him dead in the eyes. "Give me my phone or I'll give you something to really be embarrassed about."

He immediately slid the phone across the table. I put it to my ear.

"Hello?"

"Grace, are you okay?" Shane's voice asked.

"What's going on, Shane?"

"We need Tucker. Alex needs a lawyer. He's in Manhattan Central Booking."

"Oh no, what happened. Oh, forget it, you can tell me later. But, I don't think it's a good idea that Tucker drives, and you might need to call his father if you want a lawyer who isn't drunk."

"You have got to be kidding me," Shane mumbled. "Where are you? I'll come and get you," he whispered.

"We're eating sushi," I explained as if that told him where to pick me up.

"Ew."

"Tell me about it," I laughed.

"So where would you be eating this sushi, exactly?" he asked.

"Just meet us at The Time Warner Center in Columbus Circle. Wait, how are you going to get us?" The phone clicked off.

I looked up at Tucker, irritation stirring in his eyes. "That was Shane. We have to pay the bill and go. He'll be here to pick us up in a minute."

"No fucking way. What the fuck is he picking us up for? This date isn't over. I'm not done with you!" The irritation was now replaced with anger in his eyes.

Done with me? I was going to have to kick this boy's ass to teach him how to treat a woman! "Alex is in Manhattan Central Booking. He needs a lawyer."

His anger evaporated and his shoulders sunk low. "Shouldn't have drunk so much." He looked at me with sad eyes. "I'm sorry; this was such a great date."

I walked to get my coat, laughing all the way. I tried to pay for half of the meal, but he wouldn't allow me, telling me he had already prepaid for half of it and I wasn't working, so I should be broke and coming to him for a job soon.

The cold air from standing outside sobered him up enough to call his father who agreed to meet with him and Alex. I stood on the street shivering, wondering what trouble Alex could have gotten into with two broken arms.

The squeal of the Jeep's wheels as Shane rounded the corner woke me from my thoughts. He pulled up onto the sidewalk like a lunatic and jumped out of the car. Without saying a word, he opened the passenger side door, pulled the front seat forward and shoved Tucker in the car. He then took my hand, helped me into the front seat, and closed the door for me.

Shane climbed back into the driver's seat and took off towards Centre Street, downtown. I stared at him while he drove. *It's completely ridiculous that someone should look so perfect or that he be allowed to drive my Jeep.*

"What happened?" I asked to get my mind off of looking at him.

"Alex was out with that chick whose boyfriend jumped him. The boyfriend had roughed her up after the incident with Alex, and well, I think Alex went to the guy's house and I guess he stood up to him."

Tucker snapped into action in the backseat asking questions and making phone calls. I leaned my head against the cold window and sighed. On a scale of one to ten, I'd have rate the date a 0.

Traffic was light and we made it there within fifteen minutes. Tucker's father was standing outside waiting on the steps.

Shane pulled up and opened his side of the car door to let Tucker get out. When Shane got back in and closed the door, Tucker made him open the window to talk to me. "Grace, I'm sorry. I know that this was one of the best nights of your life, so I'll take you back to Masa whenever you'd like."

Is he insane? One of the best nights of my life? I kept my voice calm, "Oh, we'll have to talk about that, Tucker."

Tucker gave me his sexiest smile. "I know, it was amazing. Grace, you're amazing." He tilted his head to Shane and nodded, "Thanks for taking her home for me, you're a good friend." He pounded his palm on the door, which made me want to scratch his eyes out. "Get her home safe, this big boy has gotta play superman!" he shouted, pointing to himself.

Shane pulled away and drove without saying a word. I kept my head against the cold glass. The tingly feeling that I had before was slipping out of my body and I found myself wanting to find a way to continue the mind-blowing numbness. Shane's silence was making it worse.

After circling the block of my apartment five times, Shane finally found a spot and pulled in. We got out and he walked me to my apartment, but instead of going inside, I kept moving.

"Where are you going?" he asked.

"I need to have a drink *or few*."

"What? Now? Why?"

I looked down at my cellphone and saw that it was 8:30. I looked at him seriously. "That was just two and a half hours of my life that I will never get back. And in those two and a half hours, I have spent more time with a jerk, than all of my years on this earth." I watched a small smile play on his face. "I am kind of hoping the rest of my night will be full of regretful behavior and irreversible decisions." I stomped away from him, but he grabbed me by my arm, spinning me around to face him.

"What? So that wasn't the best night of your life?" he asked with amusement in his voice.

"Shut up, Shane, go home!" I walked away.

He threw his arm around my neck and walked with me. "I think I need a night of watching you entertain me with your regretful behavior and your irreversible decisions."

"Then we definitely need to call Lea to tell her and Conner to meet us at Boozer's," I said.

Shane looked down into my eyes. He was so close to me like this that it was hard to think straight. His whole body vibrated with sex appeal, or maybe that was me. Either way, I didn't want to have any sexy thoughts about me and New York City's Most Popular Man-whore and I wanted my best friend with me.

He must have read something on my face. "Grace, are you afraid of being alone with me?" He eyes widened and he took his arm off my shoulders. "Grace, I get it. You aren't interested in anything with me. I'm not going to try anything, I promise." He looked around and back to my eyes, running his hand through his hair. He took his phone out of his pocket. "I'll tell them to meet us there."

Boozer's was crowded for a weeknight, as Shane and I meandered our way to the bar.

Shane introduced me to Ryan, the bartender, and told him whatever I wanted was limitless and he was paying. I eyed him suspiciously and took off my coat. When he saw me with my coat off, his mouth dropped open and he froze. His eyes smoldered, giving me a slow long once over from my eyes to my toes and back up again. He sucked his breath in, but said nothing. He looked awestruck, and I had no doubt that if I were any other girl in the world other than me, that look would have made me let him take me home.

"What would you like, Grace?" Shane asked me. I hesitated. I wanted to say to be someone else, at least just for tonight; but I couldn't. I still had to find someone, someone who I'd been half a person without. "Tequila, please," I whispered.

Shane tore his eyes off me, "Ryan, the woman wants Tequila. Line up the shot glasses, salt and limes, sir," and he turned back to me with a wicked smile, "And let the regretful behavior begin!"

Everything was placed on the bar in front of me.

My eyes never left Shane's as I slowly licked the back of my hand, salted it and licked it again. Lifting the shot, I tilted my head back and emptied the glass, and then sucked on the lime.

"My God," he whispered.

I narrowed my eyes at him, "Why am I drinking alone?" I could feel a heat burn inside me.

A sexy playful smile crept across his face, "Oh, don't worry, Grace, you're not alone," he said, as he slowly licked the back of his salted hand and devoured his drink.

I wanted to ask him if he could do that to me next. *Please, Lea, get here fast before I do something I will regret*.

"Holy Shots!" Lea screamed when she and Conner walked up to us, eyeing all the Tequila that was lined up. *Oh, thank you God, she's here!*

"Lea!" I yelled, and hugged her tight. When I pulled her away, I said, "That, my friend, will be the last time that you will ever talk me into going on a date!"

Lea held up her finger, about to make a point and I grabbed it with my mouth and bit her. "Ouch!"

"Last time, Lea. It's my messed up life and if I want to waste it, I will!" I ended the sentence with another shot that Shane had handed to me; his fingers brushing mine. My breath caught, his eyes noticed, and my cheeks flushed with heat. *Crap!*

Lea grabbed a shot off the bar, "Come on, Conner. Worst thing to do is let a friend drink alone, looks like I'll be taking off again tomorrow!" She emptied her glass.

Four shots in, Shane grabbed my hand and nodded toward the dance floor. I smiled back; butterflies bursting in my stomach. I motioned for Lea and Conner to follow us.

Shane spun me around, facing me away from him, and grabbed hold of my waist. His fingers dug into the material of my shirt, pulling me closer to him. His touch made me lose my train of logical thought. All my coordination; out the window. I fell back against his body, he swayed my hips to the music; fire erupting deep inside me.

I tried to pull away from him. I wanted to run away from the heat; too afraid to get burned by the fire pulsating in my veins. My entire body ignored my thoughts; it just melted into him.

I glanced over to Lea and Conner for help, but received nothing but an impish grin from both of them.

Shane spun me back around to face him. A rush of exhilarated fear seared through me. I felt the heat of his hands through the thin material of my shirt. I wonder how it would feel with his hands on my bare skin. *Oh, shut up, Grace, do not think about Shane like that!* "Shane," I gasped shaking my head at him.

His eyes were so intense. *My God, he is sexy.* Exquisitely tempting, but too dark and dangerous, just barely out of sight beneath the surface.

He tightened his grip around my waist, pulling me in closer. Burying his face in my hair, he whispered, "You're killing me, Grace."

I leaned away from him and frowned up at him.

"I know. I know, Grace!" His hands flew up into the air. "I have absolutely no chance at a night with you. I'm not trying to sleep with you. I'm just having fun, you smell awesome, you are inhumanly beautiful, and you're making my heart beat overtime. Shots?"

I threw my head back laughing. "Shots!" I agreed.

Taking hold of Lea and Conner, we shoved through the dancing crowd to our waiting drinks. Four more shots. Numbness; the world was perfect, pure, and my life had meaning. I hadn't died a thousand times over and my heart had not been ripped from my chest.

"Hey, you okay? I have to go pee, come with," Lea demanded slurring.

I can't even remember walking to the bathroom.

Standing in front of the faucet, I held my hands under the icy cold stream until they burned. Lea had gone into a stall and she was silent, very unlike her.

She walked out of the stall; slamming the door accidentally and giggled. She came over to the faucet beside me and washed her hands.

Noticing my hands were still under the stream, she shut off my faucet and handed me a clump of paper towels. She looked at me intently in the mirror. "What's going on? What really happened with Tucker, besides Alex and his stupidity cutting your date short?"

I gave her a look, which I hoped said it all, but just to clarify, I added, "Let's just say it was the worst date of my entire life. End of story."

"And, what is going on with Shane out there? The way you guys were dancing, I thought, maybe...well, it just looked intense," she said.

I cringed. It felt intense. It felt good, but there's no way I could say that. "Lea, ever since I got here, there's been so many intense moments that I feel like a rubber band about to snap."

Lea grabbed my frozen hands and stared down wide-eyed at them. "Why do you do these things?" She rubbed my hands in hers to warm them. "You know, Grace, I haven't really known Shane for long, but I can tell you he would be great for a one night thing and that's it, he's hollow when it comes to girls. But, damn is he sexy. Sometimes, I secretly wish I met him first, let him have his way with me, and then met Conner!"

We burst out into a fit of giggles, "Lea, I can't." *Okay, so I was really trying to believe that.*

"So what do you want?"

"Right now, I just want Jacob to be here to give me a big hug and say, 'I'm sorry that the entire male gender of our species sucks.' But, more than that, I need another drink so I can forgot about everything for a little while."

When we returned, Shane was sitting at the bar with a stunning blonde. A twinge of envy coursed through my body, but I washed it away with another drink. I watched as he leaned in, brushing her long golden hair off her shoulder and whispered into her ear. She ran her fingers though his hair and giggled, sliding closer against him.

I could be steadfast in the things I wanted for myself, but I would be lying to say that the passion and lust that Shane had in his eyes for me before wasn't so very tempting. Although seeing him with this other women just proved the fact that I was nothing special. I knew down deep in my soul that I was special to the person I was looking for. Lea slid on the barstool next to me and laughed, "Do you see that? Girl, that could have been you! Just think, you gave up a night of ride 'em cowboy with Hottie McShane, for..." she looked at the empty barstool on the other side of me, "Oh, right. No one that I can see."

The blonde stood up, taking Shane by the hand and she led him to the dance floor. She was all legs and cleavage.

They danced like they were the only two people in the room and I had to look away, wondering if I had looked like that just a few minutes before her.

Lea and I slammed down two more shots. We spun our stools around and scanned the dance floor. Shane was still dry humping the porn star, but his eyes were on me.

Another shot. *I didn't want to feel this. I had no right to feel this way.* I didn't want to think of myself as slighted, I didn't want to wish to be someone else every second of every day. *Right now, most of all, I didn't want to have such a strong desire to be that blonde dancing with Shane.* Not just for the fact of getting to spend a night with him, but also wanting to run away from my past. Just to spend even a small amount of time pretending I was normal.

I strolled past them, smiling and shaking my head. I needed to run some icy water over the back of my neck, the bar was spinning and I needed to try to ground myself. *Then, I'm getting some fresh air.* I walked into the back hallway, alone.

"Don't fucking move and don't fucking yell," a man's voice hissed into my ear, "Or I swear to God I will slit your fucking throat."

I froze as I watched Shane and his new friend get lost in the dance crowd behind me from the corner of my eye. *Did he see what was happening to me?* "Okay," I replied, feeling the sharpness of the knife at the nape of my neck. The fingers of his other hand dug into my arm. *That's going to leave a bruise.*

"Move back, let's go, just turn around." He waved the knife in the air and pointed to a door near the bathroom.

He shoved me hard against the door; the hallway was spinning around me. I definitely should not have drunk so much. *And, really why does stuff like this have to happen to nice girls when they hardly ever drink? Not fair.*

He came up behind me, eased the door open and pushed me through.

Once he shut the door, he flicked on the light switch and turned the lock on the knob. I glared straight into his eyes. He stood tall and broad with short-cropped hair, his eyes so blue and bloodshot they looked almost purple. I vaguely remembered seeing him at the bar, somewhere in the background. He had a gold ring on his left hand finger, a tattoo of the name Sarah across his inner wrist. I could have belted out detail after detail, and illustrated every single inch of the man who was going to attempt to hurt me. A sliver of a thought flashed through my mind. *Should I let this be the end? Isn't this what I've wanted since the day I woke up in that hospital bed after the accident? An easy out of this life?*

No. I wanted to see *him* again. Gabriel said to live this life of mine. If this were the end of it, it would mean that I'd have already found *him* and not known it. *No. I decided to live this life.*

"I like the way you dance, now I'm going to dance with you, I want to see what's so hot about you," he said. He bared his teeth back and tried to slam into me with all his weight. "I'm gonna break you in half, bitch."

I chambered my open palm and thrust it straight up into his nose as he flew towards me. I heard a sickening crunch and smiled at myself. *After hundreds upon hundreds of years, I definitely knew how to protect myself.*

Blood poured out of his nose. "Oh yeah, bitch. You know I like it rough."

His bloody hands tried to grab me, but they were too slippery. He threw himself at me instead, trying to wrestle me to the ground. I laughed at him.

I slammed my knee into his groin and clipped him in the nose again with my elbow.

"Grace!" I could hear Lea's muffled screams in the hallway as she banged on the door. I could hear other screams along with hers and the sounds of someone slamming themselves up against the outside of the door. I kept my focus on my attacker, though. I didn't want him to catch me off my guard. He was big; *a lot bigger than me*. If I hadn't had so many centuries on this earth of learning how to protect myself, I would have definitely suffered the fate of so many young women today. As I sidestepped his attacks, I thanked God that I was the one who this brutal man had chosen to victimize. Any other girl at this bar would have probably gotten killed, but tonight this man would be surprised; there are girls who can fight back. *Especially ones that have lived since the dawn of time.*

"Get the hell off her!" Shane yelled after kicking through the door. Wooden splinters burst from the doorframe.

Before I could take my next breath, Shane ripped the guy away from me; pounding him in the face over and over. His eyes were wild.

The second Shane looked at me with concern, the guy leapt at him; stabbing the knife into Shane's shoulder and pulling it back out. Shane shook his head stunned, steadied himself and moved in as the guy lunged to cut him again. Shane dexterously blocked the knife with his right hand and hammered the guy square in the chest with his other fist. The bloody knife splattered and bounced. The man crumbled to the floor like a rag doll.

Shane grabbed my face with his hands, pulling my eyes away from watching the blood flowing from his shoulder, to his eyes. "Grace, you okay? Did he hurt you? He had blood all over him when I came in. Where are you hurt?"

I grabbed Shane's shoulder and applied pressure to it. I smiled up at him, "It was his blood, Shane. He didn't hurt me." Shane looked from the limp body slumped on the floor and back to me, his expression a mixture of relief and awe.

A dark look settled on his face. "Did he touch you? I swear to God, Grace, I'll kill him right now."

I placed my hand up to his face, laying it softly on his cheek. Even through my numbing drunkenness, I still felt the slow burning heat of him washing over me like crashing waves. "He never got the chance, you came."

He looked down across his shoulder, smiling. "Grace, I just got stabbed to save you. Can I at least have a kiss as a reward?" He wiggled his eyebrows up and down.

I leaned forward and kissed him on the forehead.

His eyes met mine, laughing, "Wow. A peck on the forehead is the equivalent to being stabbed to you? No way! I'm going to milk this one! You owe me, big time!"

I slapped him in his arm, making him wince. "Shane, you could take your blonde bimbo home or me, and you wouldn't know the difference. But, I do owe you," I said, smiling. "I'll think of something where I get to keep my clothes on."

Everyone in the bar seemed to pile into the back room at that moment. The bouncers came in, the police were called and Shane was driven to Lenox Hill Hospital a few blocks away.

I sat in the waiting area of the emergency room being questioned by two uniformed police officers. They were kind and compassionate, so different from what you always heard was the clichéd stereotypical NYPD officer. They reiterated over and over how very fortunate I had been that Shane had come in when he did. They had been on many calls where it had been too late.

The blonde Shane had been dancing with, Brianna, sat across from me, biting her fake nails. She had ridden in the ambulance with him. The two police officers in a squad car escorted me, as if I was the criminal.

I couldn't stand to be in the same room as her. I bet Shane didn't even know her name. I couldn't stop myself from the thoughts flooding through me as I watched her. Why would anyone let themselves be used by someone for one night, fully knowing that there wouldn't be another? How low could this girl feel about herself that she still waited for Shane to take her home? Was it for the sole reason to elevate her status with her friends?

Conner and Lea arrived ten minutes later than we did, both mumbling about too many run-ins with the cops in one night. We all talked Brianna into calling a cab to head home, because we didn't think Shane would be up for any more fun tonight.

After an hour, Shane strolled out into the waiting area with twenty-one stitches holding him together. He leaned his elbow onto my shoulder and smiled, "Were you worried sick about me?"

I rolled my eyes. "No, Shane. I knew your big fat ego would block the knife somehow."

The four of us walked out of the hospital around midnight. Sharing a cab, we drove home in silence, the shadows of the city falling over us as we moved along the quiet streets. Lea and I were dropped off first and the guys would continue the cab ride to their apartment. The driver pulled in front of our building and I reached inside my jacket pocket for money, but the guys pushed the money away.

"Oh, Shane. I forgot to mention it, but Brianna wanted me to tell you to call her. We made her call a cab, sorry." I looked to Conner and Lea, "We thought it would be longer, and well, she was annoying to stare at really."

Shane's eyebrows pulled together in confusion, "Who's Brianna?"

It figures! I walked into the apartment laughing at myself for how jealous I had felt over someone Shane hadn't cared enough about to ask her name.

Lea dropped her coat on the floor in the living room and threw herself on the couch. "Are you okay? Grace, that man almost... I mean, he stabbed Shane! That could have been you," she whispered, rubbing the back of her neck in amazement. Her eyes welled up with tears.

I sat down next to her and put my arm around her shoulders. "It's okay now, I'm okay and Shane's fine." I gave her a weak smile.

She brought her hand to her mouth, "I don't know what's more unbelievable, Alex getting arrested tonight, you getting attacked or Shane being a hero!" She sighed and gave me a perplexed look. "And, why in the world did you go to the bathroom solo? That's like, completely against the girl code or something."

I just shrugged. "I needed to get some air."

Lea looked at me through squinted eyes. "Why do I feel like you're not telling me something?" She sat upright on the couch and leaned forward, closer to me.

My cell vibrated and started ringing the blaring alarm sirens I programmed into it, making us both jump. The timing couldn't have been more perfect. I did not want her thinking that Shane had gotten under my skin while I was drinking.

"Gray, you need to change that ringtone. It scares the crap out of me every time I hear it. Who is it, anyway?"

I grabbed my coat off the coat rack and fumbled through the pockets. Touching the screen, I saw a number I didn't recognize. I didn't answer.

"Who was it?"

"I didn't recognize the number," I said. "Well, whoever it is, it has to be a wrong number. The only person who would call me this late is you."

My voicemail rang. Lea looked at me expectantly. I sighed heavily. If she wasn't standing there waiting, I would probably not even check the message and just go right to bed.

I touched the little voicemail icon on the screen and placed the volume on speakerphone so she could listen. She's the one that wanted to hear it anyway.

Shane's low raspy voice echoed into the room. "Grace, it's Shane. Give me a call back, tonight. Doesn't matter what time." There was a few seconds of silence and then, "Call me or I swear I'll ring this phone all night." He chuckled and clicked the phone off.

Lea shook her head and giggled. "Gray, he's not going to let up. He's going to want payback for saving you. A lot more than a little peck on the forehead."

"He is going to be relentless, isn't he?" I asked laughing. *Why was I feeling a little happy about this?*

She nodded, "Gray, the entire population of women in the Tri-State Area would kill to have Shane Maxton call their cell and give them the attention he's giving you right now. He's not used to girls not being affected by his charming ways," she laughed.

"I don't get how anyone can find him charming. It's all just about how he looks, I don't really see too much of a personality there."

Lea tilted her head, "Shane's really cool when you get to know him. I've had a ton of heart to heart talks with him. He's really smart and talented. I think he just got his heart broken once and he's just protecting himself." She yawned loudly, "There's a lot more to Shane than meets the eye, but he's definitely not someone who you could have more than a short fling with, it's not in him. Unless, maybe..."

"Don't even think another thought. I agree, Shane is um, very tempting, but I've been saving myself so long for something that is so much better than Shane. I will not let myself be led off my path. So stop it. Please."

My phone exploded with sound again. I touched the screen to see Shane's number staring back at me, again. I fingered the answer icon. "What do you want, Shane?" I asked.

"Who is Brianna?" he asked.

Lea made stupid goofy faces at me, a few obscene hand gestures, and called it a night. I listened to his breathing on the phone as he waited for my answer.

"Um, the stunning blonde you picked up at the bar and danced with," I replied, walking into my room. "She went in the ambulance with you, Shane. How could you not know who I'm talking about? Anyway, why are you calling me and asking about it. More importantly, who gave you my number so I can plot their slow death?"

"Oh, man. I thought her name was Lori," he laughed. He seemed to hesitate for a few moments, as if he was trying to formulate his next sentence carefully. "Did you get upset when I was dancing with her?"

I leaned the phone on my neck and started undressing. Rummaging through my drawers, I found the only clean sleepwear, a tiny tank top and matching panties. Thank God, Conner wasn't staying over tonight, I desperately needed to do laundry. "Shane, why in the world would I care if you danced with someone? Is that why you called me?"

He chuckled which irritated me to no end. "No," he sighed the word. "I just wanted to see how you were doing. It's not every night that someone attacks you, right?" *Not in this lifetime, anyway. Hold on. Is this his attempt at being sincere?*

"I'm absolutely fine, exhausted, but fine."

He suddenly sounded remorseful, "I programed your number into my phone when I called you on Lea's phone looking for Tucker. I didn't think you'd mind." His tone lifted immediately, "I was about to grab something to eat and then go to bed, what are you doing?"

I exhaled slowly. I didn't want him to think I was about to jump and get something to eat with him if I said I was hungry and about to get something to eat myself. "I'm climbing into bed right now," I yawned and sank into my cool cotton sheets.

"Oh." I could hear him smiling at me through the phone. *He never lets up, does he?* "That's a thought that's going to last me all night."

"God, Shane! Shut up! Why does everything have to be sexual with you? Have you seriously never had a platonic friendship with a female before?"

He laughed his low raspy laugh. "No, not really. Lea maybe, but she doesn't count. She belongs to Conner and he's my buddy. Before that, it's been a long time."

"Shane, I went on a date with Tucker and you still flirt like crazy with me!" I said exasperated.

"Grace. Don't you get it? I'm really trying to do this platonic thing here." He sighed, "I just called to see if you were okay about what happened before."

Yeah, sure and I'll buy that bridge you're selling me right now, do you take credit or cash? "I'm okay, Shane. Thank you very much for helping me to kick that guy's butt. Oh yeah, and getting in the way of the knife."

"Yeah, when I think back on it now, it looked like you were doing fine by yourself. I just saw all the blood on the guy and I thought he hurt you. I went crazy. How did you fight that guy back? He was like five times your size."

I giggled. *Yes, I giggled like a schoolgirl. I'm such an idiot.* "I had an older brother who taught me how to protect myself."

"You had a great older brother."

I smiled. "One of the best."

There was a hesitation again. Then he took a deep breath and asked, "Why didn't you have a good time with Tucker? I figured you didn't like him, but I don't understand why you went on a date with him."

I yawned again. "Lea forced me to go on the date. She has this warped vision of us marrying best friends or brothers or something." I sighed heavily, "Tucker is nice enough, but he's just not my type." I did not want to get into this with Shane.

"And your type is?"

"Not Tucker."

We stayed on the phone until six the next morning, talking about everything and anything. Nothing got too personal, and nothing even remotely provocative. He spoke to me about his music, his songs, and his words. I could have listened to him for another lifetime and then some more. We stayed talking until my phone's battery was beeping that it was about to die. I appreciated the effort he was making to try to be a friend, I accepted the fact that it was a leap for him, but I was not caving in anytime soon and I hoped he realized that. He never again mentioned that I owed him anything for saving me, but I think that it was unusual for him to lift a finger for anyone else besides his friends. He was more shocked than anyone that he'd done it. I knew in my heart at the end of our conversation that I did need to repay him in some way.

When I sat up groggy the next day at three in the afternoon from the most exquisite dream I'd ever had; I knew exactly what I needed to do. My unconscious mind had conjured up a sleep filled with me playing music, alone in never ending rapture. *I was going to audition for Shane's band.*

It would only be six weeks until Alex's casts would come off and then I could go about my own way. I wasn't sure if there would be more trouble in store for Alex after his arrest, but I figured on the court system in the city to draw out any trials for years to come. Alex most likely spent the night in jail and would be out the next day with only a desk appearance to show up to. I guessed that in six weeks when his casts were off, he wouldn't still be in jail or anything and he could just jump back in the band again.

The truth was that after listening to Shane play and listening to him on the phone, I *wanted* to play with him. Besides, this would be my way of thanking him for what he had done and I would be fully clothed while I did it!

Chapter 8

The apartment was dead silent. I tiptoed down the hallway and into the bathroom trying not to wake Lea. I showered, shaved, scrubbed, and put lotion on, every girlie thing I could think of. I even painted my nails.

Lea was standing in the hallway with her arms across her chest waiting for me when I was done. Mist from the bathroom wafted through the dim light. "Well, the boys are busy tonight with the auditions, so what trouble are we going to get in tonight?" she asked smiling.

"I think I'm about to do something stupid," I said.

Lea grabbed me by the hand, led me down the hall, through my bedroom door, and sat on my bed. "Okay, I hope to God this has something to do with a hot guy and some toys."

I gave her a wicked smile. "I guess it does. I'm going to the audition."

She jumped into action. "Here," she ripped through my closet and flung clothes at me, "Put these on, you have to look hotter than hell. They are going to flip the F out!"

I slipped on a low cut, red spaghetti strap shirt and a pair of tight low-rise skinny jeans. I pulled on my boots and dried my hair until it was pin straight. Grabbed my black leather jacket and strapped my guitar case on my back.

It was seven o'clock when Lea and I left our apartment. The auditions should have started earlier, but I really didn't know of the exact time. It was snowing lightly and the city had a beautiful soft light hue to it. The snow crunched lightly under our feet. When we got to the guy's block, Lea ran. *I figured she was excited.*

Walking through the first floor to the basement was eerily silent, and I wondered if anybody showed up at all.

Taking a deep breath, I knocked on the studio door; adrenaline surging through my body. *God, this felt good. Not only was I going to play in front of everyone, I would be playing with Shane.* There was no way I would give myself to someone like him, but I could be with him this way, which to me was just as hot. That way, I could go on doing what I was here for, looking for my other half.

Conner opened the door. A huge smile crossed over his face when he saw us. "Just in time, two beautiful girls in the studio should help ease some tension, I hope." Lea jumped into his arms.

The band sat together on the floor looking completely miserable. Shane looked up at me with a confused expression. He stood up, dusted his pants off, and started to walk over.

Tucker got to me before Shane could. "Hey, are you here to listen to me play? That's cool, my first fan." I ignored him and stepped past. I took off my coat and handed it to Lea.

Shane's mouth fell open when he saw my outfit, but not as far as it did when I unbuckled my guitar case. "I'm sorry, Tucker, but I'm not here to listen to you play. I thought I'd take a crack at auditioning; see if I could play as good as Alex."

Tucker laughed, "My fucking mother could play better than Alex right now, both his arms are broken, but she ain't here. But, damn girl, you look hot. I'd like to buy some stock in that ass later. My place or yours?"

I grimaced in Tucker's direction. I noticed a couple of six packs open where he had been sitting. I smiled sweetly at Tucker, "I think you are subhuman when you drink and talk like that, so I'd appreciate it, if when you do drink, you don't speak to me." I turned to Shane. He tore his eyes off my guitar and looked at me, waiting. "Shane, is it okay if I try?"

Shane tilted his head. "That looks an awful lot like a 1964 Gibson ES0335 TDC," he murmured.

"Yeah, an awful lot like it. So, can I play?"

"You tell me, Grace. Can you play?"

Lea giggled. "Come on, Conner, get your camera phone out. You are going to wanna record this." Conner dug through his pockets as I plugged my guitar into Alex's amps.

"Give me a fucking break. Don't let her embarrass herself like this. Shane, tell her no!" Tucker yelled. He was cut off from yelling more by one of Lea's shoes flying across the room and smacking him in the head.

I pulled the old leather strap over my head and let the beautiful heaviness of my instrument hang from my shoulder. The hardwood and course strings beneath my hands sent shivers through my body. I closed my eyes and breathed in deeply. Butterflies stirred in my insides; flapping their tiny, little wings from their long dormant slumber.

Slowly, I began playing the sweet low melody that Shane had played for me the first time in the studio, mimicking it perfectly. The beginning dynamics of the sad melody were soft and desperate, and then I increased them to a faster level, pushing and tempting the longing emotion of the music. I begin pounding out dark chords to create a sensory texture that stabbed straight into my spinal cord and bolted through every pore in my body. A warm rush of blood twisted and spiraled across my cheeks and down my torso, causing the hairs on my neck to stand up along the way.

A rich, darker sound melted into my melody. Shane had joined me, twisting our notes together in a passionate harmony. The notes we bore were like the blood that flowed through our veins feeding our beating hearts.

Our rhythm continuously got faster, truly as a heartbeat in the throes of a passionate climax within the song. The dynamics of the music were increasingly getting louder until both our instruments met at the top with what seemed like an explosion of sound. We pushed each other to new musical heights, an idea played by Shane would be finished or embellished by me and vise-a-versa. Then the dynamics of the melodies changed again to a decrescendo, a softer level, returning from the climax and passion, to the sadness and longing, until the song slowly ended with a thick heavy silence.

When we ended the song, he was breathless.

"What else can you play?" he asked almost panting.

"Anything you want me to," I replied.

A determined looked shadowed his features. "Hendrix," he answered.

I grinned wide and blasted through Purple Haze from start to finish, embellishing on Hendrix's infamous guitar solos and deliberate distortions. My fingers hummed.

Shane stared with disbelief still flooding his darkening expression. It clawed at me; my fingers flittered along the strings again.

Improvising, my goal being to make Shane's jaw drop even further, I began a soft ballad, unfolding the notes at a slow measured pace. My fingers bounced towards all genres of music, each note giving rhythm and birth to a funky piece of music that soared throughout the studio. A bleak bluesy beginning dripped from each note, transforming into a jazzy composition and weaving into a web of classical eloquence. My fingers moved faster, turning the melody into a sharp shrill rock solo and then into the heavy chords of thrash. Slowly, I returned to the low murmurs of a hushed lonely melody, like a heartbeat unraveling its beautiful ethereal essence into the heavens until there was silence.

"That girl can play," Ethan's voice cut through the silence.

Alex chuckled, "Yeah, and I think I'm in love!"

"Shut up," Shane said. He glared at me, "Play more." Sitting back against one of huge couches that were haphazardly laid out around room, he gestured for me to continue. His expression looked agonized and I was immediately regretful for showing him this side of me. This was supposed to be my thank you, something good; not something that should make him angry with me.

"No," I said shaking my head. "You seem really upset with me for some reason right now and that's not what I had wanted to happen, Shane." I slid the strap of my guitar over my head and gently leaned my guitar against the amp. I grudgingly got my case and started packing up.

"Don't go, Grace," Shane said just above a whisper.

My eyes met his. He looked tense and scared. "What did you want to happen?"

"I honestly thought you would let me play for Alex and that you wouldn't be angry. I don't understand what it was that I did wrong, but right now, you look like you want to kill me," I explained.

He ran his hand through his hair and grabbed his guitar. He paused and watched me for a moment, "I'm just thunderstruck right now, I'm not angry. That's like the third time in less than a week you've managed to shock me. What else can you do? Fly? Or," he started laughing at me, "Or, can you also play the piano and sing? Because then I'd understand Alex, then I'd be in love with you too."

I froze. "Well, we definitely wouldn't want that, would we? So let's just say that I can play guitar really well and I can't do anything else." I felt my face blush.

"Ha! Don't let her kid you. She can do it all," Lea laughed. Startled, I jumped back a bit. I had forgotten that everyone else was there with us. *Oh, that's not good.*

Shane stopped strumming his guitar and looked at me curiously.

Ethan jumped up and pulled me over to keyboard. He switched it on and stood close enough to me that I felt uncomfortable. I looked up at him timidly, but he smiled down at me and brushed the hair off my shoulder. "Go ahead, Grace, make us fall in love with you," he chuckled jokingly into my ear.

I blinked. *Screw it; I want to play*. Gabriel said live this life. This was me living. Hopefully in the interim of me living, I'd find *him*.

Not thinking any further, I bit my lower lip and closed my eyes, remembering the song that Shane had played for me on his guitar. That piece needed a piano part. I thought about the words he sang, the torment and the longing. I reached for the microphone that Alex used to sing into when he played the keyboard switching it on.

Slow and steamy, I let the lyrics fall from my lips. My fingers danced like raindrops across the keys. I tore through the haunting melody as if it was a brilliant light to help them in their darkness. I bared my soul in each word, note and breath. My soul had been on mute for thousands of years until this very moment. Tears threatened to burst from my eyes, so I kept them closed tight.

I let my voice drift to a whisper and stop. My fingers continued their feverish playing, blanketing everyone with the shear depths of the real me. I saw *him* behind my closed eyelids, pale blue angels eyes. *My angel; my soul mate.* The melody swirled around me, washing me in ancient visions. The world has been dull and unkind without *him*. I played for *him*, for how we used to sing together in the gardens, a gentle ethereal ballad.

Ethan's cool hand on my shoulder startled me into stopping. My fingers clutched at the keys. My eyes flew open and everyone was standing there gaping at me. But not Shane, Shane had never gotten up, he was kneeling with both hands leaning on his guitar; his fingertips white from tension.

"I think I can speak for everybody here, you're taking Alex's place," Ethan announced. "Where the hell did you learn to play like that?"

I could barely take my eyes from Shane's. He looked like he was in so much pain and I didn't want to be the cause of that. He seemed so broken. I shrugged in answer to Ethan's question, "I took a few lessons."

Tucker stumbled up to Ethan and looked around to the rest of the guys. "Wait a second; does this mean I don't get to play? That pretty much sucks, Grace."

An hour had passed and we all hung out in the studio, playing music and laughing at Tucker's drunken tantrums. I wanted desperately to talk to Shane, but I was too nervous that he'd already thrown away what simple friendship we had started to have. As everyone started to clean up their stuff, Shane walked to the door of the studio, grabbing his jacket on the way.

"Hey, dude. You're splitting?" Ethan asked. "Where you off to? Shouldn't we celebrate or something?"

"I have plans," he said and glanced at me. He wrenched the door open so hard that it hit the wall. Then he walked out and slammed the door behind him.

I had no idea how in the last 24 hours, I had gone from being someone you would jump in front of a knife for, to not being able to stay in the same room with.

Ethan hooked his huge arm in mine. "I say we take this gorgeous little thing out and celebrate!"

We ended up in Boozer's, which was quiet until Tucker got there. We ordered food and sodas (yes, we actually ordered pitchers of soda) and Tucker entertained us with his drunken outbursts.

In his total state of foolish inebriation, he invited everyone for a mid-week mini ski vacation in his parent's "resort house" calling them to make the plans, waking them up. Continuing his wild behavior, he called ahead to the "resort house" to make sure they would order the same champagne that I liked at Masa. His reasoning was so he could try to "sweep me off my feet." Everyone howled with laughter when I told him the only way I'd go was if he didn't, or he could just send the champagne right to my apartment so I could drink it alone.

I was enjoying myself until Shane walked into the bar at midnight with a beautiful dark-haired girl. He sat her at the bar and ordered some drinks, never acknowledging us at our table.

I watched him trail his fingers along her arm. Giggling, she leaned closer to him and kissed him. My mouth went dry and the only thing on our table was a pitcher of soda. Watching Shane kissing that girl made me want something stronger and I hated myself for it.

His strong hands ran up her thighs and she squirmed in delight. I had to turn away from them. Dragging my eyes from the scene, I found myself face to face with Ethan, who was watching me curiously.

Ethan looked over to Shane and back to me. "Hey, you okay?"

"Yes, I'm awesome," I said. I knew Shane was what he was, so why did I feel like I was drowning? Why would I care if Shane were kissing someone else? I definitely didn't want him kissing me.

Ethan smiled at me politely. "Does that bother you?" He motioned toward Shane who was now pawing at the poor girl's breasts through her shirt. "Shane and that girl?"

I smiled weakly. "I just think that Shane is better than that, but he doesn't want people to see that, does he?"

Ethan laughed. "Grace, you are adorable. That *is* Shane. Don't be like every other girl he's bagged, and fall for him, thinking you'll be the one that'll change him. It's not going to happen."

I gave him a disgusted look.

"Don't do what that girl's doing either," he pointed to Shane's date, who was rubbing him in a very private area through his jeans. "Because a night with Shane for those girls always ends the same, a little while in the Bone Room and then maybe cab fare home. Don't turn yourself into one of them, you're better than that."

I burst out laughing. I was so loud that Shane glanced up and caught my eye, which made me laugh even more. His expression looked sad for the briefest of moments and then he quickly turned back to his *friend*.

"Oh God, Ethan, seriously? I can't believe you think you have to sit here and preach to me about him. There is no way I'd ever let myself be abused like that. Although," I teased. "I have to hear all about this Bone Room."

As Ethan and I laughed about all the debauchery that occurred in the Bone Room, our small group seemed to peter out and go home; all complaining about getting up for work in a few hours. By two in the morning, Ethan and I were the only two left at our table. Shane and his date were still at the bar molesting each other.

"You should definitely come to Tucker's winter place, though. It's crazy. You'll love it." Ethan said blushing.

"Oh, will I?" I laughed.

"Would you like me to walk you home? It's two."

"Thanks, Ethan, that's sweet, but you don't have to. You live in the opposite direction."

He blushed again. "Yeah, but I really want to."

I studied Ethan's face. Was he the one I'd been looking for? I searched his features for something, anything. His eyes were soft brown with little flecks of yellow mixed in, long platinum blond hair pulled back into a low pony tail; handsome sweet smile. I wondered if he would try to kiss me and how I'd feel after.

I snatched up my coat and smiled at him. "Sure, Ethan, I'd love that." We walked out of the bar without ever looking in Shane's direction.

We walked home through the snow. He asked me questions about my family and about Lea and me growing up. The closer we got to my front door, the closer I came to realizing that he couldn't be the one I'd been looking for.

Ethan walked me up the stairs and leaned in for a quick peck on my cheek. He lingered for just a moment and stepped back smiling.

I let out the long breath that I hadn't even realized I was holding and smiled at him gratefully. "Ethan, I..."

He tucked a stray strand of my hair behind my ear and left his hand on my shoulder. "As much as I would love to kiss you right now, I won't. I can tell you're uncomfortable. Anyway, I don't think I can start a relationship with my new guitarist without screwing it up somehow in the next few days," he smirked.

I sighed. "Ethan, I can't do relationships either, I can't even muster up a one night stand. I'm sorta in love with someone, I just haven't seen him for a long time. Thank you for walking me home and making me feel special though."

"Yeah, well you are. Besides we all owe you big time for taking Alex's place. You blew us away today. Even Shane and he never gets flustered over anything, especially a chick."

"Yeah, well he seemed really ticked off at me for coming by and playing. I didn't mean to show off or anything. I just really missed playing like that. It was...something," I laughed. I unlocked the door and said goodnight to Ethan again, knowing that he would be a nice friend to have around.

I tiptoed into my room. I cursed out loud for forgetting to do laundry again, so I kept on my clothes. Looks like the spin cycle and I have a hot date tomorrow morning.

Slipping under the covers, my cell phone started blaring its harsh sirens. I jumped for the phone, stumbling through my blankets and falling with a hard thud on the floor. I didn't bother to look at the number, because I was in so much pain from how I had landed.

"Hello?" I said through gritted teeth.

"Where are you?" That raspy low sexy voice demanded. It was angry.

"I'm in bed, Shane. Honestly, right now I'm on the damn floor. Why are you calling me?"

"Is Ethan with you?" It was a whisper; a harsh painful and heartbreaking whisper. And I didn't want to hear it. I didn't want him to pretend to care about who was with me. It confused me and scared the hell out of me. I didn't want these intense hormonal feelings to overtake my sane mind every time he was in reach of me and his eyes looked at me the way they did. I didn't want to be another one of his many. *I was in love with something else*.

"No."

A long sigh floated to my ears overwhelming me. "I'm sorry, I shouldn't have..."

"Don't feed me any of your crap, Shane. I have no idea why you think you can call me at any hour and pretend you give a crap about who I leave a bar with."

"Stop, Grace. Please!" Shane yelled into the phone. "I have a whole speech I need to say and..."

"Yeah, yeah, Shane. Four whores and seven beers ago...save it, Shane. I don't care what you have to say to me. It's none of your business if I take home an entire football team. Are you just pissed because you didn't get a crack at it first? You can't even comprehend how someone isn't fazed by your rock god status. Well get it through your skull, you're not a thought in my mind. So get on with your life. And don't be pissed off at me because I tried to do you and your friends a favor by showing you I can play a few instruments. You don't want me to play with you guys; fine. I DON'T CARE!" I poked my finger hard at the end button on my phone, hanging up on him. *There's no way I'm going to let him get the last word!*

My entire body spiked with the heat of the surging adrenaline bolting through my veins. Beads of sweat burst through my pours. I pulled my clothes off. Sleeping in my bra and panties would have to do. I sank myself into my sheets and curled into a ball. Closing my eyes, I tried desperately to remember the reasons that I kept moving on. But just like it's done so often lately, my mind got muddled and I couldn't even focus myself on those ancient blue eyes. Nothing seemed to calm me down.

A soft tapping at the window jarred me to my senses. Honestly, it made me want to scream and call 911, but like the cheesy horror movie my life was, I went to the window wrapped in my bed sheet and pulled the curtain to the side. Standing there covered in snow was Shane. I let the curtain fall back. I should let him freeze out there.

"Grace, please! It's freaking cold out here." His voice was muffled from the glass. I ignored him. "Grace, I swear I will ring your doorbell until I wake everybody up. Open the damn window!"

I pushed the curtain aside, unlocked the latch and opened the window. About a foot of snow seemed to blow in with Shane, although I couldn't tell which substance was colder. He surveyed my room, no doubt looking for Ethan. The relief was visible in his expression.

Then his eyes really focused on me. "You're not dressed, are you? Is that your sheet?"

I held the sheet tighter and looked away. "What. Do. You. Want?"

Without warning, he stalked toward me. My breath caught in my throat. In the bright moonlight, streaming through the open window his eyes looked so intense, like icy glaciers. *God help me, why was the first thought in this body to find some way to melt those glaciers?*

I backed up until he cornered me against the wall, slamming his open palms against it. He smelled like whiskey and cheap perfume.

He slowly leaned his body into mine, backing me tight against the wall. Instinctively, I pushed my hands up against his chest. His shirt was wet from the snow and his body trembled beneath it. My traitorous sheet fell to the floor.

"Shane, stop," I breathed.

He rested his forehead against mine, his hands slide over my shoulders down to my waist; slow and gentle. *Oh, my God, did his touch feel good.*

Brushing his lips across my cheek, he buried his face in my hair, "Grace, all I want to do it kiss you right now," he whispered. Softly, he pushed my hair back and grazed his lips along my neck. His lips were warm and soft; I wanted them all over me. *This was too much.*

"Shane, please," I whispered. *Why was I saying please? Please kiss me? Please let me forget who I am? Please stop?*

He pulled back slowly, his eyes meeting mine. My heart was dancing wildly in my chest. His expression was full of sadness and hunger. "Just tell me why I got crazy thinking you were going home with Ethan? Tell me why I want to kill any man that looks at you? Grace, I don't want to feel this way."

His hands subtly slid to my waist, one finger hooked itself under the lace trim of my panties. I let out an audible sigh. This was too close, too tempting.

"Shane. Stop, you're drunk, you're soaking wet, you are so cold you're trembling."

He stumbled away from me, "I'm not trembling from the cold, Grace." He sank down onto my bed and hung his head in his hands. In the dim light, he looked like a defeated little boy.

Wrapping my sheet around my body again I opened my door, walked to Lea's bedroom, and knocked for her. She sleepily stepped out into the hallway and I pulled her into my doorway to look at Shane. She gave me a confused look and pushed me back into the hallway.

"What the hell is he doing? It smells like a liquor store in your room!" she whispered.

"He must have climbed the fire escape. He knocked on my window after I hung up on him." I shrugged. "He's been quite hands-on in there. I feel mauled."

"He didn't do anything to you, did he?"

I shook my head. "No, but God, Lea, the way he touched me I freaking wanted him to. That was so damn erotic and I can't believe I just said that out loud to you."

She gave me another confused look. "So, why are you in the hallway with me?"

"Lea, that's Shane in there. He's probably been with more women than I could count. The only difference I'd be to him is that he would actually know my name. Look, he's soaking wet from being in the snow. Can I have one of Conner's shirts and pants and stuff. Oh, and can I borrow a shirt and pants from you. I haven't done laundry."

Running back into her room, she emerged not even two minutes later with a pile of clothes for me. I immediately dressed in the hallway, not wanting to do so in front of him. If he looked at me with those hungry eyes again, I didn't trust this body to say no to him. *Hormones suck.*

Shane was still slumped over on my bed, but he at least looked up when I came back in.

"Did you wake up Conner? Oh, God. Grace, did you call the cops?"

I giggled at his absurdity. "Shane, you are a real ass sometimes." I kneeled down in front of him and lifted his wet shirt over his head. It stuck to him and he comically had trouble helping me get it off him. "I have dry socks, boxers and pants for you too, but you need to dress yourself."

Leaving him to get dressed, I went to the kitchen and grabbed a couple of bottles of water, then to the closet for an extra pillow and blanket for the couch.

He walked into the living room as I was making up the couch for him to sleep on. His face was drawn and broken.

"What?" I asked him exasperated. "There's no way you should be going home this intoxicated in the snow with no jacket on."

He ran a hand through his gorgeously tousled hair, "I really screwed things up with our friendship, didn't I? You're standing here looking at me the way you look at Tucker."

I stopped what I was doing to look at him. Strangely enough, I had not felt the same after Shane touched me. With Shane I wanted more, I had to talk myself out of saying yes. With Tucker, I knew I never wanted him to touch me again. With Shane, the only real reason I held back were those ancient blue eyes that I clung to looking for. *That and the fact that Shane was a man-whore.* I laughed at myself for the thought.

"Why are you laughing at me?" he asked.

"Shane, you can't ruin a friendship if you were only pretending to be my friend to get into my pants."

His face darkened. He stormed toward me and grabbed my wrist. His touch didn't match his facial expression. It was soft and pleading. He led me back to my bedroom. When we reached my door, he stopped and brought my wrist up to his lips and softly kissed it. Chills ran down my spine, his breath hot on my skin. He lifted his lips from my skin and I swear I felt pain from the separation. His hand still holding mine, he caressed the soft sensitive skin of my wrist, looking down at it. My breath caught.

"You have a tattoo?"

I said nothing. But, I watched as his features changed again; this time to drunk confusion. He'd be too drunk to notice anything but my tat. *I hope*.

His thumb lightly swept over my wrist and stopped. His eyes looked in mine, flickering in and out of focus. "It's covering up a scar?" He grabbed my other wrist fumbling for it, and I didn't fight him. *Maybe if he saw what I had done, he'd think I was psychotic and he'd leave me alone*.

"Why would you do that?" His voice was no louder than a whisper.

Taking my wrists back, I held them to my chest. "You know, Shane, the people that walk around you every day? Each of them has a life separate then you. Pasts, pains, loves and losses. You don't know me. I am a hell of a lot more than a fifteen-minute screw, and sadly, most of your other *friends* are too. You just don't ever see that from between their legs."

He softly traced the edge of my jaw with his index finger. "Goodnight, Grace," he said as he wobbled back to the living room.

I closed my door quietly and made sure I locked it.

Chapter 9

Shane was still sprawled out over the couch when I woke up the next morning at 10 o'clock. It was still so early that it would be really mean of me to kick him out, but late enough that I was stuck alone with him since Conner and Lea were at work.

I peeked out the front door to see how much snow fell. The sidewalk was already shoveled, the streets were plowed and a light feathery snow was gently falling. I grabbed the mail and decided instead of running that I'd just make coffee and curl up and play my guitar. Then I would tackle my laundry.

I threw the mail on the kitchen table, barely noticing the one piece of mail addressed to me. Maybe, the size of the envelope was what made me look twice at it. It wasn't normal size; a bit larger and thicker than the rest. It might have been the color, a creamy peach that struck a chord with me. Whichever, I picked it up and walked into my room. I stuck my head in the living room to check on Shane; he was still out cold.

Sitting down on my bed, I glanced quickly at the return address on the letter. It was from the hospice. I ripped open the envelope and unfolded a handwritten letter. Another smaller envelope slid out and fell to the floor. Bending down, I picked up the fallen envelope and read the name on the front; *Gracie*. It was in Jacob's handwriting.

My knees buckled and I sat heavily on the floor, leaning against my bed. I read the unfolded letter first. I think that's what was meant for me to do, since the other letter was still sealed. It was from one of Jake's doctors, Doctor Slaterman, whom Jacob seemed to grow very fond of while staying at the hospice.

Dear Grace,

I never got to give my condolences to you before you left. First and foremost, I wanted to write that we held a small memorial for your brother, recalling how full of love and life he was, and how amazing he was with all the other patients. What started out as a small gathering in the common room turned into a significant event. I know that Jacob did not want a funeral or wake for his passing, but I felt we needed to celebrate Jacob, the patient we had for the longest period, who fought the hardest against his disease.

Before Jacob passed, he spoke privately with me, asking me to give you the letter from him that I have enclosed.

I hope all is well with you, Grace. The patients and staff here miss your nightly musical tributes for your brother. Our halls have never been more silent.

Best Regards,

Martin Slaterman, MD.

Cradling Jacob's letter in my arms I promised myself that I would record a few pieces of music on a CD for the patients there. Looking down again at Jake's handwriting, I traced the letters with my fingers.

As I opened it, tears spilled from my eyes. How death takes everyone away, leaving me here, knowing where everyone goes, and knowing I would never be welcomed there; this is hell.

Gracie,

So, I guess I'm a goner. I wish I could have stayed with you longer, but I couldn't fight anymore, and for that, I am sorry.

I want you to know that because of you, I was not scared. I knew that there was a heaven and that I will make it my mission to get you there one day too.

After your accident, when we lost Mom and Dad and I almost lost you, I really thought you were crazy. I thought that you had major brain damage from the accident, but your doctors assured me that your head was the only thing that was not injured. It took me months, maybe years to see finally that my little sister did really die with my parents in that accident and your soul stayed. But Gracie, I'm happy that you were here and I was honored with the chance to have you in my life, because without you, I would have died with my diagnoses. You showed me what faith and what love was and if I can do anything where I am now to help you end your punishment, I will.

I love you, Gracie. I promise you that I will see you again one day.

Jake

I folded the note back up so no one could see it. I didn't know if anyone who read it would understand what Jake had implied, but I couldn't chance it. Lea was the only other person who knew my secret. They were the only two people I had ever told about my past. The reason was simple; this was the hardest life I had fallen into.

Usually, I fell into someone older who lingered on for a short amount of time. When they passed on, I would end up a lost soul in another shell. I'd lost so many people, and I'd suffered so many sicknesses and diseases, it was beyond count. I once woke up in a woman who had been attacked by a rapist. She was lucky enough to die in the beginning of his torture. *Me?* My soul showed up for the whole show. I begged him to kill me when he was done with her body and he did; slowly.

Each time that I could take no more of a person's life, I would take too many pills, or forget to take certain medicine, or like in this life, slice my wrists open when I was sixteen. I don't condone suicide, but really is it? These beautiful souls have gone and I'm just shoved into their rotting bodies. *My own personal hell, a lost soul on earth for eternity.*

Jacob once asked me if I was a ghost. I told him that I didn't know. I'm more of just a lost spirit, wandering around looking for the other half of me.

This was the only life that I had lived through while trying to end it. Gabriel once said that maybe it was because *he* was here with me somewhere. Gabriel. I think I'm his personal play thing, I think this is his sick experiment on how much an angel's heart can take before it turns its wings on the love of a human.

Two hours later, Shane's soft touch on my shoulder woke me. I had fallen asleep clutching Jacob's words. My face was still damp from tears and it hurt to blink them.

"Grace? What's wrong, are you sick?"

I sat up, the papers crinkling noisily around me. "I'm fine. How are you?" I asked curtly.

His muscular arm reached up, running his hand through his hair, a lost confused expression on his face. "What the hell did I do last night?"

Laughter busted out of my mouth. "That's great, Shane. No, really. That's perfect. Why don't you go home now, okay? Goodbye," I snapped. *Jerk. I still felt the heat of his touch on me!*

He stood there deep in thought, seemingly trying to remember any information from the night before. "Grace, I know we didn't, did we?"

I grabbed up all the loose papers around me, got up, shoved them into a drawer, and stormed out of my room. I slammed the door in his face, but he just swung it right back open.

I bolted into the kitchen and he was right behind me. I honestly thought about getting a sharp knife out of one of the drawers to scare him. He grabbed me by one arm and swung me around. My heart pounded hard and I could feel my pulse in my wrists.

"What did I do? Why have you been crying?" He asked with a soft sad expression. His face leaned in so close to me that I felt his breath on my skin.

"You didn't do anything, Shane. You called me last night. You thought I was with Ethan. I hung up on you and you climbed up the fire escape in the snow, with no coat on and banged on my window until I let you in. Now please, just leave."

"No." He shook his head vehemently. "No. I'm not leaving until I know I'm not the reason you're crying." He stopped talking and looked me intensely in the eyes. "You were wearing a sheet? You...you got me dry clothes," he said, remembering.

"No big deal, see?"

"No big deal? I leaned you up against a wall; I can still taste your skin on my mouth. I can still feel your body against mine."

For the life of me, I couldn't think of anything to say. What he just said was so intoxicating that I didn't want to say anything to make him do it again, or make him not want to.

Gently, he took my wrists in both his hands skimming his thumbs against my scars once more. My heart sped up from his touch. I turned my head away from him; waiting for the insensitive questions people always asked when they noticed my scars. *Did you just do it for attention? Did you have a plan? Was there a backup plan? Will you try it again since you failed the first time?* Instead, his soft gentle voice asked, "Why were you crying this morning?"

Dragging my hands away from his touch, I let them fall limply to my sides. "I received a letter in the mail today from the hospice where Jacob passed away. Inside was a letter that he had written for me before he died. It was just hard to read it."

Taking my hands tenderly in his, his breath caught. "Grace..."

The way he said my name made me ache. It shattered my already broken heart to dust. The tears came, streaming like rain down my cheeks. Shane pulled me into his arms and I fell into him. He gently stroked my hair as I let my sadness overtake me.

He held me until my tears stopped. I looked up at him, and smiled weakly, "I'm sorry, Shane."

I tried to move away from him, but he gently held me tighter. He closed his eyes and leaned his forehead against mine. It felt like last night all over. Only this time, he wasn't drunk.

He raised his head, just enough to look into my eyes, and breathed in softly. His blue eyes were captivating. He held himself there, almost touching my lips; just a soft breath between them. I watched the inner struggle in his eyes as they looked down longingly to my lips. Then, meeting my gaze again, he closed his eyes and trembled. He inhaled deeply and stepped back; my disobedient body followed. I had to ball my fists and force myself to stand my ground. There was no way someone could have this effect over my body; it was insane; it was mortifying.

The shrill ringing of the doorbell made us both jump. I gave him a small tight smile, thinking of the horrible mistake I could have just thrown myself into. I backed away.

"Please don't be sorry, Grace," his words were soft and gentle. "I am your friend and I'm here if you need to talk about anything or need a shoulder to cry on."

The doorbell continued ringing like a screaming child wanting attention in the background.

"Thanks," I whispered.

I spun around to walk towards the front door.

"Especially if that's the only way I'll ever get to hold you," he whispered. I didn't think it was meant for me to hear, but I looked back to acknowledge it anyway. He was looking up at the ceiling, running both his hands through his hair. No, it wasn't meant for me to hear, which made it all the more dangerous.

I opened the door to two men in suits with gold police shields held out in front of them. "Good afternoon. We're detectives from the 19th precinct. We're looking for a Grace Taylor." Shane was behind me immediately.

"I'm Grace Taylor. How may I help you?"

"Miss Taylor, may we come in. We need to speak to you about the incident with Carl Sumpton."

I waved both the detectives in and showed them to the living room, shoving Shane's makeshift bed things over so we all had room to sit. "I'm sorry, Detectives, but I'm not sure who Carl Sumpton is, unless you are referring to the man who attacked me in Boozer's late Wednesday night?"

Neither of them sat down.

Shane quietly exited the room.

The older detective, who was without a doubt the thinnest man I had ever met, introduced himself as Detective Allens and he pulled a file folder out of his soft leather briefcase. Placing it on the coffee table, he opened its contents and Carl Sumpton's arrest picture stared back on me. Smiling menacingly for the camera was the man who attacked me.

Sitting down on the edge of the couch, I leaned forward and touched the image on the paper. "Carl Sumpton? I hadn't been told his name."

The second detective, who I'd estimate to be around thirty, sat down on one of the chairs. He folded his hands on his lap and leaned forward, golden brown eyes serious, yet cautious.

"Miss Taylor, I'm Detective Ramos. Had you ever had contact with Carl Sumpton before?"

"No. That was the first time I'd ever seen him. Although, now that I look at his face without him trying to throw himself on me, he does look kind of familiar." I sighed.

Shane returned with a few bottles of water and offered them to the detectives. "I can make coffee if you'd like," he said.

Detective Ramos accepted the water from Shane, "Thank you. I'm sorry. I didn't catch your name." He twisted off the top of the bottle and sipped the water, waiting for Shane to reply.

Shane gave him one of his heart stopping smiles and held out his hand to shake the Detective's hand. "That's because I never said it. I'm Shane Maxton." He sat down next to me, placing a water bottle on the table in front of me with one hand. The other he placed on the small of my back, letting me know he was there for me. I wanted to melt into his touch.

Detective Ramos shifted in his seat and continued. "You're the one who helped to stop the attack." It wasn't a question.

Shane smiled at me, gently rubbing my back with his hand. I clamped my mouth shut, afraid that the butterflies that were wreaking havoc in my belly would fly out of my mouth and attack Shane at any moment. "Grace was doing a pretty good job of defending herself. I think she would have taken care of him all by herself if I hadn't get there in time, but I'm confused. We already spoke with the arresting officers at the hospital that night. Has something changed?"

Detective Ramos and Allens shared a glance. Then the older man nodded his head and Detective Ramos looked to Shane and me with a somber expression. "After Mr. Sumpton was arraigned, he was remanded and housed in Riker's. We don't know how it happened, but he was put in his cell at 1400 hours and at the evening head count after the meal he wasn't accounted for." He hesitated for a moment, letting the news sink in. "The cell was still locked when they went to feed him. No one understands how he escaped, since the cell hadn't been opened since his arrival. Furthermore, when questioned, none of the other prisoners even remembered seeing him inside his cell."

The hairs on the back of my neck stood up, and the pressure in Shane's hands became tighter on my back, holding me steady. "Like he just vanished?"

Detective Ramos gave me a tight smile. "No. Most likely, he found some way out with help from someone on the outside of the cell. He probably terrified the other prisoners so badly that they pretended to see nothing. He was a monster when they brought him in. They needed a few corrections officers to settle him down when he was left in his cell, but there's an even more disturbing part," he explained.

I nodded for the detective to continue. What could be more disturbing than telling me the guy who attacked me could be roaming around the streets of New York City ready to attack another girl?

"When we ran his name through our system, nothing came up. Investigating further, we found him to be an outstanding citizen until the last five months or so."

Shane looked curiously at the Detective; asking the question that was formulating in my head. "What happened five months ago?"

Taking a deep breath, Detective Allens stepped forward to answer, "He was admitted to the Sans de Barron Hospice; he was terminal. His doctors had given him only a few weeks to live. He'd been comatose and unresponsive for weeks, then sometime last Sunday, he just walked out of the hospice. Am I right in saying that you had been living at the hospice with your brother Jacob for approximately six months?"

I swallowed hard and nodded a yes. "There must be a mistake though. The man that attacked me, there was no way that he could have been that strong and dying of some disease at the same time. Maybe the guy stole the real Carl Sumpton's identity or something."

The detectives both shook their heads in agreement, but their expressions never reached their eyes. They had their own theories and they weren't going to share it with us.

Detective Ramos cleared his throat and continued, "When a perpetrator of a crime of this magnitude is arraigned, the District Attorney on the case usually requests a temporary order of protection to be issued to the victim. This is your copy of the order." He placed another paper on the table from his briefcase. "I wanted to say that I'm sure this matter will be resolved soon."

Shane's hand was still on me. It was quickly kindling a fire under his fingertips. His features were angry. "And you think a piece of paper will stop this lunatic from trying to hurt Grace again?

What should she do if he comes up to her when she's walking down the street? Should she say, hold on let me look in my purse, here this piece of paper will stop you?"

I placed my hand on Shane's knee and his eyes snapped to mine at the touch. "Stop it, Shane. I'm sure they will do everything they can to contain him again." I looked at both the detectives. "Thank you both for coming here and telling me instead of calling me on the phone. I appreciate the paperwork and everything. Is there anything that you think I could do in the meantime, while you…um…work on this matter?"

"We understand your anxiety, Mr. Maxton. For the next twenty-four hours, there will be a uniformed officer sitting outside this apartment in a patrol car. Just be aware and keep your eyes open, Miss Taylor."

After a few more words, I walked the detectives to the front door and locked the deadbolt.

Shane came up behind me and gently placed his hands on my shoulders. They felt strong and safe; I stepped away quickly. The last thing I needed was my head muddled from his touch. "I'm fine, Shane," I snapped.

He stormed off down the hallway. "Yeah, well you definitely will be, because Conner and I are staying here with you and Lea until that asshole is behind bars again."

Somehow, I thought that would prove to be more dangerous than Carl Sumpton trying to kill me.

Chapter 10

Shane thundered into the bathroom, slamming the door behind him, "I'm taking a shower! Do not leave this building without me!"

"Make sure you scrub yourself real well, Shane! That perfume you were wearing when you came here last night stinks!" I screamed, as I slammed my bedroom door. Now he was going to be Mr. Chivalry and pretend to care about me? Was he trying to prove something? Who did he think he was? And who in the world was going to protect me from him? AND, what gives him the right to shower in my apartment? *Oh, this is the perfect time to start doing my laundry with really hot water!*

Grabbing my laundry basket, I raced to the basement and started our archaic washing machine. When I did, I could hear Shane screaming from the shower above me. If he was really going to stay here for a while, he better get used to taking ice cold showers!

Overhead, I could hear him stomping through the apartment looking for me. Hearing the stairs creak under his weight, I turned to the door as he smashed it open. He strode across the tiny washroom, stopping a little more than an inch from me. His hair and skin were soaking wet; drops of water streamed down his skin.

"You really need to do your laundry right now? What? Are you mad at me for wanting to stay here? Ticked off because I might actually care if you are okay? What? Will it ruin your high expectations of me?" He cupped my face in both his hands, his breath quickening as he searched my face. "Or, maybe Grace, you want me here every freaking bit as much I want to be here and that scares the shit out of you?"

My eyes looked down. His towel was loosely wrapped around his waist. *God, please don't let that thing fall off!* My eyes rose slowly over the beautiful muscles of his stomach and chest; over the vibrant colors of his tattoos right to his blue eyes.

I tore my face away from his hands. "Nothing about you scares me, Shane. I just don't want you getting the wrong idea about us."

"I know, I know. There *is* no us. I'm not talking about staying here to..." Realization crossed his face. "Grace, you really think so little of me to think that I want to stay here so I could try to..." He stepped back shaking his head. Turning around, he walked up the stairs and continued with his icy shower.

I opened a folding chair and sat watching the machine vibrating, knowing he was right. I did want him here. Guilt overwhelmed my senses. How many years had I made it through whole lifetimes of other people, never feeling anything for another man the way I did for *him*. Now, I'm here with the Shane, the most commitment phobic person I had ever met and he's the one that peaks my interest? There was no way that I could break the vows I made to myself to find *him*, on someone as flimsy and shallow as Shane Maxton. I don't care how absolutely delicious he looked right out of an ice cold shower!

At three o'clock, Shane came down to the laundry room with a plate of food a hot cup of coffee for me. "I thought you'd be starving by now."

I smiled. "More bored out of my skull than hungry, but thank you." Grilled cheese sandwich with tomato and a banana. I dug in hungrily.

He chuckled to himself shaking his head, "You know, Grace, you don't have to stay down here. I promise you I will not bite," he smirked. "Well, unless you ask me to."

"Shut up," I smirked back at him. "I'm sorry about before," I said in-between chews. I knew it was impolite, but I was really hungry and I just wanted to apologize fast so we could forget about everything. "I guess I'm just a little freaked out by the whole Carl Sumpton thing."

Shrugging as if it was no big deal, he asked seriously, "Do you remember him at the hospice?"

"Not at all," I said, swallowing my last bite. "He did look familiar, but not from anywhere I could pinpoint." Shaking my head, I threw my hands up. "There were so many people there. I used to play my guitar for Jake every night, well, up until the last few days. There was always a different crowd of people surrounding the door listening. But if he was comatose, he shouldn't have known anything about me. I barely left Jake's room, let alone walk into other patient's rooms."

"Maybe he thought your playing stinks," he said taking my empty plate.

"Probably. I mean, I am almost as horrible as you!"

My statement was punctuated by the sound of the dryer's buzzer. Cracking up, I walked over to pull out and fold my last load of laundry.

When I lifted the last handful of clothes onto the small wooden table, I blanched, noticing Shane was holding up my bra and panties. I lunged for them, trying to snatch them out of his hands. He just held them up higher, making me stand on my tiptoes, jumping for them.

"Hey, Grace. Maybe getting an eyeful of your lingerie woke up our friend Carl from his coma. These are pretty intense undergarments, I know I'll be thinking about them later tonight!" he teased.

I shoved him in the gut, not hard, but hard enough to make him bend over and hand back my belongings.

"You are a jerk, Shane Maxton."

"Thanks, that's like the nicest thing you've called me so far."

After I was finished, Shane helped me carry my clothes upstairs. We both passed the front window and peeked out to see if a police car was parked anywhere on the street. It was. Smack dab in front of my door step. *Yeah, that's not going to scare the neighbors.*

Stretching himself across my bed, he watched me put my clothes away. Legs crossed at the ankles and hands under his head. I crossed my arms laughing at him.

He tilted his head toward my guitar, "Will you play something for me?"

I paused in thought, looking at him. I didn't want him to look at me with those intense eyes again. I ended the thought as soon as I had it. I would have to play in front of him later, next to him on stage, so I should get used to it now.

I unbuckled my case, pulled out my guitar and nudged him to move over on my bed. Well, it was *my* bed. He rolled over on his side and propped his head up with his hand to listen to me. I twisted my body around to face him, fingering some strings.

"What are you in the mood for?"

"Surprise me."

I didn't close my eyes this time, just watched as the fingers I'd come to know as my own, played. I started with the theme song to Sesame Street, which landed me a pillow to the side of the head. Giggling, I drifted into a rendition of You're so Vain by Carly Simon to Lost Cause from Beck, stopping after (I Hate) Everything About You by Ugly Kid Joe.

"Nice, Grace. What was that a montage of how I feel about Shane songs?"

I smiled wide. "Gee, am I that easy to read?" I teased.

"Play something that means something to you," he whispered.

So I did. I let my fingers go. I let my voice soar; rough and edgy. Piece of my Heart by Janis Joplin. *Wouldn't Shane get a blast out of knowing I used to practice with her before she became big?*

I matched her voice, her tone, her essence and through the whole song, I never looked away from his eyes. It was intense and electrifying. I felt more sensual and erotic than I had ever felt in this skin.

"You are simply the most amazingly talented person I've ever met," he whispered.

"Eh. I bet you haven't met too many people then."

*   *   *   *   *

Lea and Conner arrived back at the apartment within five minutes of each other. Both of them came barreling into the apartment, demanding to know why there was a police car parked in front of it.

After Shane told them about our visit with the detectives, Lea became very upset, crying and hugging me. Then she spent a good twenty minutes locking all the windows, pulling up the ladders to the fire escapes and looking under all the furniture.

Conner agreed that he and Shane should stay with us. He also thought that Ethan should too, since he had some sort of martial arts training. However, Shane was completely against it. *He wasn't drunk anymore, yet he was still against Ethan being with me?*

"Well, I hate to say it, but Tucker had a really great idea last night," Conner said, wiping Lea's tears away with his hands. *Oh, he's a keeper!*

"That drunken fool had a lot of ideas last night, most had to do with Grace and him on the pool table, so which idea are you taking about, Con?"

Shane glanced at me and made a tight smile.

"We should definitely go up to his winter place for a few days to get away from here," Conner explained.

Lea shook her head and cried harder. "I can't take off of work next week. My boss is going on vacation and needs me to hold down the fort while she's away."

Shane was staring at me. "Tucker invited you to his winter house?"

I scrunched my face into a frown, "Yeah, Tucker thinks I will fall in love with him because of his house, his money, his jaguar, and his expensive bottles of champagne."

"And what do you think?" Shane asked me.

"I don't think about Tucker at all."

I loved the way he smiled back at me.

The guys sat for the next hour trying to formulate a plan to keep us safe. Lea cried and whined, and then cried again. She was terrified. I eyed Conner. He caught the hint and ran over to Lea, who was by then in hysterics, soothing her with kisses and soft whispers.

I grabbed Shane's hand and pulled him into the kitchen. "Leave them alone for a minute. She needs to calm down and he really seems to do it better than me lately."

"Are you okay with everything? I didn't know the right stuff to say to you before. I just tried to take your mind off it, but are you scared?"

"No. I'm not scared of Carl Sumpton hurting *me*. I'm scared of him hurting Lea, Conner, or even you."

His mouth curved into a concerned smile. He lifted my hands and held them wrists up, between us. I raised my eyebrow at him. "You're not scared of much, are you?" He rubbed the scars on my wrist again. "One day, I hope we become close enough friends that you'll tell me about these."

"That would be real close, Shane. I think you're missing that get close to a women chromosome in your DNA," I laughed. "I have to take a shower and get ready for the show tonight. Why don't you call ahead and let those bouncer friends of yours know about Carl and let's take the picture of him too?" I said, walking away.

I jumped into the bathroom ready to transform myself into *Rock Goddess of Mad World*. I was insanely excited and all the thoughts of Carl Sumpton and his secret whereabouts washed away from me the more I thought about going on stage. I showered with the most scalding hot water I could stand, relaxing every muscle in my body. I wrapped myself in a towel and bolted through the hallway to my room, hoping I wouldn't be seen. I dried my hair and added a streak of temporary purple hair dye to it for a little funky feel. I polished my nails a deep purple to match the streak in my hair. While I was sliding a denim mini-skirt over my hips Lea knocked on the door and came in with a black bag.

A little time alone with *The One* and she'd forgotten all about the scary monster, she looked content and relaxed. *Oh, I envied her*.

"Wow. Your hair looks hot! And, I'm glad you're not fully dressed, because I brought you a little surprise today on my lunch hour," she beamed.

"Oh no, should I be afraid?" I giggled.

Lea tossed herself and the bag on the bed and gave me a naughty smile. "Before you open this bag, you have to promise that you will wear what I have in there! You cannot say no, because right now, I'm so freaked out about this stalker of yours that I want you to cancel the show. So any little thing you say might set me off crying."

"Oh, shut up!" I laughed grabbing the bag. "You know that I won't let anything happen to you or me." I stopped talking the minute I pulled the tiny garments out of the bag. There was a black lacy see-through bra with matching underwear. Well, it was more like a piece of dental floss than underwear. I held it up to her, "What is this supposed to cover, really?"

Another wicked grin is all she offered me.

The last piece I unfolded was deep purple, and it was the most perfect top ever made in existence. The neckline daringly plunged to show more cleavage than I'd ever seen on one of Shane's ladies. The back was almost bare and it just provided a thin lacy piece of material across the back to cover the strap of the bra perfectly. The material was silky and soft and I hugged my best friend as tightly as I could. "This is the most insane shirt I'd ever seen." Yanking off the clothes I had on, I pulled on the new sexy undergarments and slipped the luxurious shirt on. It fit perfectly.

When I looked at myself in the mirror, I gasped loudly. "This is lethal. This outfit is going to cause a riot. Lea, don't you think this is too much?" I frowned at my reflection; a part of me really, really wanted to wear this outfit, but another part was terrified.

"You look like a Rock Queen! It's perfect. Besides, I think my outfit is even worse than yours!" She dashed out of my room, came back with another bag, and started undressing and throwing clothes everywhere.

I stood in front of the mirror spinning around to get the full view. My shoulders were bare and the way my hair cascaded down in shiny black waves, I felt almost naked. But, I think the worst of all of my thoughts at that moment was the excited idea of what Shane would think when he saw me. *I needed to stop these alien thoughts when I was around Shane.* I needed to focus on finding *him* and not worry about meaningless urges I had for Shane. Besides, it's just this body's hormones that were acting up, nothing more.

All thought flew out of my head when I turned to see Lea's outfit. I looked like a nun compared to her. A deep red skin tight, shorter than short dress. It looked like it was made out of spandex and had huge openings to show off her waist. The color was brilliant, and the red accented her sandy blonde hair making her look like a vixen. Conner was going to be shocked.

We applied our make-up, giggling as if we were thirteen and up to trouble, and oddly that's exactly how I felt. Lea did my eye shadow, because she was always better at it than I was. She made them look smoky and sensual; my light grey irises looked like they could glow in the dark.

Holding hands, Lea and I walked out into the living room. All I heard was Conner curse and start demanding that Lea take the dress off, but when I looked at Shane, all the commotion seemed to get lower and fade away.

He had been leaning against the far wall and then pulled himself away, standing at attention when I walked in. His eyes greedily examined every inch of my bare skin. He lingered on my eyes and lips the longest, which I did not expect. He slowly walked over to me and gently reached for my hand. He entwined his fingers in mine, lifted my hand over my head, and twirled me around slowly.

"I have never seen anyone more exquisite in my entire life, Grace. You seem to have this knack of making me completely...breathless." He seemed shocked at himself for saying the words. He spun me around again, brushing the hair off my shoulders, his gaze sending shivers along my neck. His breathing stopped, caught somewhere in his lungs. Lightly touching the skin on my shoulder, he inhaled deeply, "You have another tattoo," he exhaled in a whisper. I felt him trace the lines with his fingers. *My most special piece of artwork, my broken angel's wings.* The very reason behind why I needed to step away from Shane's warm touch.

The corners of my mouth quirked upward. "I bet that's your signature line to try to pick up women, huh?" I stepped away; keeping the smile on my face, but inside I was dying. *How could it be that every time he touched this body and I pulled away, it ached all over?* I shook my head free from my thoughts and placed my hand on the back of my shoulder. "They are my angel wings. To remind me and to honor what I've lost."

Shane flinched and drew his hands back when I said the words. He tucked his head down and looked away, "Your family," he murmured.

I didn't correct his assumption. I tucked my lips between my teeth and clamped down tight. What would I tell him anyway? Gee, Shane, I was born thousands of years ago when the world was first created, in what people today call biblical times. When a small band of angels called the Watchers were placed on Earth to watch and protect the humans. *Yeah, sure, that would go over well.*

Should I tell him also that these angels, even though it was against their laws, took human women to be their wives? Each wife bore the angel's children; the Nephilim. These creatures, part angel-part human, grew to be giants in our world. Giants of pure evil. They wreaked havoc on the Earth, tearing humans apart, and eating their flesh.

Should I tell him that *I* was one of the girls who fell in love with one of the angels and I was the only one who didn't have a child? That we never got further than a kiss? The Watchers were exiled from the earth, thrown into the Abyss until Judgment Day. The punishment I was given was this existence. A lost soul searching for my angel on earth, forever banned from heaven.

Yeah, sure, and the next thing I'd see is the view from the back of the silly bus as they hauled me off to the funny farm. I could never tell someone like Shane my secrets.

The next few hours flew by as if someone had pressed the fast forward button on my remote control of life. We met up with the rest of the band at the bar; it was more packed than I'd seen it the first time I stepped foot in it. Conner was absolutely right when he said the auditions for a new band member would get them a lot of publicity. Everywhere you turned in the bar, people were talking about who would take Alex's place. Alex sat in a booth as if his was royalty; his fans coming up to him, paying their respects.

Tucker walked in with his head held high. His Gucci suit was still on with his tie undone and the first two buttons open. He brought an entourage of people from work, escorting them all right to me and introduced me to each one. There was red headed Jimmy, who spoke with an Irish accent. There was also Cameron, who upon meeting me said, "Your girl has a great ass, Tucker." Lastly, there was Bradley, who elbowed Tucker and called him the luckiest guy in the world.

From the corner of my eye, I could see Shane grimacing. His foot started tapping wildly against the chair he sat in and he had his eyebrows pulled together. When Tucker placed his unwanted hand on the small of my back and began moving it quickly downwards, Shane jumped out of his chair. Pushing himself between Tucker and me, he grabbed my waist and pulled me forward, "Okay. Almost time to go onstage, so let's have a band meeting before we do this!"

Ethan and Brayden looked at him with raised eyebrows. Ethan chuckled and shook his head. Brayden froze in surprise, "Huh, why?"

"Just shut up and let's go!" Shane snapped.

"You guys go ahead; I'll be there in a few minutes. I think I need to talk to Tucker alone," I said. Shane's eyes widened and his lips pursed, and all I wanted to do was laugh at how beautiful he looked even when he was angry. "Go ahead, Shane. I'll be right there."

Tucker stepped forward and pulled me away from Shane, "Yeah, Shane. Give us a few. She'll still be able to play when I'm done with her, I promise. She just might not be able to walk straight," he laughed.

My face burned. Lea stepped closer to me, knowing exactly how hard I wanted to hit Tucker in the face. I stopped myself before I could pull my fist back. He was not going to ruin this night for me. I grabbed him tight around his forearm, digging my nails in. I didn't stop, even when I heard him groan in pain.

I yanked him with me.

"Whoa, she definitely wants me right now!" Tucker disgustingly called to his friends.

Shane stalked off to the stage, followed by Ethan and Brayden.

I stopped only a few feet away, making sure we were still in view of everyone. I balled my fists tight and grabbed his suit jacket. I dragged his face a few inches above mine. His breath smelled like whiskey. "You are the most conceited, self-centered ass that I have ever met! Don't you ever put your hands on me again, and do not talk to me about how you want to sleep with me, because it ain't happening. Now, Tucker, I had enough class not to smack the skin off your face in front of all your friends over there, but if you disrespect me one more time, I will not stop myself from hitting you. Got it?"

His shoulders slouched down. "I really like you. You're so beautiful."

Feeling guilty, I let go of him. "Tucker, when you drink, you have a nasty habit of making people feel like they aren't worth much. I'm more than someone who is just beautiful and you haven't even tried to get to know me. I'm sorry, Tucker, you're a nice guy when you're not drinking, but I gave you a chance and I didn't like how you treated me." I walked away.

I got to the stage and looked back. Tucker was already talking to a group of other girls. *Yes, I was just a pretty little bauble to look at.*

Shane was plugging our guitars in when I climbed up. His eyes quickly scanned over me. "I guess Tucker's pretty fast, huh?" he sneered.

If Shane were any other person, I would have said he was acting jealous, but this was Shane, and he'd never had feelings for anyone. I watched his expression. His forehead was scrunched together and his lips were tight. Four full shot glasses were on the amp next to him. He knocked back one and slammed it down empty, next to the others, glaring at me.

I shoved him lightly against the wall of the stage, behind the tall speakers, where no one could see. I left my hand on his chest were I had pushed him. His heart raced below my fingertips.

He looked down at my hand and slowly raised his eyes to mine, his hands reached out softly to keep me at a distance.

"Are you angry with me or Tucker, Shane?"

He shook his head and said nothing, but the hands that were keeping us apart were losing their pressure. "Did you fuck him?" His heart sped up. *Was he afraid of my answer?*

I bit my lower lip and smiled. "Yeah, right in the hallway to the bathroom. I just let him have me against the wall."

His heart stopped, and then it started wildly drumming under my hands. Beads of sweat formed on his forehead. *This can't be right. He can't care about me.*

He pushed against my hand, eyes desperate to get away from me. I almost let him pass, but I slammed my arms into his and pushed my lips to his ears.

"Is that what you think of me? Is that what you need to hear? That I'm like all the other girls? Tell me, Shane," I whispered, pulling my head back.

We stood inches apart, breathing each other in. My whole body was on fire.

Glancing down at my lips, he gave me a small smile. His hand traced the contours of my jaw and down my neck; I shivered under his touch.

"No. I want you to tell me why you have a pair of broken angel wings on your shoulder. I want you to tell me why you cut your wrists and I want to know why and how you play and sing the way you do, but most of all I want you to tell me what I need to do to be a good enough man for you."

I stepped back immediately, not expecting any of what he said. I grabbed one of the remaining shots and gulped it down, loving the burn. "Shane..." My mouth opened to say the words, but I couldn't form a complete thought. "I don't want to be just another one of your girls. I have other...things, too many things in my life." *Why couldn't I just tell him I was with someone else? Because that would be a lie, I was alone, searching for someone else.* "I really just need a friend right now."

"Hey!" Ethan's voice called from behind us. "You guys about ready?" he asked, coming over to stand next to us. Brayden followed. They took the last two shots and drank them. "Next time, we do them together," Ethan said holding up the glass. "That will be how we start each show with Grace."

I laughed. "Sounds good to me. Shall we amaze them?" I said, looking out into the crowd.

Shane smiled down at me. "Grace, trust me, they were amazed just by you walking in."

I shook my head giggling and I walked to pick up my guitar, but not before I overhead Ethan say, "Shane, you break that girl's heart and I swear I'll rip yours out. She's off limits."

"Dude, I don't know what the hell is happening to me, but trust me, right now we're just friends," was his reply.

The manager of the bar, Kelvin, was standing in front of us at the microphone as we walked out. His voiced echoed, "...new guitarist we've all been dying to see, and gentlemen, if any of your clothes make it up here, I'll personally kick your sorry asses outta here! Here's Mad World!"

The crowd roared when we were all visible. I ducked my head and laughed as a hot pink lacy bra sailed onto the stage. I plucked it off the floor and flung it at Shane, "I believe this is for you?" I teased into my mic. Howls erupted and Shane wore his sexy woman-eating smile. He tucked the bra into his jeans pocket, letting it hang down his leg.

"Hey, everybody!" Shane addressed the crowd. "I'd like to introduce you to the gorgeous Grace Taylor on guitar!" *I never heard so many catcalls in my life.*

Shane's perfect lips stretched across his face and when he nodded to me, something danced behind his eyes. I locked eyes with him. Tilting my head, I took the cue and my hands started flying all over my guitar. The crowd detonated into shrieks and screams. Shane joined in and our harmony made us both breathless. We played as one, staring at each other, neither one of us looking away. The crowd was somewhere in the distance, but we were in a place all our own. If we weren't careful, the fire in our eyes would cause an inferno, so I laughed and looked away. We matched each other's intensity. It overwhelmed my body and made me ache; *this friendship would kill me*. Right at that very minute, I wanted to die a thousand deaths for it. Truth be told, I hadn't felt this alive in years. My fingers pulsated along the strings and then my voice burst out in song, alongside Shane. It was more intoxicating than any drink or drug. It burned through my veins and blazed into my heart, giving it a reason to beat. Rapture enveloped my body and soul.

We performed all the Mad World songs we practiced until Shane put his hand on the small of my back and whispered into his mic, "Let's introduce them to Janis."

Something in the tone of his whisper made my knees weak. I could almost picture Janis by my side with her haunting laugh. *Come on*, she called to me.

I slid up against him, our backs touching and his body quivered in tune with mine. Leaning my head against his shoulder, my hair washing over him, our eyes latched on to each other's. Changing her words, I sung to him.

Oh, Come on, Come on, Come on, Come on!

Don't I make you feel, Shane, like you are the only man,

And don't I give you nearly everything that I possibly can?

Baby, you know I do!

All the time I tell myself that I, well I think I've had enough of you, Shane,

But I'm gonna show you that a woman like me can be tough.

I want you to come on, and just take it,

Take another little piece of my heart now, baby,

I watched as my words showered over his body; he sang back to me, eyes blazing.

The set ended in a riot of noise and applause. Shane bounced off the stage, but instead of emerging himself in an army of girls, he turned and reached both his hands out for me to jump down. Without a second of hesitation or a thought in my head, I dove into his arms. His strong arms caught me, cradling me like a baby and kissed me on the cheek. The lines of friendship completely blurred out of focus as I scanned his flawless face. *What am I doing? Is one night worth it?* Not in any lifetime.

"That was...intense. I think I need a drink," I breathed.

"Yeah, well, I need another ice cold shower. Tequila?" he asked.

I glided out of his embrace and nodded vigorously. I gave him a little friendly jab in the arm, "I'm sure in a few minutes any one of these girls will cure you of your need for a cold shower," I teased. I needed him to walk away and go find some meaningless one-night stand so I could remember what kind of man Shane really was.

He didn't respond to my statement, only tightened his smile and escorted me through the screaming crowd to the bar. Lea was the first to meet us there and she hugged me tightly, lifting me off the ground. "Oh. My. God! You guys rocked!" She held me closer and whispered in my ear, "Was that as hot as it looked?"

I leaned my head back, bit my lip and nodded a yes. We fell over each other giggling.

Conner grabbed me up next in a bear hug. He reminded me so much of Jacob. "Thanks for helping my friends out."

Then after that, everyone just started hugging everyone. Brayden hugged me awkwardly around the neck like I had a contagious disease, Ethan hugged me and swung me around like a five year old, and Alex desperately tried to grab me by the waist with his casts. I playfully shoved him in the chest, telling him I was afraid he'd hurt himself by hugging me and he placed a kiss on my cheek. "Thanks for taking my place, Grace. I can't wait to take these things off and play beside you!" he said holding up his casts.

"Yeah, well just don't go and get yourself arrested again. What's going on with that, anyway?"

His face turned red. "Yeah, I know I'm an idiot. I shouldn't have gotten involved, but he roughs her up, Grace. You're not supposed to hurt girls like that, you know."

I nodded my head at him.

"My court date is in three months, they released me on my own recognizance. I'm sure everything will be fine. Tucker and his father are pretty slick lawyers. His dad spun a great story about me coming to her rescue. Which is sorta true, it was just a day or two after the jerk beat up Cara."

Behind the bar, Ryan lined up the shot glasses and set out salt, lemons and limes. An onslaught of beautiful girls surrounded us, and our conversation ended when Alex noticed them. Tucker and his work buddies also walked over to take advantage of the crowd of ladies that was forming.

With the swam of busty bimbos bombarding us, I felt claustrophobic. Lea seemed to feel it too and she yanked Conner and me out of the middle of the crush of bodies. She elbowed me hard in the ribs and pointed to the far end of the bar. *Shane*.

He stood alone, leaning his elbows back against the bar. A bottle of tequila stood beside him with a single shot glass. His hair was tousled, messy and incredibly sexy. His dark tee shirt was tight and a tad raised from the way he was leaning. A perfectly toned stomach peeked out. He looked like a Greek god. A Greek god whose eyes were glued on me.

A dark haired girl slithered up to him and brushed a piece of hair from his forehead, blocking his view of me. They spoke for a few seconds and I watched his head shake and the girl walked away. My guess was that she was ugly, but when she turned around to walk off, I saw that she wasn't. Another girl followed in her wake, a platinum blonde this time. She also walked away with a rejected look on her face.

Lea gripped my arm and nodded towards Shane, "What do you think that's about?"

I shrugged and looked to Conner for an answer.

Conner's eyes squinted. "Maybe he realizes that he wouldn't be allowed to take someone back to your apartment, since that's where he says we're staying until that nut is caught." *Now, that made sense.*

Lea eyed me. "Nah, I don't think that's it at all. I think he's got it bad for his new guitarist. Did you see them up there, Conner?"

"No way," I said. "I like Conner's explanation much more than yours. It's much safer for everyone involved!"

The three of us walked over to him. He reached over the bar and pulled up three more shot glasses. He slid them over the bar to us and reached over the bar again for the salt shaker and a handful of limes on a napkin.

The four of us each salted the back of our hands, took a shot and popped a lime in our mouths. Lea pinched my waist and patted me on the shoulder. She pushed Conner away from us and started a private conversation with him in whispers. Giggling to each other, they walked off a bit down the bar to be more alone.

I knew exactly what she was up to; she wanted me to be alone with Shane. *Nice best friend, throwing me to the sharks*.

Shane poured me another shot and gently took hold of my hand. He stuck his pinky into my shot glass, slid his wet finger over the back of my hand, and then salted it. I watched his hands on mine. *This is going to go from bad to holy crap in a minute*. My eyes rose to meet his. I licked the back of my hand and tilted back my drink.

"I bet you make that taste like heaven," he said.

I placed my glass back on the bar and looked down at it. I turned back to him, tilting my head up, our faces so close. "Shane, I watched you before. You didn't have to say no to those girls because you think you have to stay with me tonight.

You don't have to stay over to babysit me instead of doing your usual thing."

His face paled. "That's what you think?" He turned around to face me; shifting his body closer to mine. He blinked back a sullen look.

My cheeks burned. "It's what Conner said when he saw you standing here letting those girls walk away from you."

"You didn't answer my question. Is that what *you* think?"

"I didn't think about it at all. I just don't want you to do something you don't really need or want to do."

Shane leaned in closer, our cheeks brushed against each other. His breath tickled in my ear, "Funny thing is, Grace, needing and wanting is exactly what I am doing. And, just for the record, it is not those girls I need or want."

Without saying another word to me, he delicately took my arm and sprinkled a small pinch of salt on the soft skin of my inner wrist. He raised my arm to his mouth and I watched him lightly press his tongue against my skin, skimming it across the surface. My breath caught. He downed his tequila and squeezed the lime into his mouth, smiling. *Oh. My. God.* "God, Grace. You do taste like heaven," he whispered breathlessly.

I felt a delicious heat rise all over my body. "I think I should go home now. I'm...really...tired." I whirled around and practically ran towards the bathroom. I had no idea where Conner and Lea had gone. They were probably headed home already. I just needed to splash cold water on my face.

"Then I'm going too," he yelled after me.

I pushed through the crowds of people and ran into the back hallway. I headed for the women's room, but hesitated when I touched the handle of the door. Dread crept over my body. The hairs on the back of my neck stood up, eradicating all of the burning desperate hunger Shane's touch invoked. Of course, I opened it and walked in anyway. *I am in a bad horror movie.*

The only window in the bathroom was wide open, and a fine layer of snow covered the tiled floor. I scanned the room. I heard a soft movement in the one stall that was closed.

"Are you really stupid enough to believe, Gabriel? Do you really believe after thousands of years, all the lifetimes, he'll get his little human prize?" a voice growled.

The door slowly swung open. My heart thudded to a stop.

Looking intensely at me was Carl Sumpton, or at least Carl Sumpton's body staring at me though ancient blue eyes. His hands clung to the sides of the stall as if he needed the help to stand.

"No human has eyes the color of an angel, who are you?" I whispered.

"Shamsiel always did say you were a smart one," he hissed. His body tried to step closer to me, but it only managed to slump back and fall against the toilet. Its flesh was transparent and bluish. The skin around its eyes was bruised and swollen; its cheeks were sunken in.

"It looks to me like that body is about to send your soul elsewhere, who are you? I've never heard of an angel who shared the same punishment as me."

The body trembled, taking great pains to continue breathing life through it. "Azazel, child, and my punishment was far worse than yours, and I've grown too tired of the burning fires of hell," it coughed. A fine trickle of deep red blood spilled from the corner of its mouth.

I lurched forward, grabbing his face in my hands, searching his eyes. Blood splattered on my arms. "A Grigori? One of the Watchers? That Azazel? Where is Shamsiel? I've been in hell here searching for him!"

"You will never find him. I won't let him get what the rest of us can't have. Do you really think, child, that we could possibly be forgiven? We have fallen, and there are no second chances. And I sure as hell won't let him get what I can't have, when his sin was no better than mine."

"We did nothing wrong. Our only crime was in loving each other. You, the rest of you, you're the ones that created the Nephilim! You're the ones that tore the earth apart and helped bring chaos down. You taught the humans war! Shamsiel and I were children; all we did was fall in love. He never even touched me, but for one kiss!"

"Child," he cooed. "He was thrown into the abyss with the rest of us. Do you really believe with a punishment of that magnitude he'd still want the love of a human?" he sneered. "Besides, do you think he knows you still exist here?"

I stepped back, wiping the blood from my hands on his shirt. "Why are you trying to kill me?"

The body convulsed. "You're the only one," it seethed. The body collapsed in on itself and stilled. I was the only one of what?

Someone in the hallway knocked on the door to come in. I stood above the dead body, confused and needing a hell of a lot more answers then what I was just given.

I didn't want to be found in the bathroom with Carl Sumpton's body, so I hoisted myself up to the open window and jumped into the alleyway below. Thank God, the bar was on the first floor or I would have broken a few bones. I ran through the darkness trying to carefully step in places where I'd leave no footprints in the snow. There seemed to be enough garbage and crap strewn throughout the alley to make that possible.

My mind ran in circles. Why in the world was Azazel around? Wasn't he stuck in some supernatural prison somewhere? I was the only one of what? *And really why was the freaking place on my arm that Shane licked still making me tingle and giddy like a kid in a toy store?* I needed to talk to Gabriel.

I ran to the apartment, praying in my mind that Gabriel would be there waiting.

I could hear Conner and Lea murmuring and giggling in the living room when I opened the front door. I locked the deadbolt behind me, which echoed a loud click throughout the apartment; silencing their sounds. I quickly walked through the hallway without stopping to speak to them.

"Gray?" Lea called out.

"Yep, just me. I'm beat. I'm calling it a night. Goodnight, guys!" I called back as I closed my door. My room was empty.

I leaned my forehead on the hard wood of the door. Tears stung at my eyes, but I blinked them back. I pressed my hands against the door and spread my fingers across the grain of the wood. I felt the coarse grooves, ran my fingers over the knotty uneven surface of it. My head spun. *Shamsiel.* Would I truly never see him again? Azazel? What would he get out of killing me, and how would he, when I'd only be thrown into another body? Gabriel? Could I trust him? He was one of the angels who helped to destroy the

Nephilim and helped bind the fallen ones to their prisons. Last one? Am I the last of the human souls? I thought it was just me, I hadn't known any of the others were punished along with me. I thought they were destroyed along with the Nephilim. *Shane? Why did I keep thinking about him when he had nothing to do with any of this?*

Someone started banging at the front door. Shane. Voices raised; footsteps thundered down the hallway.

I heard the floor boards creak on the other side of my door. I could hear his breath, "Grace..." Then something hard thumped against the door right above my head. I pictured Shane in the same position as me with our faces almost touching but for the inch of wood between us.

"Grace. Please let me in. I'm...sorry."

I lifted my head and walked away. There was way too much...intensity, too much tension between us; this body was not capable of handling Shane. He'd probably eat me alive. *Unfortunately, that sounded so very delicious to me.*

I heard his foot kick the door and his body slide down to the floor. "I'm sleeping on the floor then. Right here." His head thumped against my door again. "Oh. Man. This is so comfortable, Grace. *Really. Very.*" His sarcastic tone made the butterflies in my belly flip around again. There was no meanness to his voice. It was raspy and silky and somehow made all the crazy thoughts in my head blur and only focus on him.

I walked to the window and pushed the curtain aside. The walkway below was pristine white and glistening. I clicked off my ceiling light and clicked on my bedside lamp. I rummaged through my drawers and found my tank top-boy shorts sleepwear. Pulling off my rock goddess outfit and pulling on my sleepwear, I wished I could wash my makeup off in the bathroom.

From out in the hallway I heard some rustling. *Maybe he was leaving?* A few bumps and curses. Laughing at the noise, I settled myself under my covers and closed my eyes.

Shane cleared his throat, kicked at my door again and the sound of my guitar filled the room. I sat straight up in my bed. Those beautiful caged butterflies were thrashing their delicate wings against my harsh dark insides. Every single thought of Azazel's visit flew from my mind, each note embracing a thought and hiding it in the darkness.

Shane played a slow melody I had never heard before. Its beginning was low and wistful, transforming into a passionate yearning melody. His awe-inspiring voice hummed along with the tune, whispered words tickled against my ears.

I opened the door.

Shane stood in the hallway, eyes wide, devouring me with his stare. The music faded or stopped, I had no clue. I focused my eyes on my guitar, my divine instrument in his hands.

He pulled the strap over his head and carried the guitar into my room, closing the door behind him.

"Please, look at me, Grace."

Sliding the guitar out of his hands, he leaned it against the wall. My eyes stayed on the instrument.

"Grace, please look at me." He stepped closer to me, blocking me from staring at the guitar. So I stared blankly at his crotch, *or where the guitar was located behind his crotch.*

I couldn't even say how he got so close to me. I hadn't noticed his movements. I tried not to even notice him, but there he was so close that I felt the heat from his body. He touched my chin with his hand and I finally lifted my eyes to his.

"Grace...I'm sorry. I didn't mean to..."

I suddenly felt the cool wall press up against my back. I hadn't known I was backing away from him, but I leaned against it for moral support. And, just like he'd done twice before, he rested his forehead against mine.

"Tell me. Tell me, Grace, that you don't feel this. Please. Tell me and I will walk right out of here." He touched his lips to my jaw; his words were hot on my skin. My heart skidded in my chest. No reasonable thoughts came to my mind, only the warm sensation of his lips moving gently down my neck.

He pressed his body against mine, one hand slowly sliding down to my waist, tracing his fingertips along my skin.

"Talk to me, Grace, please," he begged pulling back.

My body moved with him. I placed my hands on his chest and grasped his shirt in my fists.

His hand tightened on my waist and with his other, he twisted fingers through my hair. "Grace...One kiss, please. Let me taste you," he pleaded, pushing his body harder against mine.

A small moan escaped from my lips. "Shane..." I stood on my tiptoes and brushed my lips past his. Both of us hesitated, breathing in each other.

"Say my name again," he begged, as he slid his hand down my hips and pulled my leg up around him. My body ached, pounded, and spasmed; I was almost delirious.

"Shane," I whispered, moving my lips over his mouth. He trembled.

He growled low, crashing his lips into mine. Every single inch of my body pulsed against his. His fingertips skated beneath the lace of my panties. I grabbed at him, sliding my hands through his hair.

I dug my fingers into his shoulders, which only made him kiss me deeper and harder. I spun out of control.

He pulled his lips away, panting, as he stared into my eyes. His fingers slipped deeper under the lace. I stopped his hand before his fingers could press inside me.

"Shane. Stop. I can't..." I felt the tears brimming in my eyes. *It was killing me to tell him to stop.*

He let my leg slowly slide down his hip from where he had placed it. His soft fingertips traveled up to my neck, until both his hands cupped my face, searching my eyes.

"Grace...I think,"

I stretched my fingers across his chest. "Please. Shane...don't. This was a huge mistake." Even though I pushed my hands against his chest, my body still arched towards his.

His eyes frantically searched mine. One foolish tear escaped down my cheek. I quickly turned my face, not wanting him to see anymore. Both his hands flew up to his hair, grasping at it. "Grace...please. You would never be a mistake to me."

Turning my back on him, I walked to the window and pushed the curtain back. "Shane, drop it. I'm not one of your groupies that you just met at the bar, I wasn't screaming for you and throwing my clothes at you, and I don't give a crap how good you play or how sexy you look on stage, none of it will make me sleep with you. So just keep the normal line you feed to your skanks to yourself," I snapped.

Grabbing me by the waist, Shane lifted me easily off the floor and tossed me on my bed. He dove on top of me, straddling me, pinning my arms above my head. *Dear God, I wanted to scream, but it was so freaking erotic that every inch of my body screamed for his.*

His face hovered over mine. "Shut. Up. Don't. Just don't say anything else." He moved his body next to mine and gathered me into his arms. "Just sleep, Grace," he whispered and he pressed closer to me, softly laying one single kiss on my angel's wings.

Chapter 11

Someone slowly traced their fingertips down my spine, leaving trails of burning fire in their wake. I woke up in sheer panic, my heart fluttering wildly, while I was tangled in my sheets next to Shane.

He gave me a mischievous grin and a steaming cup of coffee. "Hey, I got you some coffee."

Without hesitation, I grabbed the coffee. I held the cup up to my lips, with the bitter aroma pleasantly filling the air, and I took a sip. *Shane knew how to make my coffee?* "Thanks. Did you make this or did Lea?"

His eyebrows burrowed together and his face darkened. He stood up and yanked off his shirt, the same one he'd worn last night, and threw it in my hamper. "Don't worry, Grace, they're still sleeping. No one will think we had sex, and if anyone asks, I'll make sure everyone knows you don't want me," he snapped, as he rummaged through a bag near the door. *Did he actually have a bag of clothes here in my freaking room, as if he was moving in?* He pulled out another tee shirt and held it in his hands, standing there waiting for me to reply. His muscles were taut and tense. *He really is too sexy for his own good.*

I sipped my coffee and placed the cup on my nightstand. I started wrapping the sheets around me to get up, but then figured that it really didn't matter if he saw me in my sleeping attire, since he had practically seen me in it every day. "I didn't ask that to see if Lea or Conner thought we slept together. I was just wondering if you or Lea made the coffee, exactly like I asked." I stood up from the bed and stretched my arms over my head.

His lips parted. His eyes dilated, following my every movement. His expression tightened and his body stiffened more with tension. He charged toward me, eyes blazing with anger? Fear? Longing? Hate? "Right, sure. Well, why not, let's talk about shit that doesn't matter. Lea is sleeping and I made the freaking coffee! What is it, too strong for you? And let me just put this out in the open, so that I don't get accused of playing games or whatever the hell your warped mind thinks I do. I am so freaking glad I didn't sleep with you, Grace, because you and me would be horrible. The sex would suck and I wouldn't have to look at you and pretend you were more than a hole to stick my dick in for the next six weeks!" Contrary, to his words, his expression flooded with hurt and he turned away from me, grabbing my robe off the closet door and then throwing it at me.

Catching the robe, I walked passed him and dropped it at his feet. When I got in front of him, I looked him deadpan in the eyes. "Thanks for the heads up on how sex would have been with you. But, honestly Shane, I just wanted to know if you actually had gone out of your way to know the exact way I take my coffee, because that just would have been...sweet."

I spun on the heels of my feet, grabbed an armful of clothes from my dresser drawers and grabbed the doorknob.

"Grace, stop."

"Go screw yourself, Shane." I turned the doorknob and stood in the doorway. "Consider your duty to babysit me done, since you stayed here last night to protect me and I still ended up hurt." I walked out of my room, closing the door softly behind me, more confused than ever. I didn't understand why Shane had said what he did, but whatever the reason, it was over and I needed to figure out what to do with the rest of this existence.

I changed into my running clothes in the bathroom and finally got the chance to wash the makeup from the night before off my face. When I shut the faucet off, I heard the sounds of hushed voices in the kitchen. I couldn't help but put my ear close to the wall and listen. *Well, I am only human.*

"...is driving me crazy, I can't take the shit I said back. She's fucking killing me."

I opened the door, not wanting to hear anymore, it didn't matter if he wanted to take back anything he said, he wasn't important.

I rushed through the kitchen and grabbed a bottle of water from the refrigerator.

"Where are you going?" Lea asked.

"For a run," I said.

"Alone?" she asked looking from me to Shane.

"Lea. This is New York City. Eight million people live here, I won't be alone," I said walking out the front door.

I ran. I ran and then ran some more. I didn't stop. I lost count how many times I circled the park. I lost track of time, as I just ran looking for Gabriel.

When the sky had been dark for a while and my body could take no more, I sat down on an empty bench. I knew I had a show to do with the band at ten. The thought swam distantly around in the back of my head. I held my head in my hands and the tears finally broke free.

A warm hand touched my shoulder and a sublime feeling crashed through my body. *Gabriel.*

Without even looking at him, without even a hesitation, with all the innocence of a child, I threw myself into his arms. I felt him smile. Calmness washed over my body.

"I don't understand what's going on, Gabriel," I sniffled.

"The fallen ones do not want you and Shamsiel ever to be reunited." Gabriel's always-stoic face gave the smallest impression of sadness. "I'm sorry, Grace. I had no idea he had escaped. I won't ever let anything hurt you." His beautiful hands cupped my jaw in a human way that made me want to jump and run. This was Gabriel, though. He was one of the archangels. He had no human emotions, no lust, and no needs.

I let him hold me until I thought I could face this existence again. I didn't ask him anymore questions, because I knew he wouldn't give me answers. I didn't want to tell him about Shane and the feelings that he stirred in me. I didn't want to beg for him to tell me where Shamsiel was, because I knew he'd never tell me. He kissed my forehead softly when I said goodbye.

I walked home and without talking with anyone, I jumped in the shower and got ready for the gig at Boozer's. I expected there to be news about finding Carl Sumpton's body in the women's bathroom last night, but Lea and Conner didn't mention anything to me.

Lea knocked on my door as I was getting dressed. My clothes were hanging over every surface of my bedroom, flung to their spots by anger. I wore an old pair of jeans and a huge black sweater. "There is no way I'm letting you out of this room looking like the Frump Queen. What's going on with you?"

I shook my head and collapsed onto my bed. I wasn't about to get into any serious conversation with her about my visit with a fallen angel who was trying to kill me, or an archangel who I hoped was trying to help me, or how I just wanted Shane to be a monogamous-liking guy who could make me forget everything. "I have nothing to wear."

She picked through the piles of my clothes and handed me the perfect outfit, *of course*. "I'm talking about you and Shane, Grace. What's going on?"

I gave her the most disgusted look that I could muster up. "Nothing. Abso-freaking-lutely nothing."

She walked right up to my face. "Really? Because, Grace, since your accident, when you woke up swearing off all boys unless they come packing wings, I've never seen anyone sway your resolve but Shane. You let him stay in your bed last night, after *kissing* him. You didn't kick him out."

"I tried to, but he wouldn't leave." I clenched my teeth. *He told her we kissed?*

"Yeah, well explain it to me then how when you and him are on stage in front of a crowd of hundreds of people it feels like we are all invading your privacy. The way you both look at each other is unreal, Grace." She sat down next to me and placed her hands on mine. "Did you feel anything when you kissed him?"

"Lea, this body blurs all the edges of reality for me. Of course, *it* wanted him. But for what? One single night? So the next day he could pick up some other chick at the bar and I'll have to watch? Besides, the last thing he said to me is that we'd be horrible together, sex would be lousy and I'd just be another hole to stick his dick in for the next six weeks."

"That's what he said?"

"His exact words."

Her mouth fell open, "He said he was really mean to you, and that he..."

"Stop, Lea. It doesn't matter. He doesn't matter," I said getting up. "Come on and make me look like a rock star."

We did our makeup in silence. I didn't have anything more to say about Shane, the subject was closed. I needed a way out of here. I needed a way to find what I was looking for without being in Grace's life. Grace was supposed to die in the car accident ten years ago, so she shouldn't be here any longer. And my soul should not be in a body that was consumed with a hunger for some idiot who could kiss me so passionately that I could forget who I really was.

It was snowing again when we walked to the bar; big giant chunks of feathery ice. Conner looked up at the sky, "Looks like the angels are having another pillow fight." The old expression warmed my heart.

The bar was packed again; I'd say five times the amount of people than the night before. For the first time that day, I felt a smile creep across my face.

Again, I waited for someone to mention finding a dead body in the bathroom the night before, but no one did. *Maybe he wasn't truly dead yet.*

Ethan waved us over to a table filled with everyone. Ethan sat next to a beautiful red headed girl named Vicki. Brayden had a shorthaired girl on his lap and Alex was with Cara. Tucker was also there and smiled a curt hello to me. Shane was nowhere to be found. I figured he was in the back room catching up on his sexual escapades. Jealously burned through my body. *No way is this good.*

Tucker pulled over a chair for me.

I must have given him a curious look, because he felt like he had to explain himself.

"Yes, I'm an asshole. I have so much to apologize for." He patted the seat of the chair and handed me a beer.

I sat down, placing my guitar between Tucker and me, just to make sure he wouldn't be able to touch me.

Tucker offered small talk after his apology, but I didn't respond too often.

Everyone else chatted, but I heard nothing. I searched around the bar for Shane, and then wanted to hurl myself off a building for doing it. The more I thought about him with someone else the antsier my body felt. As the minutes passed, it got worse. I jumped up and lugged my guitar and myself into the bathroom. Lea was too busy in some sort of heated discussion with one of the other girls to notice.

I half expected to see Carl sitting on one of the toilets, but the room was empty. "Azazel?" I whispered. No one answered. If he knew how to get me out of this hellish punishment, then maybe I needed another talk with him, just for *informational purposes*.

I washed my hands and put on some more lipstick, and then made my way back through the crowds. I glanced over to the stage and saw Shane sitting by himself in the back, just out of view. I didn't know if he was alone, but I jumped onto the stage anyway.

He sat on a metal folding chair with his legs up on another chair, playing his guitar. He lifted his head only slightly when he noticed me, but he didn't stop playing.

"Hey," I said. "What's doing?" I brazenly pushed his legs off the second chair and sat down.

His expression was guarded. "Oh, are you talking to me? I thought we hated each other." His lips curled down, his sadness peeking through.

I wanted to kiss those lips desperately. *Shit! This is getting worse!* I smiled at him. I didn't even mean to, it just burst from my lips. My cheeks burned.

"Stop smiling, Grace." He leaned forward, a smile appearing on his face that matched mine. "A smile like that can give a man hope."

But I couldn't stop smiling and neither could he. We sat there smiling, staring into each other's eyes, until Ethan walked up to us and cleared his throat. "What is with the two of you?"

My eyes snapped from his and I couldn't quite catch my breath. This is too dangerous. I needed to find Azazel before I give myself, body and soul to Shane. I shivered; I needed to end my time here. It's not like me to want someone or to need someone, especially when I knew it would only be for a few hours.

The crowd screamed for us to play, and when we emerged from the back of the stage, the sound was deafening. Shane struck a chord and that silenced the audience. The rest of us took his lead and the crowd roared back to life.

The music was intense and electrifying. It pulsated along the walls and through the stage rocking me to my core. I played as if it was the last time I'd ever hold my guitar.

After the set, we all jumped off the stage. Sweaty and on fire, we ran to the bar to try to quench the flames.

Laughing and singing our last song, Ryan lined up shot glasses of Kamikaze shooters for us, fruity and sweet. I gulped one back and slammed in on the bar.

Someone leaned against the bar next to me, "May I buy you a drink?"

I lifted my head to the voice.

"Hi, I'm Steve," he said, and then pointed to my empty glass, "May I buy you a drink."

I smiled politely at him, "Thank you, but the band has a running tab at the bar, so there's no need to."

Ryan slid over another Kamikaze shooter to me and the irony of name of the drink and my life made me giggle.

Steve smiled down at me with sexy green eyes. "You were amazing up there," he said to me, nodding to the stage. "I'm sure you hear this all the time, but you are incredibly sexy and your eyes...I've never seen a more beautiful color."

Before I could thank him, Shane stepped between us. "Hey, excuse me, um, Steve was it?

Yeah, well Grace and I have band things to take care of, so goodbye." Shane stood there glaring down at him until he backed away. "Walk the fuck away from her right now; she's not up for grabs, Steve."

Steve held my gaze, "She's not up for grabs? Calm down, jackass. I just wanted to buy this beautiful woman a drink."

Shane stepped in closer to Steve, blocking my view of him. "Just walk away, dude."

Steve shook his head laughing and held his hands in the air. He leaned past Shane and spoke directly to me. "Listen, my friends and I will be here for a while, so if you'd like to dance or something, come and find me."

I watched Shane's knuckles turn white as he balled his hands into fists. I slid off my barstool, smiled at Steve and placed my hand on Shane's chest, softly holding him back. "Thank you, Steve, but I'm wiped from the show, so I'm calling it a night. I'm Grace by the way. It was nice to meet you and I'm glad you enjoyed the music." I turned to face Shane letting Steve know that our conversation was over.

I kept my hand on Shane. "I am leaving now. Don't ever do that again to me. Don't ever stop someone from speaking to me. I'm not your property. I'm barely even your friend."

His eyes bore into mine, "Do you want to go home with him?"

"What the hell is wrong with you, Shane? Are you serious right now? You're the guy who has slept with almost every girl in this bar, and I can't have someone buy me a drink?"

"You told him no thank you and he didn't listen. And Grace, I haven't slept with anyone since you walked into this bar that first Friday."

I raised my eyebrows. "Liar. You've been here with girls, sucking their faces off right in front of me."

"I haven't slept with any of them, Grace."

"Please don't say anything else. Please don't. I have to get out of here. I'm exhausted and I don't have the energy to fight with you."

"Then, I'm taking you home and I'm staying."

I folded my arms across my chest, "Excuse me?" That's what came out of my mouth, but my mind was high-fiving myself, trying to think of the sexiest thing I could wear to tease the hell out of him.

We grabbed our equipment and headed for the door without saying our goodbyes. I texted Lea when I got outside, because I didn't want her to worry, and I knew she and Conner would come home when she read the message.

We walked through the snow in silence. The only sound in the streets was the sounds of our shoes crushing the snow beneath us.

When we reached the apartment, Shane went in first and searched all the rooms, while he made me stay in the front hallway. When he felt that Carl Sumpton was not hiding somewhere, we raided the refrigerator.

Shane settled on making pancakes, while I jumped in the shower to wash the night's show off. When the hot water ran cold, I jumped out, wrapped myself in a towel, and walked out into the kitchen.

The spatula fell to the floor splattering pancake batter all over. Shane's eyes widened, "Pancakes are almost ready," he whispered.

"There should be more hot water in about five minutes, if you want to jump in the shower," I said.

He turned the burners on the stove off and lifted his shirt over his head. My body hummed. Every single nerve ending trembled with want.

He gave me a crooked smile, "Why Grace? You think I'm dirty?" He walked towards me slowly.

"Oh, no, Shane, I'm betting on you being *filthy*," I teased.

He moved closer until I could feel his sweet warm breath on my face. My body wanted to lurch forward into his arms and be over with it. Just one night with Shane, get it out of my system and then I'd leave. I'd leave and find Azazel and ask him to help me end my eternity.

The front door opened, spilling voices into the apartment. Shane's expression turned desperate with longing. I turned away, walked into my room and closed the door. Leaning against it, I exhaled the breath that I'd been holding in. I couldn't even begin to understand the hold that Shane had over me. It terrified me and it made me hate myself. I didn't want to be the same as all those other girls and I was. I changed into a simple pair of jeans and tank top and made my way to where everyone seemed to be.

Lea had invited a few people from the bar and they were all hanging out eating Shane's pancakes when I ventured in. Shane sat on the arm of the couch laughing with Ethan when I came in. His expression softened when he saw me, and my heart ached. How I wish that I could really have *been born* Grace and not know what heaven felt like.

Within a few minutes, Shane made his way towards me and placed his hand on the small of my back. I didn't flinch, I didn't move away, and I leaned into him. I wanted him to think that Grace would have loved him, because she would have. And I made up my mind that, in the morning I was leaving, and nothing would stop me.

"Are you okay?" he asked looking down into my eyes.

"I'm just tired. I think I'm going to call it a night." I smiled up at him. "Goodbye Shane." I felt his eyes follow me down the hallway, but his body never moved.

Chapter 12

That night, I dreamt of a prison of fires that bound the fallen angels deep beneath the heavens. I could smell the burning toxic fumes as if they were real. They weighed down heavy on my skin and grabbed hold of my lungs, squeezing the life from them.

Far away in the distance, I could hear a frantic voice calling my name, screaming for me, and pulling me to the surface.

The body of the voice slid onto my bed, pinning me down. "Grace," it whispered. "Grace, please wake up!" The voice shook me violently.

I wanted desperately to answer the beautiful voice, but the air was too thick and my throat burned with sweet noxious flames, crushing me from within.

My eyelids were heavy and stung with burning tears. It took all my strength to pry them open.

"Grace," the voice whispered, as I was taken up and cradled into its arms. A deep red burst of fire exploded across the ceiling, flames stretching toward me like fiery hands calling me home.

"Grace, baby, please, please wake up. Grace, please don't leave me, please. I love you."

The strong arms nestled me into its chest and it carried me into oblivion.

I heard glass shatter and felt its icy sharpness rain down over my body. Ice-cold air exploded in my lungs and the blackness came.

I awoke, strapped to a gurney in the middle of the street with an oxygen mask covering my face. I breathed in greedily and coughed up putrid black ooze into the street.

The emergency medical technicians unstrapped me from the gurney and helped me sit up. The world spun around me in a torrid array of vibrant colors. Lea was next to me with tear streaks running down the black soot caked on her face. Conner was behind us talking to a firefighter as black smoke billowed out of our apartment windows.

Tucker, Ethan and Brayden ran down the street followed by others, but I didn't know who they were. Voices were running over each other and I couldn't make out any of what had happened. I still wasn't sure if any of it was real.

Lea sat on the gurney with me and held me in her arms. Shane stood in the distance with his eyes fixed on mine.

"They are saying this is definitely arson," Lea whispered. "The fire started in your room."

"What?" I croaked.

She grabbed me tighter. "Oh God, Grace, this is the scariest thing ever. Somebody wants to kill you. Kill you!"

Ethan ran up to the gurney, grabbed me in his huge arms, and cuddled me close. "What would we do without you? Are you okay?"

I shook my head. Shane was still watching me.

Tucker grabbed me in his arms next, but he sat down on the gurney and pulled me into his lap. I was so tired that I had no energy to even stop him. Shane turned his head.

They talked me into riding in the ambulance to get checked out for smoke inhalation at the hospital. I just wanted to jump in my Jeep and leave as I had planned, but Lea and Tucker practically threw me in the back of the ambulance, strapping me on the gurney on the way in.

Lea rode with me. She just sat next to me holding my hand and crying.

"How did I get out of there?" my voice cracked.

She looked at me and tilted her head, weighing if she should tell me. "Shane carried you out. But, I don't think he wants you to know."

"What makes you say that?" I coughed.

"Because, he told me not to tell you."

I was rolled into the emergency room where I waited a total of fifteen minutes until a doctor saw me. Lea and I decided that was some sort of record. We weren't even finished with all the paperwork they asked for.

The nurse that checked all my vital signs was a horror. However, when the doctor on call walked in, Lea straightened herself up and tried to wipe my face of debris.

He introduced himself as Doctor Tanner and began a monotonous speech about smoke inhalation. "Smoke inhalation contributes to the total number of fire-related deaths each year for several reasons...the damage can be serious...life threatening...its diagnosis is not always easy, since there are no sensitive diagnostic tests...you may not show symptoms until 24-48 hours after the event," he droned on.

I knew I was fine, because I was picturing him completely naked with only a stethoscope around his neck.

Waiting for my release papers to be signed, Lea and I sat around the emergency room and told dirty jokes to two elderly men who had been waiting to be released along with me.

Within ten minutes, the entire emergency room was silent, listening to our banter. Curtains were pushed aside and laughter could be heard down the hallway.

Tucker walked in right before I was released and gave me another hug, holding me a little longer than was needed. "Here's your superman to break you out of here," he whispered in my ear.

"Where's Conner and Shane?" Lea snapped.

Tucker chuckled, "Conner was still talking to the fire chief and the police. Shane probably met a hot chick in a uniform and got sidetracked, you know how he is." He helped me down off the bed that I was sitting on and hooked his arm in mine.

"How bad is the apartment? Can we stay there tonight? Do we need to get a hotel room?" I asked.

"Whoa, sweetheart, calm down. Don't worry about anything. You girls can stay with us and we are definitely getting you out of town for a little while, Grace. The way it looks is that this was done on purpose."

Tucker drove us back to the apartment he shared with Brayden and Alex. "Grace, you can stay at my place. It's no problem, since we have an extra bedroom. My cousin Blake is staying in it now, but he won't mind sleeping on the couch. Or you can just sleep in my room, whatever you're more comfortable with."

I looked at Lea in the backseat and cringed. "I really want to stay with Lea. That's how I'll be comfortable."

He gave me one of his condescending smiles. "Don't you think that Lea would want to be with Conner? The Bone Room is the only room they have there, and trust me; the sheets in that room will *stick to you*."

I cringed again.

Lea moaned. "Ew that's disgusting. I have no problem being at a hotel. How about we stay at the Waldorf for a few nights?" Lea's tone became excited with the thought.

"That's absurd," Tucker snapped. "Grace has no job. You work, for what? Minimum wage at that little publishing house? And your apartment just caught fire. You can't afford the Waldorf, let alone a roach infested seedy pay-by-the-hour motel. She's staying with me tonight, and then we are going to my winter place. We'll leave tomorrow before the snow starts really coming down."

"Tucker, I thank you, but I'm not staying with you tonight. End of discussion." I said.

When we reached Tucker's apartment, he pulled his jaguar in behind a huge shiny black Cadillac Escalade. He pointed his finger at the monstrous SUV and gave a smug look. "That's my cousin Blake's ride. He just started working with me in my father's firm and he already bought a shiny new toy. It's hot, right?"

"Sure, if you're attracted to giant things made of metal that mess up the environment and suck you dry for gas," Lea quipped.

We followed Tucker into his apartment, where he threw his coat on a chair and hurried out into another room. He left Lea and me standing there, still full of ashes and soot, and feeling oh so very welcomed.

Tucker shared his apartment with Brayden and Alex. It was a stereotypical bachelor pad, if said bachelors were all fourteen and just hitting puberty. Posters of half-naked schoolgirls lined the walls and empty beer cans were lined up along the coffee table, artfully holding up fifteen pizza boxes. The smell of cologne and stale beer seemed to be their brand of air freshener.

I jabbed Lea with my elbow, "And you wanted to stay at the Waldorf, when we could have this," I giggled spreading my arms wide.

"I rather stay in the burnt apartment. This is ridiculous. I don't feel like you're safe here, and I really want Conner and Shane with us at all times."

"Shane?" I whispered.

"Grace, if it wasn't for him, you'd literally be toast right now!" she hissed. "I'm calling Conner to get his ass over here. Tucker gets all creepy when he's around you!"

She yanked her phone out of her bag and started talking in hushed whispers with someone on the other end.

Tucker strode out of one of the back rooms with a bottle of his precious champagne. "Would you like some of your favorite?" he asked, holding the bottle up for me to see.

Without waiting for either of us to answer, he busied himself with trying to find clean glasses to pour the champagne in.

A knock interrupted us at the door. Tucker cursed and opened it and cursed again. "Yes, Ethan. What do you need?" he snapped.

"I need Grace and Lea," he said. He looked at the bottle of champagne Tucker was holding and threw his hands up in the air. "Hey, lover boy. They were just in a house fire, so why are you trying to give them champagne? Look at them, they need a shower and a good night's sleep!" he yelled as he ushered us out and down the hallway.

Ethan walked us to the next apartment. "Don't mind Tucker. He's usually not such a jerk when it comes to women, but Grace, you seem to bring the idiot out in him. Are you guys okay? That must have been terrifying."

"What? Being in the fire or the thought of having to sleep over at Tucker's? Because both seem like a nightmare to me," I whispered.

Ethan paused as he pushed his key in to unlock his door. He turned, hugged me tight and patted Lea on the shoulders. "Conner and Shane are coming back and you'll be safe here. You both need a nice hot shower and sleep."

Their apartment was the exact opposite of the one we were just in. It was impeccably clean, with lovely soft leather furniture, and actual artwork framed on the walls, all with a musical theme. There was not one naked schoolgirl poster to be seen.

I walked in and cracked up laughing. "No way. You, Conner, and Shane live here? This place is..."

"Surprising?" Ethan offered.

"Grown up?" Lea giggled.

"Um, yeah, both." I answered.

Ethan nodded, "It's the reason we live together. The three of us are neat freaks and I think Shane is a closet interior decorator, because he put this place together. Come on and I'll give you the grand tour, Grace."

Lea walked herself into Conner's room and closed the door behind her as Ethan led me around. He left the bedroom doors closed though, and only pointed to each one saying the names of the owners. My stomach lurched when he named the Bone Room and a surge of jealousy crashed through me at the thought of how many girls Shane had been in there with. *Jealous? Am I admitting this to myself now?*

Ethan noticed my apprehension to the Bone Room and placed his arms around my shoulders. "Don't worry; you can sleep anywhere you want if you feel weird about being in there." He handed me a towel from a closet in the hall. "But, you do have to take a shower right now, because you smell like hell." With that, he shoved me in the bathroom. "Use whatever soap stuff you like," he said as he closed the door.

I looked around the small bathroom. It was clean, *I mean really clean.* The toilet paper roll was even on its little roller on the wall and not just sitting on the sink because no one could insert it.

I opened the shower curtain, turned on the water, and stuck my hand under the stream to gage the right temperature. *Ah, scalding! That's the perfect temperature.*

I peeled out of my smoke scorched clothes and stepped under the jets, letting the water wash away the evidence of my almost death by fire incident. I used some sort of herbal flowery smelling soap and scrubbed the black ashes off my body.

Inhaling the warm steam made my already burning throat worse, but it made me focus on what I really needed to think through. Why would someone be trying to hurt me? Someone like

Azazel? Was it just jealously? He didn't want Shamsiel to be with me because he couldn't be with whomever he was with? Or was it more? After all these years, how did he find me? Was he roaming the earth? I thought they were all sent somewhere...Was he like me and could only possess a dying body?

The door to the bathroom opened, putting a halt to the inner dialogue I was having. "That better be Lea," I snapped.

I heard Shane's raspy low chuckle, "No, sorry. Just me. But, if you want me to get Lea to come into the shower, that's a really entertaining thought."

"Shane, get out of here!"

"Relax, Grace, I'm not going to jump in with you. I just came in to give you some of my clothes to wear. Unless you want to traipse through the apartment with just a towel on in search of clothes, because that's just...Hey, you know you are absolutely right, that's a *much better idea* than me giving you something to wear...I mean, I clearly remember the first time I saw that at your place. That image is definitely burned into my skull. I wonder if it would have the same effect on everyone else here."

"Okay!" I yelped, poking my head out through the shower curtain. "Thank you! Please just leave the clothes and go!"

Shane stood leaning against the sink with his arms folded. The expression on his face didn't match his teasing; he looked worried and exhausted. "Are you okay, Gray?" His using Lea's nickname for me made my belly do a flip-flop. *What am I, twelve again?*

I stuck my face back in the shower and reluctantly turned off the water. There were a lot more tears that needed to be washed away. I held my hand out to him, "May I have the towel, please?"

He placed the towel in my hands and I dried myself behind the curtain. I wrapped the damp towel around myself and stepped onto the cold tile floor. "You're still in here."

"Yeah. I'm having trouble moving," he whispered.

"Did you get hurt before?"

"No," he murmured. He took the shirt he had brought in for me and smoothly pulled it over my damp hair. I lifted one arm at a time into the sleeves, strategically keeping the towel wrapped around my body. When the shirt fell to my knees, covering me fully, I let the towel drop. "Well, that's something I've never done before," he sighed.

I tried to smile, but I was beyond exhausted at this point, "I guess you do mostly the undressing of women, huh?"

Shane reached out his hands toward my face. *I really should stop him; he really shouldn't touch me. But man, do I want him too!*

He laid his hands against my cheeks and gently wiped the moist skin below my eyes, as if wiping away my tears. "You were crying," he murmured, as his thumbs trailed softly along my skin.

"Well, I was just in a fire that Tucker says someone purposefully set, so yeah, I've been crying."

His hands stilled on my face, "Tucker said that, huh? That ass couldn't just give you one night of rest?" He glared at me, "I swear, Grace, I will not let anything happen to you here, and tomorrow we'll all go up to Tucker's place and get away from Carl Sumpton and his sick twisted games. No one will know where we are."

So, everyone still thought this was Carl Sumpton trying to kill me, just some sick delusional guy that's been stalking me for the last six months. I wished it were so simple. I felt myself shudder and Shane's expression softened.

He drew me into him, slid his hands around my back, and held me close. Every point of his body that touched me sent shivers down my spine. The shivers became much worse when my hands, all on their own accord, slid up the length of his arms and gripped his shoulders. Far worse was the thought that there was only a thin layer of material covering me and it was riding up as I lifted my arms, and I didn't even have underwear on!

As if he had read my thoughts, Shane leaned back, reached for something, and shoved it into my hands. "Here, I can't stand here with you like this, so wear a pair of my boxers, please."

Without taking my eyes off him, I slid the boxers up my legs. Ripples of heat surged through me as his jaw clenched tighter and his eyes dilated into huge pools of blackness. *My God, did I want to dive in.*

We just stood there, face-to-face, eye-to-eye until I felt the room start spinning.

"I'm really tired, Shane. In fact, right now I kind of feel like I'm going to pass out." I leaned my hand on the sink to help myself stay upright. Before I was even aware of what was happening, Shane picked me up and cradled me in his arms. My eyelids were so heavy that I automatically wrapped my arms around his neck, slumped my head on his shoulder, and closed my eyes.

I felt him open the bathroom door and the cold air from the hallway sent goose bumps up my arms; I could have sworn he held me tighter. I heard Ethan's voice mumbling near us.

"She just conked out in my arms," Shane said.

"Yeah, Lea just passed out on Conner in the living room. He had to carry her into bed. Where are you going to put her to sleep?"

Shane was moving through the hallway with me, the motion rocked me gently. "Open the door to my room," Shane said.

"Shane, that's not the best idea. She's going to wake up pissed at you."

"I'll sleep in another room. I'm not putting her in the Bone Room, Ethan."

I opened my eyes as Ethan flicked the light on in Shane's room and I lifted my head off his shoulder.

Ethan smiled at me sweetly, "Hey, Grace, can I get you anything?"

"No, Ethan, thank you. I'm just wiped out. I don't care where I sleep, I just need to sleep." I looked around the room quickly. A beautiful dark cherry wood bed took up my view, and my guitar case was leaned up against it. I turned my face into Shane's, "You saved my guitar?"

Pulling back the covers of his bed, Shane delicately laid me down and sat beside me. His bed was soft and smelled like freshly washed linen; I closed my eyes.

"Get some sleep, Grace. We'll be right outside if you need anything," Shane whispered.

I reached my arm out and tugged his arm toward me. I can't even say why I did it. I was tired, scared, and angry, and it was the only thing that felt right. "Don't leave, Shane," I whispered back.

Shane squeezed my hand softly and moved off the bed. I opened my eyes to see Ethan close the door and Shane stroll across the room to his dresser. He pulled off his shirt and jeans and threw them into a large wicker basket in the corner. I watched the tattoos move against his muscles as he looked through his drawers wearing only a pair of boxers. He pulled on a pair of pajama bottoms and nothing else.

He switched off the light and crawled under the covers right beside me. He ran a single finger along my arm from my shoulder to my elbow. "Are you okay?" he asked.

"Yes, I just didn't want to be alone. I'm sorry," I whispered.

He pulled me closer to him and my body fit into his perfectly, "Don't be sorry. I get to hold a beautiful woman in my arms all night, so I'm definitely making out on the deal."

"Thank you," I said.

I could feel his raspy chuckle against the back of my neck, "For what, saying you're beautiful? Like you don't hear that from every freaking guy that looks at you."

"No, not that. For saving my life tonight. You could have gotten killed, Shane. Don't do anything like that for me again."

He softly placed his lips on the nape of my neck, just below my ear, and kissed me. "Shut up and go to sleep, Grace."

Chapter 13

The very first thing I was aware of when I awoke was Shane's body against mine. His hands were snuggled around my stomach and his face was buried in my hair. His breath came out in smooth even puffs along my shoulder.

I nudged him and tried to escape from his grasp, but he only smiled and held me tighter. I tried to roll over and fling my legs onto the floor, but that only got him to roll on top of me and start a full-fledged wrestling match. I finally pinned him down and freed myself from him and the bed, only to have him tackle me to the floor; both of us laughing.

There was a knock at the door and both of us bolted off the floor as if we were just caught by our parents, which only made us laugh even more.

Ethan came in holding a steaming cup of coffee, "Hey, I got coffee and bagels inside!" His eyes looked back and forth between Shane and me, his face reddened and he looked down at the floor. "Ah, sorry, I didn't mean to interrupt anything."

It was my turn for the heat to rise to my face. "Ethan, you didn't interrupt anything. We were just wrestling to get to the door first. There is absolutely nothing going on between Shane and me."

Ethan shrugged and nodded his head. "Well, breakfast is inside anyway. Everybody is packing up now, so we should be heading out soon." He didn't even wait for another response. He just turned his back to us and left the room, closing the door behind him.

I felt Shane's glare as if it was a burning laser on the back of my head. I turned to face him. "What's that look for?" I asked, already knowing the answer. *I just damaged his ego*.

"Why do you do shit like that?" He was pointing to the door.

"Like what?"

"Pretend that you don't give a shit about me. You're the one that asked me to sleep in here last night. I get a lot of mixed signals from you, Grace."

It killed me that he was right. Shane wasn't one to beat around the bush, he said things straight. I needed to tell him something to make sure his attention would go on to the next girl and I wouldn't feel so tempted by him. I wrapped my arms around myself, because telling him just a small part of my truth made me feel like my insides would burst and I'd be nothing more than dust. "Look, I was with someone for a long time. We had to go our separate ways, but I'm still in love with him. I don't...want anybody else. So...this is weird for me. I'm sorry, if I'm giving you any signals. I really don't want to be with anyone but him."

Shane's expression didn't change.

"Ever. Especially with anyone who would think I was only worth one night of their existence," I whispered. I looked down humiliated. I could feel the blush on my face heat my cheeks and spread down my neck. *I wasn't special, was I?* Maybe Azazel was right, maybe *he* wouldn't want me anymore. I looked back up to Shane; his lips were turned down and his eyebrows pulled together as if I had hurt him. Like I could ever hurt someone like Shane. I needed to get away from this life. It confused me and bothered me and all I wanted to do was to crawl back into bed with this man and pretend that I was really Grace. Grace would probably hate herself in the morning when she left the Bone Room, but I bet he would have made her feel loved for a few hours.

I walked out of Shane's room and exhaled. I walked into the bathroom and ran the cold water over my hands until I was numb. I shouldn't care what Shane thinks or what Shane feels, but that was the problem; *I did.* This life was too confusing and I was losing sight of what I set out to do, *and Azazel was trying to kill me*.

Lea's muffled calls through the door snapped me out of my thoughts. She knocked once and came in. "How did I know you'd be doing this?" Grabbing my hands from under the icy stream, she wrapped a towel around them and held them to her chest. "Is this really the only way you can let off steam? Or whatever it is you're trying to do?" She didn't wait for an answer. "I called my boss and told her everything that happened last night and she gave me the next two weeks off, can you believe that? I hope it doesn't take two weeks to find that lunatic. I'm so freaking scared."

"I think maybe I shouldn't go with you guys today. Maybe I should go someplace else and..."

"Shut up! Shut up! I don't want to hear about want you want," she snapped. "There is somebody out there who has tried to kill you. *Twice!* I know you think you have some sort of in with whatever supreme beings there are out there, but this is the real world and I don't want to hear any of your bullshit! You can't go off the deep end with me here. Don't do stupid things because Jacob and your parents are gone and now you think you're alone. I'm still here, Grace! You promised me that you'd never do anything to hurt yourself again, you promised me!"

I did. I did promise when we were sixteen and she found me after I tried to end my life. She not only found me, but she also saved me. She had said she dreamt about a beautiful angel with giant golden wings that told her where to find me. I couldn't doubt her dream, and I couldn't doubt it was an angel, because that would have been the only way anyone would have known how or where to find me.

I had left early for school that snowy morning, before Lea had even woken up. I had been involved in an early morning music program, so she should have never doubted me being there. Instead of taking the bus to school, I hopped on the train and got off in a remote area that was surrounded by the Jamaica Bay wildlife refuge. I walked at least two miles into the thick forest. There was about three to four inches of snow covering the ground. I brushed my footprints over with a large pine needle branch that I yanked off a tree. Leaning up against a cold tree, I took a razor to my wrists; no tears, no regrets. I didn't want Grace Taylor's life; the life of a teenage girl who had just lost her parents, and needed to learn to walk again after her body was mangled in a car wreck. No more damage was evident on the outside of her body, but the inside was messed up and I didn't want to be in there any longer. I couldn't be inside the body of a teenager; all the heartache, all the need and hunger was constant. The worst part was her memories, so vivid and so real, I hated the fact that Grace was gone and I was there. She would have been something amazing one day. Instead, I was there, searching for someone.

I knew that Grace's soul was gone, I knew, as always, that day when I got shoved in her body that there was no way I could save her, but I tried. For the first time, I tried to fight the pull of my spirit. I wanted her to live. *My God, she was only fourteen years old.* Her parents were driving her to buy a dress for her very first dance. She even had a date with the cutest boy in school, Lucas Fraser.

I fought against her body, but it consumed me; devoured me. I fought while her body laid in a coma in a hospital bed for a little over six months. It was then that Gabriel had come to me, the first time in lifetimes. I had thought I was forgotten, but he held my soul in his arms until I woke up as Grace, calming my spirit.

Gabriel had told Lea where to find me that day. He woke her up five minutes after I had left, so I wouldn't have too much time alone. She followed his instructions exactly, bringing along a first aid kit complete with Steri-strips and surgical dressings.

Lea stared those terrified brown eyes at me in the bathroom, repeating her mantra, *"You promised me."*

"I know I did, and I'm not doing anything to put myself in Carl Sumpton's path. I don't even know who he is, but I'm sort of thinking that he's really not Carl Sumpton. Like maybe he's something...else."

Her eyes widened and she immediately started to hyperventilate. "What?" she panted, grabbing at my shoulders.

"Come on, Lea. Carl Sumpton was dying in a hospital last week, and now he's running around trying to kill me?" I didn't want to scare her with the story of my little talk with the dying body of Carl Sumpton. Lea was too good, too innocent to be involved in this. "I just think that there's something else going on and I don't want you and Conner involved. I just want to get you guys far away from me and whatever or whoever is after me."

"No. No, no, no," she was shaking her head so hard I thought she might snap it right off. "You are coming with us and Conner, Shane, Ethan and even Tucker. They are going to protect us." Grasping my shoulders tighter, she pleaded, "Promise me."

Hesitating for only a second, I sighed heavily, "Sure, I promise."

Her shoulders relaxed and she exhaled long and slow. Grabbing me in her arms, she hugged me tight. "Gabriel would never let anything happen to you. He always gets someone to save your sorry butt anyway."

I wondered where her strong faith had come from. "Why do you think that?"

She stepped back and gave me a curious look. "Every time you come close to kicking the bucket, someone is always there. Me, Shane. I wonder if Shane had a dream about the fire. We were all asleep; he was on the couch, so how could he have known?"

I stepped away from her and opened the bathroom door. Turning back, I looked at her from the doorway. "What you don't seem to understand is that I will go on, and I don't want you guys to get hurt. This is your life, Lea. Mine was over centuries ago, but you have a future, things to hope for and look forward to. I'm just here for one thing. I don't want anything to happen to you or Conner, even Shane or Tucker, because you're all trying to save *me*." I walked into the hallway.

"But you did promise me, so you're coming with us," she called from the bathroom.

The living room had a mountain of duffel bags piled on the middle of the floor. Hushed voices were coming out of the kitchen, along with the sounds of plates hitting against each other; everyone was eating.

I lingered a bit in the hallway before entering the kitchen. I hated that everyone thought they needed to save me when it wasn't their problem, or their fight. The truth was that I needed to find Azazel; I needed to figure out why he wanted me gone. I needed to find Gabriel and see if he could tell me anything, and I could do neither with everyone around me trying to watch out for mad men.

"Hey, there she is! Good afternoon, Beautiful! It's about time you got up!" Tucker sang. He was sitting at our small kitchen table shoving a bagel in his mouth. Ethan and Conner sat around the table doing the same thing. Shane sat quietly on the countertop and didn't even lift his head when I walked in. Another guy leaned against the counter closest to me, holding a bagel and coffee in his hands, I didn't even look up at him, I guessed it was Tucker's cousin Blake. Lea walked in behind me.

I nodded in Tucker's direction and walked straight to the *Box of Joe* that Ethan had bought and poured myself some coffee.

Tucker cleared his throat and started barking out commands, "So, Grace, we are going to be taking your Jeep and Blake's truck. As soon as you are ready, we can leave. I'll drive your Jeep and you can just sit and enjoy the ride."

I looked up from stirring the sweetener into my coffee. "I'm driving my Jeep, Tucker. And I have no clothes, since my bedroom somehow caught fire last night, so before I go on your little trip, I'd like to stop at a store and buy some clothes, so I don't have to stay in Shane's tee-shirt and boxers the whole time I'm there. When you guys are ready, you can leave, and I'll be about an hour behind you. Just give me the address. I have a GPS, so I'll be fine."

Lea started to argue, but a voice I'd not heard before interrupted her, "Well, that sounds like a plan then. If you'd like, I can stay behind and keep you company, and make sure nothing else happens."

I snapped my head to the direction of the new voice. It was soft velvet and sweet; reminding me of melted caramel.

Blake stood there casually leaning his back against the cabinets. His skin was so pale it was almost white, until my eyes met his and a splash of crimson shot across his cheeks. He was very handsome, with a lean muscular build. Light brown hair hung messy and sexy over his head, but I barely saw any of it. I fixated on his eyes, his ancient pale blue eyes, which were looking profoundly back into mine.

"Hi," he said with his cheeks turning brighter. "I'm Blake, Tucker's cousin."

I froze, unable to speak. I held his gaze. It was all I could do to keep myself composed and not throw myself at him. I hoped no one noticed how fast my heart was pounding against my chest or how my hands clammed up and balled into fists, trying to hold myself back from reaching out to touch him.

Tucker shot up and leaned into the space between Blake and me, folding his arms. His face was tight and possessive. "Thanks *cuz*, but I don't want to be responsible for your brand new truck," he said eyeing Blake. "Besides, Grace doesn't even know you, so I don't think she'd be *that* comfortable driving with you, since her feelings for her safety have been questioned lately." *Crap, I hated lawyers. It would look completely horrible for me to drive with someone I just met, but I needed to be alone with him somehow. I needed him to know who I really was. Finally. He had to be Shamsiel!*

Blake pushed himself off the counter and looked down at Tucker as if he was trying to scare him. I could smell the testosterone in the air.

Everyone in the kitchen had stopped talking and watched the exchange between them.

Shane jumped off the counter and strolled passed us as if nothing was going on. When he reached where I stood, he turned to Tucker and Blake, who were standing toe to toe with each other fists clenched. "Wow, this is like mating season at the zoo. Why don't I go with Grace later after she picks up what she needs? After all, everyone knows there will never be anything between Grace and me. *Ever*." He emphasized the word ever and looked at me through his icy blue eyes.

Shane's words seemed to do something to Blake, because he seemed even angrier, but he backed off Tucker all the same.

Blake stepped towards Shane, but Shane sidestepped him and ignored the advance. Shane just walked closer to me and gently escorted me out of the kitchen and back down the hallway to his room, "You have a strong effect on people, don't you?"

I could still barely speak. I just stood in the center of his room and stared at the door. My mind tried to formulate coherent thoughts, but I was just grasping for straws. I couldn't think logically, because all I could see in my mind were those ancient blue eyes.

Lea walked in Shane's room and jolted me back to reality. She shot me a wide-eyed look that expressed her concern about what had just happened. "What in the world was that about?"

Forgetting Shane was in the room with us, I grabbed at her hands, my heart beating wildly. "Did you see the color of his eyes?"

She gave me a perplexed look. I heard Shane behind us stop what he was doing and he turned to listen. I glanced at him and just shrugged my shoulders like nothing mattered. I leaned in close to Lea and whispered softly, hoping Shane couldn't hear, "He has the exact color that I've been looking for."

Lea's eyes danced with understanding, "Are you *effing* serious? Are you positive?" She started pacing and dancing around.

"What are you two whispering about? What have you been looking for?" Conner asked walking in. He nodded to Shane after, "Someone has got to talk to Tucker, he's obsessed. And did you see him and Blake? Dude, I thought it was going to come to blows."

Shane said nothing; he just stared at me, waiting for me to say something. I let go of Lea and tried to act calm and restrained. "I just think that everyone is a bit nervous and out of sorts because of what's going on, that's all. Everyone's on edge, so we definitely should get out of the city and up to Tucker's as soon as we can. It'll make everyone relax and we won't have to look over our shoulders for a while." I watched Shane for a reaction.

"Do you want me to stay here and drive up with you? It's up to you, nobody should make the call for you," Shane said.

"That's fine," I answered. Turning my head to Lea, I continued, "I'll just run to the store quickly, I promise I'll be right behind you guys."

My choice seemed to settle everybody down, even Tucker and Blake. I couldn't keep my eyes off him as they packed his truck with the duffel bags in the falling snow. He couldn't keep his eyes off me either and before he left, he walked past me and looked right into my eyes. "Be as quick as...humanly possible," he grinned. I almost fainted. I toyed with the idea of just grabbing a handful of Shane's clothing, or sharing Lea's, but none of it made sense. Just a few more hours, it wasn't as if it would be a few more lifetimes. My heart catapulted through the air.

I took exactly thirty minutes in the department store, grabbing whatever I could, not even trying anything on. Shane just walked beside me wherever I went, holding bags and cracking jokes that made me laugh out loud, literally.

We rushed home and I tossed everything I bought into the huge backpack I had purchased along with my clothes. My phone ringing its sirens, alarming me of a text message, was the only thing that slowed me down.

New Text Message

Lea: 2:45 pm

Are you sure this is him? He's an a$$hole.

Me: 2:45 pm

IDK! Not like anyone gave me a chance to talk 2 him!

Lea: 2:47 pm

Bad feeling. Rethink ur options

Me: 2:49 pm

WTF are you taking about?

Lea: 2:51 pm

U decide...

The next message was a multimedia one sent from Lea's phone. I left Shane in the living room watching the news about the slow moving snowstorm, while packing his belongings as slowly as he could. I locked myself in the bathroom and clicked on the message.

She had recorded some of their conversation in Blake's truck. The conversation was between Tucker and Blake placing bets on who would bag me first, and they were up to one thousand dollars. Lea's caption read: Isn't Acting Like Much of an Angel.

The second multimedia message was from Conner's phone. I pressed the icon and immediately heard myself playing my guitar. Conner's camera phone scanned across the studio to Shane's expression. It was an awestruck Shane. I had brought him to his knees. Conner focused in on Shane's face, tears welled in his eyes; desire and love shining over his face. It made me breathless, watching his perfect features watch me with such intensity and longing.

Shane banged on the bathroom door bringing me to my senses. I needed to get to Blake to see if he was whom I'd been searching for. *Yes, God yes, I loved the way I had just seen Shane look at me, but we all knew that look would only last one night.* Even if Blake wasn't my angel, I couldn't settle for someone like Shane. Grace was worth more, *I was worth more.*

Chapter 14

I tilted my head up to watch the hushed fall of the feathery white flakes blanketing the earth. Delicate snowy crystals seemed to dance around the air in front of me; moving to music that only they could hear.

Snowcapped windowsills and fluffy snow covered branches made the city look picturesque and hopeful.

Shane brushed off the snow that had collected on the front and back windshields. I was amazed at how much had already fallen and the news said that the storm wasn't even near us yet. There had to be about a foot of snow on the ground already. Before we left the apartment, we watched as warnings scrolled along the bottom of the television screen to stay indoors and to drive only in cases of emergency.

I didn't know by whose standards we would call this an emergency, but I would have sprouted wings myself and flew to see those ancient blue eyes if I couldn't drive.

Shane opened the passenger side door and knocked his boots on the side of the well, spraying snow all over.

"Hurry up, just get in, I want to get out on the road ahead of this storm if we can."

Shane gave me an exasperated look. "We could just stay here, Grace. We don't have to go to Tucker's place. I promise, I'll keep you safe."

"Shane. I'm going. If you want to stay, then stay."

The inside of the Jeep was still cold, and mist drifted from our lips each time we spoke. I shivered and turned on the heat and defrost, and tried to blow some warmth into my hands. When the air seemed warm enough not to cause my fingers to shake, I plugged in my GPS system and keyed in our destination. Outside the snow fell faster.

I pulled over the snowdrifts with my four-wheel drive; the wind howled against the car. "Looks like the angels are having one hell of a pillow fight!" I laughed.

"Pillow fight?" Shane whispered.

"Yeah, it's an old saying, but Conner said it when it started to snow the other night." I glanced at his expression, his head hung low and his arms were folded tight across his chest. "What's wrong? You don't believe in that stuff or just not in old wives tales."

I stopped at a red light and waited for his answer.

He shrugged and looked out the snowy window. "I don't give much thought to angels," he said and shivered.

I took the Lincoln Tunnel and emerged into a wintery wonderland worse than what we came from, nothing that side of the tunnel seemed to have been plowed. Shane buckled himself in his seatbelt, but still sat at the edge of the passenger seat; knuckles white clutching my dashboard.

Shane's phone went off. When he answered it, I could hear Conner's voice on the other side. The howling winds hitting against the Jeep made the rest of the conversation hard to hear.

After a brief conversation, Shane clicked off his phone. "They made it there okay. Conner says the roads are getting worse. They are talking about white out conditions on I-80."

Thick chunks of snow collided with the windshield; the wipers could barely stand against the attack. "We can't go back now. It's fine. Look," I pointed through an almost opaque windshield. "The roads aren't so bad." *Who the hell did I think I was kidding? I was insane driving in this!* I gripped the wheel as tightly as I could.

Shane glared at me openmouthed.

I pressed harder on the gas pedal to stop him from looking at me and it worked. He snapped his head forward and crossed his arms glowering out the window. "Lea is right, you *really do* have some sort of a death wish," he whispered.

I let the statement go. Fighting with him right then would cause me not to concentrate on the road that I could no longer see. All I needed to do was stand in front of those ancient blue eyes. I needed to know if Blake was who I'd been looking for.

"Do you want to explain to me why you are driving in this insane blizzard to get to someone you don't want to be with? Or am I wrong about you and Tucker?"

He would never understand. "I don't want to be with Tucker. Let me just concentrate on driving."

He kicked the floorboards with his foot. "Whatever."

We continued the drive in hours of eerie silence; nothing but the muted sounds of the snow closing down and suffocating the earth. Would this be what death would be like for me when my eternity was done? Silent, cold and empty; no heaven at all?

We both jumped, startled, when the voice from my GPS called out for me to take the next exit.

The Jeep skidded onto the off ramp and almost into a snow embankment, but I somehow managed to straighten out. Shane cursed under his breath.

"We're almost there," I said. "The GPS says we'll be there in three minutes."

I drove slowly, my blood pumping fiercely through my veins. The GPS announced to the world that we had reached our destination. Outside the windshield, it was pure white.

"Tucker's driveway is right off this main road, so we are probably at the entrance."

I turned in, only to hit what seemed like a four-foot wall of snow.

"Looks like the drive is plowed in," he said. "Try to pull up to the right more so you're off the main road in case another plow comes by and doesn't see us."

I pulled up more, hands shaking. "Should we get out and walk from here?"

Shane grimaced. "Tucker's driveway is at least three miles long. Its got its own name, so there's no way we can walk in this. I'll call them and see if he can get to us with the snow mobiles."

He tried calling, so did I, but he got no reception at all and mine went right to voice mail so I left a message.

"What should we do?" I asked anxiously.

"We should stay in here until we can get them on the phone. That way, Grace, we won't die out in the pretty white stuff," he teased. "Kill the ignition, don't waste the gas."

A tremendous gust of wind tilted the Jeep, so I frantically tried my cell phone again. No service. *Craptabulous!*

Shane started shifting around in his seat, "My ass is asleep from sitting so long. Is that even possible? Wanna rub it for me?" he laughed.

"Shut up," I laughed back.

As he tried to make himself comfortable, he skimmed his hand lightly across my knee, sending shivers throughout my body. *Of course, he noticed.*

Bending forward he sprang the handle on the seat and pushed it all the way back. "You're cold already, climb over here."

I looked at him as if he had just grown another head. "That's not necessary." I mean seriously, if a brush from his freaking hand sent shivers all over my body what would his whole body on me...I refused to finish the thought. To keep me from jumping on top of him I thought about my Jeep being mauled by a bear looking for food in the blizzard.

Outside, the wind screamed louder, and inside, the temperature was dropping faster. "What's in your glove box?"

"My glove what?"

He pointed to the dashboard in front of him.

"Oh, you mean my glove compartment. Trust me, there's nothing in there you'll want to see," I explained.

"*Glove BOX*. And is that supposed to make me *not* want to know what's inside it?" Shane laughed. "Because, trust *ME*, it doesn't."

We both reached for the glove COMPARTMENT/box at the same time, but he was quicker. About half a dozen tampons flew out at him.

I laughed uncontrollably. "I told you it's nothing you'd want to see, why do you always have to try to get your way?"

He reached his hand in and felt around, throwing the last tampon at me. "Because I was hoping you had one of these," he said smiling, holding up a flashlight. His eyes studied mine as he dropped the flashlight back into the glove *whatever*. He tucked a loose piece of my hair behind my ear. Another shiver rocked my body. A small flicker of sadness passed over his eyes.

He unzipped his jacket and peeled it off. "Come here, Grace, you're freezing." He gathered me into his arms and easily pulled me onto his lap. Of course, it would be an easy task, my mutinous body helped him right along. He held me in his arms and draped the coat over us.

Not having any control over my body, I nuzzled into his chest under his jacket. It was as if I floated on warm tropical waters. Somewhere in the back of mind, I thought about those ancient blue eyes, just three miles away. The image blurred and faded in and out. I clung to Shane, not wanting to move a muscle, for fear the friction and heat between us would spark a fire. I laughed at the thought.

Shane moaned and held me tighter, "What are you giggling at under there?"

I poked my head out from under his jacket, our faces so close to each other I could barely breathe. Our lips so close.

"I'm losing it," I muttered. "I'm desperate for some hot cocoa; you know the thick and creamy kind with those sweet sugary little marshmallows. I want to sit near a roaring fire with my hands wrapped around the warm cup and I want to feel the velvety heat coat my mouth and slide down my throat," I ranted.

His breath pitched. "God, Grace you can seriously make anything you say the sexiest thing I've ever heard." His eyes lowered their gaze to my lips as he unzipped my jacket. We locked eyes as I slipped my arms out of its sleeves. Wrapping both our jackets over us, he pulled me closer and nestled his face into my hair, his breath sparking flames down my neck.

I gritted my loudly chattering teeth. *Traitorous body!* I wasn't the least bit cold.

He slid his warm hands under my shirt and slowly traced his fingertips along the small of my back and up my spine. His touch was killing me, killing my soul; just leaving the body of Grace wanting and needing.

I slid my hands up the front of his shirt, telling myself it was for the warmth, but I was never a good liar. His body was soft and deliciously warm, and the restraint was torturous.

A low moan escaped from his lips. He pushed himself up against me and gently pulled me into a sitting position; my legs straddling him. *This is too dangerous, too toxic; too beautiful.*

I glanced down at him and immediately I wished I hadn't. He was watching me closely. He hesitated and fixed me with his intense icy blue stare. He raised his beautiful hand to my face and traced his thumb softly against my lower lip.

"One kiss, Grace, just one simple kiss. Baby, please," he begged. "Just one." His hands reached up, grabbing my hair and pulling me towards him. His smell was intoxicating; I inhaled deeply.

He ran feathery fingers through my hair and around to the nape of my neck. I trembled under his touch. I was a complete dripping hot disaster; falling into pieces wanting him to fill me and put me back together.

"Do you have any idea what you do to me, Grace?" His voice was low and husky, and he gazed at me, ice blue eyes concentrating hard. It took my breath away. "Just one. Grace..."

His slow deliberate hands moved over my skin, fingers trembling. It unleashed an inferno that coursed through my body. Every move he made was so freaking erotic.

"Just one," I whispered. Then his lips touched mine. It was barely a kiss; his lips hovered over mine, taking the briefest of moments to savor the intensity.

I told myself, just one, a little one, then that would be it. I would stop myself from going too far.

"Grace," he sighed and his lips devoured mine. I fell completely apart in his arms, his touch unraveled me, and his kiss brought me back together; complete. I wanted all of him; I wanted to taste every inch of his body. I moaned desperately into his mouth and he pulled me closer.

He clasped my hands above me and yanked the tee shirt over my head. He tilted his head back appraising me, and then let out a long faltering sigh. He trailed kisses over my neck and shoulders, and across my torso, leaving a burning sensation in their wake. Gently, he grazed my skin with his teeth, biting me softly. Every place he touched me echoed in my groin, making me breathless.

Yanking the cup of my bra down, he licked me in circular motions; my nipples hardened, I could feel the moist sensation all the way in my groin. He touched me as if he couldn't get enough, like I was the first woman he'd ever touched, I shuddered in response to his fingertips.

My fingers ran down the lean muscles of his chest and settled on the button of his jeans, undoing them with the snap of my fingers. His hands slid over my legs up to the button of my jeans, unbuttoning it slowly. He leaned back and grinned wickedly, which made the deep parts of me ache with want even more. Thick hot desire burned in my belly.

Watching me, he laid his hand flat against my belly, dipping his fingers slowly between the material of my panties and my skin. My body hitched up towards him with longing. His fingers kept traveling down, ever so slightly, and my body throbbed for them. I quivered and his breath faltered again, as he watched my breathless reaction. Our breathing amplified in the small confines of the Jeep. He dug his teeth into my bottom lip and moaned; I rocked against him.

I slipped my hands past his waistband and tugged gently as my hands grasped his smooth hard skin. He closed his eyes, his breathing caught.

When he opened his eyes again, his gaze was scorching, wanting, needing. I felt his legs tense under me; he throbbed in my hands.

His lips touched mine again, breathing me in like I was his air, then he tore his mouth from mine; panting. "Please, Grace, whatever it is you're going after, please try to find it here in me. I will try my best to be the man that you need me to be." His words brought me back to earth, and sent me reeling, as I realized where our hands were. I pushed against him and leaned back.

I cupped my hands over my swollen lips and tried desperately to get off him. I was astounded by what I had almost let happen, what I still wanted to happen. "Shane, I'm sorry." I felt my eyes go wide and filled themselves with tears. I looked out the window, I looked up, down; I was frantic. I started the engine and blasted the heat; ice-cold air filled the small space. My body convulsed and raged against my decision to stop kissing him. I squeezed my hands around the steering wheel just to keep them off him.

Shane lightly placed his hand on my chin and pulled my face towards his. I flicked the heater even higher. The noise from the vents was a welcoming distraction from the hunger in Shane's gaze.

"I lost myself in you that night, lost myself somewhere in that kiss," Shane said.

"I told you *I can't* do this. I told you I was in love with someone else."

"An ex-boyfriend, right? Not Tucker or Ethan or Blake?"

I nodded my head and wiped the humiliating tears from my cheeks. I wasn't crying about the kiss, *because my God, that was freaking amazing.* It was the fact that he could make me forget something that I've been after for thousands of years with just the tips of his fingers. *Oh my, what would the rest of his body do to me? It's killing me that I want to find out!*

"Let me help you erase his memory," he whispered.

I almost threw up on him. In fact, I know I definitely would have if there were any food in my stomach. I literally dry-heaved. Then I smacked him across the face. I wanted to punch him. I wanted to punch him with a fully closed fist.

He didn't even flinch from the slap. He just arched his stupidly perfect eyebrow at me, as if I was a joke to him.

"You cold fucking bastard! What will you erase it with, your dick? You really think sleeping with you is that fucking awesome? I love someone, Shane, with my whole heart. Don't you understand what that means? Do you even have a heart inside that body of yours?" I cried. Hot tears poured down my face. They came down to defend my angel, the one I could never seem to find.

He drew his hands back and leaned against the door, looking right into my teary eyes, expressionless. "No, Grace. I don't have a heart. I did once, but I gave it to a girl and I let her keep it when she died. That's why I am the way I am, why every girl is just another piece of ass to me. No one has ever come close to making me feel the way she did. But shit, Grace, I would do anything to erase her, to not feel that fucking hole in my life."

I couldn't look at him any longer. I would have bet my life on him lying to get me to have sex with him right there out of pity. Like I would be the one that could tame him. I wondered how many poor girls got their heart crushed by those words. I'd burn in hell before I became someone's piece of ass! "Let's just keep trying our cells, so we can finally get out of this box, forget everything that's happened, and move on with our lives. You can go back to your adoring *Pieces of Ass*, and I can go back to being alone. Everyone gets to live happily ever after."

"Holy shit, Grace! Do you not listen to anything? Grace, that's not a kiss I'm ever going to forget. Looking at the way I fucking make you cry, I wish like hell I could forget it, but I freaking can't! I want *you*!" He grabbed my hands and pinned them together.

"Don't do this, Shane."

"Why? Lie to me and tell me you don't fucking feel that need between us," he yelled.

"Really, Shane? You want to go there? What are you asking me for exactly? You just want me to spread eagle for you right here, let you have your way with me, get me out of your system? Then we get out of this and you get to treat me like nothing but a PIECE OF ASS? You can have a great story to tell the guys-all about how you tapped that ass stuck in a snowstorm."

He had nothing to say, because I was right. "This is a nightmare, Shane, me and you. I woke up crying the other night thinking about how you kissed me!"

"Really, Grace? Why don't you go ahead and ask me what wakes me up sweaty and trembling every freaking night! Go ahead, Grace, ask me!" he demanded. He pulled me closer.

"Get away from me, Shane!" I moaned, moving away. I clawed his hands off me and I yanked open the Jeep door. It wouldn't budge, so I shifted my body and kicked at it until it opened enough for my body to climb out. All the while, Shane was screaming, cursing, and pleading for me to listen to him. I pressed the mute button and yanked my shirt back over my head. "I'm a fucking novelty to you, just because no other girl has ever had the self-esteem to say no to you!"

I pulled myself out of the car. The snowdrift we were parked in was so high that I was able to climb right onto the roof. Underneath the hardtop, I could feel Shane kicking the passenger side door open to come after me.

The roof lurched beneath my feet and Shane grabbed my flailing arms, dragging me off the Jeep and into the snow. "Get away, Shane!"

He lifted me up and tossed me over his shoulder, forcing all the air from my lungs. Carrying me, he climbed the snowdrifts, as I pounded my fists against his back. When he found an area sheltered by a tree, he eased me off his shoulder, sliding me down the front of his body. *Oh, holy horror was that freaking hot!*

I tried to wrench free, but he held me tight against him with one hand on the small of my back and the other grasping my neck through a fistful of hair.

He gently tugged my hair back and pulled his head down to mine, kissing me once on the lips. He brushed his lips along my cheeks to my ear and whispered with the heat of his breath, "Go ahead, Grace, ask me what dreams I wake from at night." He pulled his head back and his eyes assaulted me with his fierce intensity. "I wake up with you as the last thought in my dreams. I dream about your lips, the smell of your skin and hair, and the freaking fire that burns inside of me to be inside you. I want to bury myself inside you and never climb out, *my sweet death.* Grace, I'm fucking in love with you."

I stopped struggling and let him hold me. One, I was freezing because I had left my coat in the Jeep and two, well, for a minute; I so badly wanted this to be my real life.

I blinked back tears. "In another life, Shane, if I was anybody but me, I would have loved to be loved by you."

Shane stood there holding me, eyes pleading, when we heard the roar of the snowmobiles. *Finally, one of our messages got through!*

Shane stepped away from me and raked his hands through his snow-covered hair. Two snowmobiles appeared out of the blinding whiteness and skidded to a halt in front of us.

Tucker lifted his visor to exclaim that my Superman was finally here, giving me a wink.

Blake lifted his visor and rolled his eyes. He jumped off and reached his hand out to me. I took it and he helped me straddle the snowmobile, then he got on behind me.

Rage shadowed Shane's features and his hands balled into fists.

Tucker looked rejected. I cared about neither at that moment. All I cared about was Blake.

With a disgusted sigh, Shane waded through the deep snow back to the Jeep and yanked the passenger side door open. I watched him effortlessly pull our packs and jackets out and sling both our guitar cases over his shoulders then climb back over the snowdrifts to our waiting snowmobiles.

Glaring angrily into my eyes, he handed my jacket to me when he passed, "Here you go, wouldn't want you to get any colder than you already are."

The words stung, because I knew he wasn't talking about the temperature. He was just stating how cold of a person I was. He was right, but I had no other choice.

After I pulled on my coat and zipped it up against the wind, Blake wrapped one strong arm around my waist and the other on one end of the handlebars. He took off without even waiting for Shane to jump on Tucker's snowmobile.

Chapter 15

Blake skidded to a stop near an enormous wrap around porch where Lea, Conner, Ethan and Brayden sat together waiting. When I climbed off Blake's snowmobile, Lea flung herself into my arms, "Oh, thank God, you're okay!"

I looked back toward Blake, "Thank you," I said.

He grinned back at me. "Get inside and warm up, we'll talk later. Then we can think of a way you can properly thank me." *What?*

"Come on, let's go inside. We'll get you warmed up and changed, and then we're going to the bar at the resort. I need a drink," Lea said, moving me away from Blake.

I was shuttled away from Blake as he drove away blasting snow out of his path. Lea dragged me by the hand through the front entryway of an enormous log cabin style ranch. When the warmth of the inside hit me, I realized how wet and cold I was. My jacket was soaked through, and so was the shirt and jeans I wore beneath it. It felt as though a layer of ice was forming on my skin. I began shuddering uncontrollably.

Shane strode in after us and looked far worse than I did. He dropped all of our belongings in front of him, closed his eyes, leaned back and rested his head against the wall. "Lea, get her out of those wet clothes."

"I'm fine," I shuddered. I was lying through my teeth. I could barely move and icy chills rocked my body.

His eyes snapped open and gave me a challenging glare. "You're impossible!" He stomped towards me, picked me up with one hand, and flung me over his shoulder like a sack of potatoes, *again*. "Bring the bags for me, will you? My hands seem a bit full," he said to Lea.

He marched with me through the house, down a long hallway and into a dark room. Lea switched on the lights for him and he threw me down on a beautiful king-size four-poster bed. "Get out of your clothes!" He walked through another door and came back with an armful of soft white towels. He lifted his eyebrow at me, "Do you know what hypothermia is? Get out of your clothes!"

I gritted my chattering teeth and began taking off sneakers and socks. My eyes never left his harsh stare, but I did notice when Lea quietly slipped out of the room. *Oh, was I going to kill her for that!*

Shane tore off his shirt and pants and stood in his boxers, leaning over his bag, searching through it for dry clothes.

With my bag slung over my arm, I slowly walked through the door where he had gotten the towels. I didn't care if it was a closet or a bathroom, it was where I would be getting changed so I wouldn't have to do it with Shane's eyes on me.

When I changed into dry clothes and blew dried my hair, I walked out of the bathroom into an empty room. My guitar was in its case, propped up against the bed, but all of Shane's things were gone. Throwing my bag on the bed, I walked out of the bedroom and into the rest of the house.

The entire house was filled with bright lights hanging decoratively from high vaulted ceilings. The walls were made of deep cherry colored timber. The smell of pine needles and wood chips filled the air; it was a real log cabin. Walking into the living room area, I discovered Lea, Conner and Ethan sitting on soft brown leather sofas; antique wooden furniture lay sporadically throughout the room.

"How are you feeling?" Lea asked.

"Fine. Thanks by the way, for leaving me in there alone with Shane. Remind me to pay back the favor one day," I sarcastically sneered.

"I guess I got the wrong idea about the whole situation, sorry," she pouted. "If you feel up to it, everyone is snowmobiling down to the resort bar for some drinks. Blake, Tucker, Brayden and Shane are already there."

"Yes, I'm definitely in need of a drink, although I have no dry coat to go outside with."

Ethan bundled me up in his gigantic coat and stood back to laugh at me. "Let's go get drunk, shall we?" He hooked my arm in his and curiously smiled down at me, "And you must let me know what you did to get Shane all fired up, so I can repeatedly tease him about it."

I shook my head, "Oh, I'm sure he'll forget all about whatever it is I did or didn't do once he finds someone to occupy his time. I think I just got on his nerves on the long car ride here." I didn't like how easy it was getting for me to spin a lie.

He tilted his head down towards me and tightened his lips. "I hate that you think that you need to lie to me."

I jumped on the back of the snowmobile and I sighed, "Well, hurry up. Now I really need a drink."

There seemed to be a good size crowd in the resort bar, despite the blizzard raging outside. People were dancing to someone horribly singing karaoke, the bar was lined with people ordering drinks, and every table was full with laughing noisy patrons.

The inside of the bar had the same sort of ambience as Tucker's house and any other time, I would have probably stopped to appreciate the atmosphere, but Blake was waiting for me at a crowded table. His beautiful blue eyes locked onto mine and didn't let go; a sweet smile beamed across his face.

Shane sat across from him and watched our exchange. We walked up to the table and Blake's smile beamed brighter. Shane tipped his head back, draining the last of his beer and then he slammed the bottle on the table. Everyone at the table stopped their conversations at the jolting noise it made. He stood up and grabbed some girl's hand that had been sitting at the table with them. His eyes watched mine as he led her to the dance floor. The girl looked back at her friends as if she'd just won the lottery.

I watched them walk away and practically have sex with each other on the dance floor. I squeezed my eyes shut and turned away. It hurt like hell, but I needed to remember that was the exact reason Shane was not a good choice for Grace, if Blake wasn't who I wanted him to be.

Blake stood up and smoothly slid next to me. He held out a shot glass for me and I grabbed it, gulping the golden liquid down. He tilted his head towards Shane and his friend on the dance floor, "I bet we could put them to shame," he smiled wickedly. Leading me to the dance floor, we grabbed onto each other like there was no one else around, like there was a thousand years since we'd seen each other last.

Everyone at the table swarmed us on the dance floor. Immediately, the temperature rose and sweat glistened on our bodies. Blake held me close and I danced with my arms wrapped around his neck. I closed my eyes and melted into his body, we danced close and hot until the music turned slow. Someone started singing Karaoke to Adele's Someone Like You, and Blake roughly grabbed my chin and pulled my lips up to his. His tongue attacked my mouth like a hungry animal, and then he spun me around to face the crowd.

I whirled in his arms to stand face to face with Shane. He looked like a stone statue, frozen in the middle of a crowd of slow dancing bodies, eyes wide; staring right through me. His lips parted as if he meant to say something, but thought better of it. The girl he was with had stopped dancing along with him and just waited beside him for his next move, as he stood waiting for mine.

Blake pulled me closer against him and kissed my neck, pulling my hair back, trailing a thick wet tongue along my skin.

Shane swallowed hard, intently focused on every spot of my skin that Blake touched.

Blake slid his hands around to the front of my shirt. He lifted the fabric, placing his hands on the bare skin of my stomach and dug into my skin roughly.

Shane's eyes dropped to watch Blake's hands and back up to my eyes. His lips pressed tightly together and shaking his head, he held his hands up to wave me off. He turned around and melted into the slow dancing shadows of the crowd.

When the music ended Lea, Conner and Ethan lugged me up to the microphone. My mind reeled. Blake stood in front of the stage cheering me on with them. Shane's beautiful back was walking to the door with the girl he had danced with in tow.

Lea talked to the Karaoke DJ and the pop beat to Katy Perry's The One That Got Away thumped through the speakers. *How appropriate.*

The first word I sang caused the entire crowd to stop and stare, and the rest of the words had them looking at me dumbstruck. When I got to the chorus, Shane stopped at the entrance to the bar and clenched his fists and raked them through his hair. I sang the song right to him. The crowd screamed over my voice and when the song ended, they chanted for me to sing more, but Blake walked up on the stage and carried me off.

He carried me through the crowds who were yelling for more and booing Blake for hauling me off the stage.

"Put me down!" I snapped.

"I haven't seen you in lifetimes, and you would rather sing for a room full of sweaty strangers?" My heart thudded to a stop. His features were taut and set, and then after a few seconds, he nodded his head and a smile radiated on his lips.

He walked me to the table, picked up his coat, and left Ethan's, the one I wore there, on the back of the chair. He nodded to Tucker who was sitting down talking with a pretty redhead. "I'm taking her back to the house. See you tomorrow!"

Tucker's jaw hit the table as Blake put his coat on me.

Blake took a full shot glass that was sitting in front of Tucker and gulped it down, and then he drank the redhead's, who wore a disgusted look on her face. I just laughed. His eyes watched me, sheer naughtiness danced in them when he heard my laughter. He took hold of my hand and ran with me through the bar, right out the front door.

Giant snowflakes still fell in heavy white sheets making an eerie silence surround us. He swept my feet out from underneath me and sat me on the snowmobile. He leaned over me and covered my mouth with his, thrusting his tongue in almost painfully.

He ripped his mouth from mine and smiled a slow sexy smile down at me. "Selah," he called me, making my heart pound hard against my chest. *My name*.

He straddled the snowmobile and offering me a sly smile, gunned the vehicle until we were practically airborne. We catapulted across the great white expanse and glided into the front area of Tucker's porch, almost colliding with the steps.

Blake jumped off his seat and helped me off and into the cold knee-deep snow. He kissed me again and tugged me up the stairs, unlocking the front door with his lips still attached to mine.

Shane's brooding dark expression was the first thing I saw when I stumbled in. He sat next to his *friend* from the bar on the couch, elbows resting on his legs and his hands dangled between them. He glowered at Blake and jumped to his feet.

Blake laughed as his eyes darted from Shane to me. "Crap, I thought we'd have the house to ourselves," he sneered.

Shane stormed over and stepped between us. "I want you to come with me, Grace."

I baulked at him. "Are you serious, right now? What am I supposed to join you and your friend over there?"

Shane leaned in closer, "Don't do this."

Blake pulled me by the hand and nodded to Shane, "Take a step back, Shane, this has nothing to do with you. You have a pretty girl over there," he said, pointing to the girl quietly sitting on the couch.

Shane touched his hand to my elbow and I froze to the spot, pretty much damn near shocked at how he was acting. Even more so, I was shocked about how the simple little touch of his hand on my elbow reverberated throughout my body, like Blake the one who I've searched for, for lifetimes, wasn't standing in front of me.

His blue eyes blazed into mine; probably waiting for me to just up and leave with him. *Ha! Like that was going to happen.*

Blake stepped closer to Shane, moving me forcefully behind him. "Back the fuck up, Shane, she's with me," he growled. My mouth went dry and my heart thrashed against my rib cage. I hated Shane at that moment. He was the only thing keeping me from what I'd waited for.

Shane stepped even closer to Blake, starring him right in the eyes. "Let her decide," he snapped back. He leaned past Blake and grabbed me by both wrists. His beautiful eyes so intense, so real. "Come with me." I knew at that very moment that I should run. I should bolt into Blake's arms and leave, and never come back, but I couldn't.

"Okay, that's enough. Get the fuck away from her," Blake said as smooth as silk. He yanked me back hard and I fell back against him with a loud thud, but my eyes never faltered from Shane's.

I pushed myself off Blake, "I'm not a fucking pretty little shiny toy, both of you get the fuck off me!" I spun my face to Shane's, "I'm going with Blake into my room. You seem to have a visitor with you that you've forgotten about."

Shane narrowed his eyes at me and got right in my face, "If you do that, you're like every other girl that you fight so hard *not* to be."

"You know what, you're a fucking asshole!"

Then he laughed at me! "In the past few weeks that I've known you, you're called me a hell of a lot worse." He raised his hand to my face and gently touched my cheek. "Call me anything you want, as long as you don't do this."

I recoiled away from him. "What? You're here to save me, Shane? I'm sure the answer to all my problems is to lower my standards and go with you and your friend."

Blake yanked me violently away from Shane again and it felt like I was being ripped in two, as if being away from Shane was tearing Grace's body apart. *My God, Grace would have chosen him. He was the one she would have fallen for*.

I grabbed Blake's hand and walked down the hallway towards the room that I left my belongings in before.

Blake locked the door behind us and I heard a loud crash of broken glass down the hallway. I tried desperately to ignore the fact that Shane was probably trashing the house, and fought the urge to run right back to him.

Before I could formulate a single thought in my head, Blake slammed me painfully against the wall. One hand wrapped itself in a vice grip around my throat and the other yanked a fistful of my hair back, bringing my face to his. He bit my lower lip so hard that I tasted the thick rusty saltiness of my own blood. Thrusting his tongue in my mouth, he pinned his hips against mine to restrain me more.

"I need you right now. It's been too long since I've had you," he moaned into my mouth. He pressed his groin into mine, as if he was trying to step right through me.

Fear rocked my body. Dread seeped through each and every one of my pores. *Had me? Shamsiel had never had me. We never. We had one single kiss.*

I bit him so hard that I felt my teeth meet each other in the middle. I pushed him off me as hard as I could, but he only squeezed my neck tighter.

"Yes, baby. You know I like it rough." His smile was wicked and his chin dripped with the blood from his lips.

"You're not Shamsiel." I could barely breathe the words. *Just let me die.*

"Yes I am," he hissed. "You don't...remember me?"

"Oh, I remember him. There's not a day that goes by when I don't think of him, every single heartbeat that pumps in this body does so in anticipation to see him again. But, *you are not him*."

He brought his lips down to my throat and raked his teeth relentlessly against my skin. "Let me remind you of our crimes," he whispered as he raked his tongue up to my ear. His free hand undid the buckle of his belt, the sound of his zipper opening sliced through the air like a sharp knife.

My mind raced frantically. I couldn't let him do this to Grace's untouched body. I knew it wouldn't matter to Grace wherever she was, but I couldn't let him. "Gabriel!" I yelled.

Blake's breath caught and he squeezed my throat harder, blocking the air from my lungs. I felt his body convulsing with laughter. "All you humans are so ignorant," he said leveling his eyes to mine. "Do you really think he'll save you?" He brought his lips to my ear and exhaled deeply, "He'd love to watch you burn, so he could roast marshmallows in your burning embers. Go ahead, call him, listen to the silence of your prayers."

I closed my eyes and let my body go completely limp in his hands. I let my arms swing down to my sides and dangle against my body.

"I'd forgotten how weak these human bodies are," he chuckled. "I always envied him because of you; this body looks so much like her. I'm going to enjoy ripping you open. Unconscious or not, although, I'd give my soul to watch your face as I do it."

The second his hands loosened on my neck to take himself out of his pants, I grabbed the first thing I could grab, which was a snow globe on the dresser that was next to us. With all my strength, I slammed in against the side of his head. The cracking sound was almost sickening, but it honestly made me feel powerful.

Blake's body flew against the wall and I smashed the globe at him again. He only looked stunned, but he leaned heavily against the wall with a confused look crossing over his face.

"You forget I have nothing to lose. I've been sentenced to hell, just like you!" I ran for the door and fumbled with the lock.

Blake thrust his arms out for me and stumbled towards the door.

I opened it hard and thrashed it against his body. I bolted down the hallway and screamed for Gabriel. The house was empty, even Shane had gone. *Shane*.

I'll never forget the look on his beautiful face when I walked away with Blake. What I just did was unforgivable. He would never forgive Grace, and he shouldn't. If I lived through this night, I would tell him. Tell him everything; because what secrets should I hide anymore? Why had I kept these secrets? Was it because people would think I was crazy? Or, because I didn't want everyone to know how truly cruel the world was? I screamed for Gabriel again, but Blake was right. No one answered me.

I thrust open the front door to the cold muteness of the snow; the angels continued their pillow fight. "Gabriel! Don't do this to me! Gabriel!" Silence answered, heavy and smothering.

I searched for a place to hide. There was nothing but snow as far as I could see. I held my breath and plunged my body into the cold wet snow. I waded in the thigh high drifts and made it to what I would have guessed about twenty feet from the front porch, when I heard Blake cursing from the porch behind me.

My clothes became icy and stung my skin, burning my flesh every time I moved. But, I wouldn't stop. *Ever*.

I could hear Blake as he grunted through the snow after me. I pushed ahead, beyond freezing, exhaustion had already set in. The more I moved, the more my mind fogged and my body staggered. My entire body numbed.

I dragged my body further, but it was too much time out in the cold snow, the end of my vision blurred and the world spun around me. *I couldn't give up, I couldn't let Blake have her*.

I didn't know how fit Blake's body was, but mine was trying to shut down. It screamed against the cold and begged my soul to give up.

I stumbled again when a shattering pain jarred my body and spiraled through my head. Something jerked my body violently, causing agony to surge through my veins. The faint hum of a snowmobile gave me the smallest bit of hope.

I blinked at the falling flakes of ice as they blanketed my face and eyes. I tried to move my body, but there seemed to be an excessive weight pressing down around me. That's when my eyes focused on him. *Blake*.

He had pinned my arms underneath me, straddled my body and crouched over me. His mouth was a mere inch from mine. I stared into his ancient cold remorseless eyes.

He slowly lifted his left hand to my face, exposing the long sharp blade of a knife. I could hear myself moan in panic. The sound made his lips turn up in a smile.

"Go ahead and kill me," I whispered.

He lifted the knife from in front of my eyes and slid it slowly down my torso to my waist. I was so numb from the ice and snow that I couldn't even feel if he had cut me yet.

"I didn't really want to kill you, Selah, I wanted to love you. Wanted you to be mine and take over the heavens. Think about it, because I won't stop until you're mine. Until everything is mine."

He placed his lips on mine as he pierced the knife into my skin.

I tried to speak, I tried to scream, but his mouth stifled any noise I could have made.

He pressed the knife through my side as if I was warm butter and leaned away to assess his work.

Calmness covered my body, as I floated away from the pain and stared into his eyes.

"Never. Never will I be anything but his," I whispered.

The world unfocused and everything became darker. After the heaviness of Blake on my body lessened, I could hear only the voices of angels, and the warmth of someone's arms.

I could hear someone yell for 911. Background noises of screams and curses melted into the blowing winds. But louder than anything, I could hear a whispered voice near my ear; warm and pure. "Don't be scared...heaven is breathtaking."

I tried to move my lips to smile, but I could no longer feel my body. I'd never get to see heaven, but at least I got to feel it once in a kiss.

Chapter 16

A moment after the world went black; I was suddenly standing in an old Victorian style coffee shop. The walls were pale green and decorated with antique framed etchings. Thick bitter smells of coffee and cinnamon drifted through the air.

Gabriel sat at a table in the middle of the empty room. He cradled a large cup in both his elegant hands and leaned his head over the steam that eerily rose from it. His eyes were closed as he blew gently over the dark surface of the caramel colored liquid.

I gingerly walked towards the dark wooden table and sat in the empty chair opposite him.

His broad shoulders rose slightly as he inhaled the aroma and slowly sipped a tiny bit through pursed lips.

Before me, out of nowhere, appeared a large mug covered with frothy white whipped cream; strands of sweet caramel crisscrossed the top. I cupped my hands around it and shivered at the warmth. Even though I wasn't in the snow any longer, I could still remember the iciness in my bones.

I lifted the heavy mug to my lips and tasted the creamy sweetness. Across from me, Gabriel opened his eyes. We stared at each other through the rising steam of our coffees without speaking.

Coming somewhere from out of the dark silence, hummed a low hissing sound and the all too familiar beeps of a life support machine. The faint sounds surrounded us and set a morbid mood against the beauty of the lovely soft Victorian style ambience.

I looked down to notice my fists were clenched tightly around my coffee mug. *This was different. Much different from any other time I'd died.* "Are you going to tell me what's going on or are you still playing your cruel games with my soul?"

Gabriel's face was expressionless as always. His features were more angelic than I'd ever seen, his skin was pure ivory and his eyes were the reflection of heaven itself. His form hummed with an invisible current that made me yearn to touch him. I clenched my cup tighter and focused my eyes on the dark wood of the table; the dark patterns of the knots of wood twisting and turning in their stillness.

His eyelids lowered and he tilted his head nodding to the side of us.

I glanced over to where his eyes had directed me. There, through a now transparent floor, was the image of a stark hospital room; Grace lay on the bed attached to machines and tubs. *Just like before.*

I felt my shoulders slump when I saw Shane and Lea occupying the seats in Grace's room. They seemed to be in a heated discussion. As always, Shane was raking his hands through his hair. Even out of Grace's body, I felt a tingly heat rise to my cheeks when I saw him. He was beautiful, *perfect*. I tried to swallow, but the emotion got caught in my throat and tears rolled out of my eyes.

"I hate you, Gabriel. I hate all of you," I whispered through my tears. I could no longer hold back. "Humans have more goodness in them then angels. You have such emptiness in you." I slammed the chair against the table and walked to the transparent part of the floor, brazenly sitting and hanging my feet over the side of the abyss. I would no longer go by anyone's rules but mine.

I could hear his beautiful raspy voice. It echoed through the foggy opening and traveled right to the core of whatever was left of me.

"I pushed her, I pushed her too far. I practically pushed her right to Blake," he murmured.

"No. Shane, trust me. She didn't sleep with him. You don't understand," Lea's tears manipulated her words.

Shane leaned his forehead in his hands, "I told her I was in love with her."

Lea looked up at him, shocked.

He slid his hands through his dark hair and gazed at the ceiling exactly where I sat. I couldn't catch my breath as his eyes slide over mine, wishing he could see me.

"What?" Lea gasped.

"I messed up. I thought she felt it too, I didn't know she was really into her ex-boyfriend. I messed up and we fought. I pushed her away and now she's here, I wasn't there to protect her."

"Ex-boyfriend?

Shane wiped at his eyes. "Yeah, that's what she said in the Jeep when we were stuck in the snow. She didn't want anyone but him." He laughed roughly, "My fucking luck, the only time I let myself feel something for someone and there's no chance, and now she's got fucking machines breathing for her."

"Do you think she'll make it, Shane? Do you think..."

He stood up abruptly. "No. Life isn't made of miracles, roses and cotton fucking candy, Lea. She's in a coma. That sick bastard knew exactly where to cut her to make her bleed to death, to weaken her entire body before we could get her to a hospital. Think about what she felt! Think about what she suffered the whole time. How many times did they have to revive her? Even the doctor said to pray for a miracle in the same sentence he said how long we should wait before stopping the machines breathing life into her! There's no such thing as miracles. Life doesn't work that way, there's no beauty in it, there's no hope."

He walked over to the bed that Grace's body laid on and sat next to her. He leaned forward and brushed a dark lock of hair off her face.

Lea walked to the other side, took Grace's hand, and held up her wrist. "Hope. It's what's tattooed on her wrist."

"Love on this one," Shane sighed.

"Faith is on the back of her neck," Lea whispered. "Do you believe in heaven, Shane?"

His features changed from angry to agony. It twisted my soul into knots.

"She'll go right to heaven, Lea, and I bet it's the most beautiful place ever created. She'll sing and all the angels will turn their heads to listen."

Lea's tears fell faster, and her body started shaking with sobs. "No, she won't. She doesn't ever get to go to heaven!"

My essence vibrated, shimmers of heat washed through me. *Oh my God, she was going to tell Shane!*

Shane brushed a finger over Grace's cheek and I could swear I felt the heat on mine.

"She was a good person, Lea. She'll go to heaven."

"No, Shane. You don't get it!" Through her tears, Lea rambled the almost incoherent explanation. "She was there, before Noah and the Ark and the flood. Her soul was there when the angels fell in love with the humans. They called them the Watchers, The Grigori. They made a pact together to marry the human women, to teach them to see clearly, there were like two hundred of them. They became fallen angels and when they married the women, they gave birth to the Nephilim, and they were all punished. She was the only one who never had a child. That's her so called ex-boyfriend, Shane. She's been looking for an angel for..."

"Stop," Shane whispered. He didn't look at Lea, but her mouth clamped shut, astonished that she said everything she did. Her hands clasped her mouth and she sobbed even harder.

Shane slid up to Grace's face and cupped her chin. "That's fucking impossible! Grace! Wake up!" He shook her body.

Lea pulled him away, "What the hell are you doing! Get off her. You're going to kill her faster!"

He bolted up, looking suspiciously at the ceiling, hands covering his mouth; he dropped to his knees. "Gabriel," he whispered.

My mind reeled. *He was calling for Gabriel? He knew Gabriel?* I tried to jump down through the hole to him, but the ceiling of the hospital room, even though transparent was solid. I stomped on the invisible floor, suspended somewhere between heaven and hell.

I watched Shane run through the hallways of the hospital yelling for Gabriel.

Through my tears, I set my focus on Gabriel, as he remained stoic, drinking his still steaming coffee. I ran to the table and pushing it with every ounce of strength I had, propelled it into the air. Coffee and cream flew through the air, but Gabriel stayed unaffected.

I stood in front of him and dropped my eyes to his level. "Shane? Gabriel, it was Shane?"

The edge of his stupid lips curled up the slightest bit, as if he was laughing at me inside. "Not really the most intricate plot twist, Grace, you should have seen it coming."

I pushed him. Of course, he didn't move, but I pushed him again anyway. "Go to him, Gabriel!" I grabbed at his shirt and balled the material into my fists. "You are going to go to him. Then you are going to come back here and tell me what I need to do to be with him again! Put me back in that body!"

His gaze stayed steady on mine.

"Don't tell me that was my one chance. Tell me the truth. For once in your existence, do what's right, and tell me what's going on!" I kneeled down in front of him.

Gabriel gasped my face and pulled me forward, placing his closed lips on mine. He kissed me and held me there. Calmness rolled over my spirit in slow circling waves, my eyelids closed.

"Selah, see the truth," his voice whispered. "Forgive me, I've always loved you."

My eyes flared open; his lips still on mine. Lying in front of me was my garden. My father sat beneath the almond blossoms, waving to me in the sunshine. From somewhere behind the trees I could not see, my mother called for him. "Enoch," she sang his name.

My insides retched. How I missed the innocence. Before I knew, what evil was. I felt my heart rip in half when I saw Shamsiel calling for me along the dirt pathway near the water, touching his hands against the bulrushes. Gabriel walked alongside him, best friends, always together.

My heart soared as I watched myself run into his arms. I leapt at him and laughing, he caught and twirled me. My feet tickled from the tall bulrushes that he swung me through. Gabriel stood back and watched quietly, smiling tightly. He hugged me next and brushed my hair from my face. "How blessed he is to have found you first," he whispered. He caressed my lips with his thumb and then he left us and walked towards my house to greet my father. The touch had made the small hairs on the back of my neck stand up.

Shamsiel and I walked holding hands and found a place near the waters to sit and sing. For hours, we'd sing, sometimes we played the lyre and laugh, other villagers would come to listen, we never minded; we never really noticed.

I watched with bated breath, as the sun began setting and he held me in his arms to say goodbye. He looked down into my eyes with such innocent love that hot tears burned my eyes. Our lips met and I remembered how it felt falling off the end of the earth right into heaven. I saw Gabriel hidden off to the side watching us, and tears filled his eyes.

Gabriel pushed me back, violently wrenching me from my heartbreaking vision. I collapsed backwards, crashing my bottom into the flipped over table. Heat spread over my cheeks, down my neck and traveled to the tips of my toes. It became hotter and boiled into rage.

"Why did you show me that! Because, *that* Gabriel is what I've been punished for all these years! An *innocent kiss*, we did nothing more!"

He moved closer to where I was sprawled out on the floor and hovered over me. "Did you ever wonder why you saw heaven in that kiss? Did you ever stop to wonder why everyone was wiped out but you?"

I sat up and crossed my arms waiting. "Please enlighten me. It's only been two thousand years or so."

The skin around his pale blue eyes tightened as if he were in pain. "We had to stop the suffering on earth, the fallen corrupted EVERYTHING! Nothing was right; nothing was whole with them here!" He inhaled deeply. As if he really needed air to breathe! "He made the oath with them. He was one of the fallen ones and he needed to be punished along with the rest of them! And I needed to get him away from you!"

"His crime was a kiss!"

"His crime was a kiss with you! The daughter of Enoch! Grandfather to Moses! You had pure blood in your veins and innocence branded on your soul! You were no mere human child! And now Azazel and the rest of the fallen know you exist and they all want to own you!"

"Why?" I screamed.

"Because you have more power than all the angels put together. When you prayed as a child, God *answered*. You have a will of your own, where as we can only do what is sanctioned by God!"

"What does that *mean*?" I screamed again.

"A fallen like Azazel can take over the heavens with you by his side. Any of the fallen, even Shamsiel." He sighed, "You and your father were favored by God."

"And you thought that Shamsiel searched for me all these years to take over heaven?"

Gabriel fell to his knees and hung his head low. "He never knew you existed. He thought you were escorted right into heaven. I don't even know if he'll believe me, he hardened himself, until he met Grace."

"Is he like me? Does he jump into dying bodies and get the ass end of life? Or what?" I snapped.

"Most of his existence he was imprisoned in hell. He doesn't deserve you, Selah. Look what he has done in his human form! He tried to erase the thought of you," he whispered.

My body turned cold. *He was right.* Shane was nothing like the angel I kissed that day. I had thought my heart was broken before, but in that very moment, I knew true and utter despair. How would I ever get through this?

I slumped to the floor right where I stood. Gabriel sat down next to me and embraced me in his warm arms. He held me close and gently rocked me back and forth. "Stay with me and I will always take care of you, I will never hurt you."

I wanted complete nothingness. I wanted all of this to end. I had enough. "I'm done, Gabriel. I can't do this anymore."

"You can't forgive him for what he's done. He is an angel, he was supposed to be the one to never falter, and the human was supposed to fail. I would have never left you, if you had chosen me."

"You know nothing of love. You don't get to choose who you fall in love with. Shamsiel would have never done the things he did, if he believed I was here waiting for him. You are not the hero here, Gabriel. You are one of *them*. And I hate all of you."

Gabriel grabbed my face in his hands and I didn't fight back. Why should I?

"Let me show you the truth then, so you will always know what he has done and how much and how long I've loved you," he whispered and placed his lips back on mine.

Visions of Shane's lips on nameless women, Shane's dead body lying on the floor in a bathroom stall with a women sitting next to him giggling and Gabriel always in the shadows watching me, longing for me; loving me. His love turned into obsession. All the others shunned him. He set the fallen ones free to capture me, he never set Shamsiel free and he had no idea how he'd escaped. All he wanted was for the fallen to capture me and make me his own. He wanted to rule the heavens more than all the others. It was harsh and painful. I tore my lips from his and shoved him away as hard as I could.

"You fucking asshole! How can you say you love me and show me pain like that? Gabriel, I'm done. It's over. Put me wherever you need to; end this punishment. If you have any love for me, end my suffering."

"Tell me you'll never love him again. Promise me that you will..."

"Shut up! Just shut the hell up! I will never promise you anything. I will always love Shamsiel. I may never forgive Shane for what he's done, but that is none of your business. You hurt me far more than he ever will. You kept us apart and you lied to me all along. You were the one that made our punishment."

He glared at me fiercely; his entire body glowed with power.

I smirked at his audacity. "Gabriel, do you think after everything that I have been through, I would be afraid of you? I have lost everything. I have lived dozens of lives. I have lost so many children, siblings, parents...there is nothing that you can do to me that I haven't already been through. I've lived in hell all these years. An idiot with wings won't scare me!"

He stood over me. Giant steel colored feathery wings silently emerged from behind his shoulders and reached to the ceiling and walls of the coffee shop. The edges of each feather looked as sharp as razor blades. They glistened and reflected the café's lights as if they were made of metal. *Maybe they were*.

I folded my arms across my chest and stood my ground. "Yeah, um. So what, is that supposed to scare me?"

His features turned hard and his skin became marbleized with veins of gray spidered across it. Each strand of his hair thickened and hardened into a razor sharp spike. His hands turned into talons, baring serrated claws that tore through the thick wood of the table as he scraped across it.

Slowly, he advanced toward me until he hovered so close I could feel the coldness of the metal and stone that he transformed into. I still was not afraid.

When the ancient blue colored irises of his eyes turned into blazing fires of reds and yellows, I raised my hand and touched his cheek softly. The flames turned to embers, and then back to oceans of blue. When I placed my other hand along his torso, where a human heart should be, his skin softened and he became human-like again. *I did have power over him*.

"You can't begin to imagine how long I've waited for you to touch me," he whispered.

"To what avail, Gabriel? I have been punished for centuries for just kissing an angel.

What would my punishment be if I gave myself to you now? Shamsiel was thrown in hell, what would *your* penalty be?"

I moved even closer into him, touching my body to his. *God help me, I wanted to hurt him and make him suffer for everything he'd done.* "Tell me, Gabriel, as an archangel, I mean you are the messenger of God, what would happen if we were to..." I brushed my lips against his neck. *If I could take him to hell, I was going to.*

He swallowed, his throat moving and constricting under my lips.

"He hasn't spoken with me. I've been on earth with you. I would suffer the fires of hell for you, but with us together we could rule the heavens."

I slid my lips along his jaw right to his lips and kissed him. I could still hear Shane in the hospital room below us screaming for Gabriel to help him. I slowly pulled away and looked right into Gabriel's eyes. His features were soft and wanting, his breaths came out heavy and lusty.

"Go to Shane, Gabriel, tell him everything. Then come back to me. Do that one thing for me, Gabriel, and I'm yours."

He stood there looking at me.

I closed my eyes and hung my head in my hands. Everything just seemed to swirl around in my mind, memories, and lifetimes. The only thing that never changed was the perfection of that one long ago kiss.

When I reopened my eyes, the table and chairs were back where they belonged and I was alone. My coffee stood on the table waiting for me.

I sipped the warm caramel flavored coffee as I watched Shane crawl onto Grace's bed and tenderly hold her in his arms.

For my sake, this better be a long coffee break, because I needed to get the hell out of here before that lunatic rogue angel came back for me. I stormed out of the coffee shop and into a dusty desert road, taking my coffee with me.

The End...*for now*...

Shane and Grace's story continues in ***Saving Grace***, the sequel in ***The Mad World Series*** by Christine Zolendz.

Come visit me on my blog http://christinezolendz.blogspot.com/

Or friend me on *Facebook!*

Or drop me a line at ChristineZolendz@aol.com

Don't forget to check out Saving Grace in the Mad World Series! I promise there won't be a badass cliffhanger again! And, thank you, thank you, ***THANK YOU*** for reading and joining me in Grace and Shane's story!

-Chris :)

Printed in Great Britain
by Amazon.co.uk, Ltd.,
Marston Gate.